LAY GENTLY
ON THE COALS

By the same author

Sir Percy Sillitoe
Sons of the Brave
Winning the Radar War (with J. Nissen)
Emma on Albert Street
The Charity of Mars

LAY GENTLY ON THE COALS

a novel by

Art Cockerill

AESOP Modern Fiction
Oxford

AESOP Modern Fiction
An imprint of AESOP Publications
Martin Noble Editorial / AESOP
28 Abberbury Road, Oxford OX4 4ES, UK
www.mne-aesop.com

2nd edition, 2011, published by AESOP Publications, UK

1st edition, 2010, published as *The Fulthorpe Children's War*
by Black Cat Press, Canada

ISBN: 978-0-9569098-2-4

A catalogue record of this book is available
from the British Library.

Cataloguing in Publication Data: Cockerill, Art 1929-

Printed and bound in Great Britain by
Lightning Source UK Ltd,
Chapter House, Pitfield, Kiln Farm,
Milton Keynes MK11 3LW

Contents

To Oliver

This novel includes many facts that are beyond dispute. In contrast, many works of non-fiction are full of fantasies and fabrications. Many familiar with the events here related will tell you that this record is nothing but a pack of lies, which may be true, but it's my version of what happened. That means I choose what to tell. Those who believe they have a more accurate version can write their own account. However, a check of the dates, times and places, and one will find enough wheat among the chaff to make a loaf of bread.

Your Gaffer

1   Every Friday Night

MAM'S HAD enough. 'If you don't shut up,' she snaps, 'I'll clip you one straight across the chops.' She says it without malice but doesn't mince her words. She can't afford to; there are too many of us.

Mam is a small woman with an ample bosom. She is rather overweight, but she is our mother and there's no more important person on earth. Her legs have troubled her as far back as I can remember. She suffers terribly from varicose veins. On the other hand, she has a magnificent head of thick, luxuriant black hair that cascades down her back when unravelled and left hanging loose. Washing and drying it is an afternoon affair because she has only the heat of the fire in the kitchen with which to dry it. She uses towels hung on the clothes-horse before the fire to warm. She rubs and rubs away at her tresses with furious intent. Then one of us children spends an hour or more combing, brushing and plaiting it, which Mam then pins up in telephone buns over her ears.

In a fading, brown photograph hanging in the living room, taken in her early twenties, she is a handsome woman in a snow white blouse, a seated Britannia regal and imperious in a stiff-backed studio chair. I easily imagine her holding a trident in one hand with a Union Jack shield at her side. She has soft, unblemished cheeks and hooded dark eyes that look directly at the camera with chaste, aristocratic calm. Yet under that serene composure, she is tough, fibrous, steely. You can see it in those penetrating eyes.

Every Friday night, she prepares for Dad's homecoming by dressing in 'her fainest', as she calls her Sunday best. In this summer of 1937, her choice is a dress of Mediterranean blue, belted at the waist, given to her by Lady Boldwell, the Colonel's wife. It is a stylish plain blue garment of high quality Egyptian cotton with short sleeves that show her white arms, smooth as lard. Its open collar lies flat against her neck and shoulders. Over the dress, she wears a full-length, yellow daisy-patterned apron.

We children are seated at the kitchen table in good time for Dad's return from the gasworks where he's a stoker. We're a rambunctious lot and Mam has her hands full maintaining order while she makes last minute preparations for the evening meal. Unlike other days when Dad's on the day shift and one of us delivers a cooked meal to him at the coke ovens at noon, on Friday we all eat a cooked dinner together in the evening.

'Mam! Our Fred's pinching the bread!' squeals my eldest sister, Mary. My brother Fred is next but one in line to me.

'You young bugger!' Mam shouts and spins round from the black range on which the vegetables are cooking, the pot lids dancing a jingle in clouds of steam. 'I'll tan your bloody hide for you!'

'I haven't done nothing, Mam.'

'Anything! It's time you learned to talk proper.'

'Anything, Mam,' says our Mary, sucking in air with her 'Oooh! He's such a little liar.'

'That's enough from you,' says Mam. 'Tale bearers are no better than tale tellers.' She has a homily for every occasion though she often misapplies them.

She opens the oven door, revealing the brown-crusted steak and kidney pie, and leaves the door ajar so the pie won't overcook. Soon the kitchen is filled with the delicious aroma of meat and pastry.

Mam rules with a rod of iron and the nearest handy implement. She once grabbed a razor- knife by its blade to threaten one of us and cut herself so badly that she'll probably carry the scar for the rest of her life.

The kitchen-cum-living room of our house in the garrison town of Northampton barely has enough space for the deal table and chairs that fill it wall to wall. A white tablecloth over a tessellated green covering the table is spotless and the table is set for a feast. The assortment of bone-handled knives, sharp-tined forks and spoons are set out with military precision. A plate heaped high with freshly sliced cottage-loaf bread dominates the centre. Sugar bowl, cups, saucers, dinner plates, the pepper and salt shakers stand guard around the bread plate.

Mam's and Dad's upright armchairs are in front of the black-stove fire on which most of the cooking is done. Behind Dad's chair, a sash window overlooks the red-brick backyard where, in the far corner, stands the outside privy. Mam sits with her back to the scullery, which is equipped with a sink, a wooden mangle, gas stove and open copper boiler with a wooden top in which we boil the weekly wash.

We children are ranged around the other three sides of the table in order of age. Whoever is the youngest sits next to Dad while the eldest, Jack, sits on Mam's right hand. The rest of us, in ascending order, are seated between the youngest and eldest. A door behind Jack and Harry opens on to a long passage leading to the front door. On the opposite side of the room is a walk-in pantry jutting into the backyard.

Numbering seven in 1937, we're the product of a mixed marriage – Mam is Catholic and Dad is Protestant and there's nothing worse. Beginning with the eldest, we're Jack, Harry, Mary, Ada, Arthur (that's me), Fred and Malcolm. Three more sisters will come later – Margaret, Kathleen and Theresa.

Mam is a staunch Roman Catholic, one of fourteen children. Her mother was a Scottish Highlander, her father an Irishman from Dublin. Bigotry was so strong in her family that no Protestant was ever allowed to step over the threshold. Not surprisingly, therefore, the day Mam left home in Preston, Lancashire, to journey alone to India to marry our Protestant soldier father Jack Fulthorpe, was the last contact she had with her family. Dad is Church of England, one of the passive kind who go to church only on Armistice Day and Easter Sunday to march in the ranks of the old soldiers.

All noise ceases the moment he comes through the front door and stomps his way grinning into the kitchen, greeting us with his laughter and infectious good humour. We greet him with beaming faces, though we're wary of his wrath when we've done something wrong. He is a well-proportioned man of medium height with strong shoulders from years of wielding a coke shovel, for he stokes ovens at the gasworks. His hair, light brown, has thinned over the years but he's not gone bald.

Born in the early 1890s, he was a comedian in his younger days and twice performed at the London Palladium for the Prince of Wales, later King Edward VII. He fought in the trenches on the Western Front and served as a soldier of the British Raj on the North West Frontier as it was before the partition of Imperial India. He left the army in 1927 when Mam contracted recurring malaria. It was a bad time to leave on account of the General Strike of 1926 and its aftermath, but he was a survivor and so, in turn, became a miner, navvy and stoker.

Always a happy-go-lucky beer-drinking working man, he will entertain us for hours with a stream of stories, music hall songs and riddles.

'How d'you weigh a whale? Take it to the whale way station.'

'Have I told you the story about the pencil? No, I'd better not. There's no point to it.'

'And the one about the kettle? No, not that. You'll get all steamed up.'

He troops out these old chestnuts so often we recite them along with him under our breath.

Dad has a fierce temper when roused and fights many a battle of words with Mam. He will never strike her, though he often raises a threatening hand, to which she will respond with a lashing tongue.

The thought of anyone striking Mam is terrifying, but she doesn't care. 'Go on, go on,' she'll goad him. 'Make it a good 'un,' and she laughs defiantly, which calms him down soon enough. Laughter is the salve that heals the wounds on both sides; it may also be her way to teach us to stand up for ourselves.

Friday night, however, is never an occasion for dissension. Flush with the fruits of his week's labours, Dad brings good fellowship into the house. Whatever the week's vicissitudes, peace reigns when he comes home with his pay packet. Mam always has a splendid meal ready: it could be steak and kidney pie or shepherd's pie, or Irish stew and dumplings, toad-in-the-hole, tripe and onions, or steamed bacon roll in a pudding cloth. Rich aromas fill the kitchen. Mounds of fresh vegetables, thick gravy – and piping hot tea to slake his thirst – are made ready. Mam takes care to look after him like a conscientious investor maintaining payments on the premium, for he is the family's sole breadwinner.

'Hello, Mag,' he'll say, kissing her, his face grimed with traces of coke dust. 'Any trouble?'

Silently, we wait for her reply. Will she turn him loose on us for playing her up? She casts a look at our anxious faces and says, 'Trouble? What trouble?' With the back of her hand, she shoves her steamed-up glasses back on to the bridge of her nose. 'There's bin no trouble, Jack, unless you mean this lot,' and she gestures vaguely around the table.

'You been playing your mother up?'

'No, we haven't! Have we, Mam?'

'Oh, no Dad.'

'No, honest we haven't, have we, our Mam?'

She never offers support, but lets us sweat it out. She feels, I suppose, that we should learn to defend ourselves.

'I'll just wash my face and I'll be with you,' he'll say.

There'll be more waiting while he goes to the cold water tap in the yellow sandstone sink in the back place to wash away the last layer of coke dust from the day's work. Though he's scrubbed and lathered before coming off shift, he always washes again before sitting down to his meal.

Feverish whispering from Mam. 'You bloody well upset me any more, our Mary, and you'll wish you'd never been born.'

'Me, Mam? I haven't said a word.'

'Well, you know what I always say, don't you?'

This brings a chorus of 'What do you always say, Mam?'

Up comes the serving spoon, flicking water on to the
tablecloth. 'Don't be so bloody lippy you lot' and, to Mary,
'It's in your eyes.'

'What's in me eyes, Mam?'

'Bloody cheek, that's what.' Laughter. 'All right, shut
up all of you. Don't go upsetting him.'

I'm certain Dad hears every word but you can't tell
from his manner when he comes in and sits at the table.
Then, with a flurry of movement, Mam will bring the
steaming pie from the oven and place it on the table. We
can feel its radiant heat. She serves the meal according to
size, need, and order of seating, beginning with Dad. No
one can begin until all are served. She serves herself last,
with a generous portion because of her energy demands.

When all is ready, Dad proclaims, 'Right! Now let
battle begin.' The clash of arms as we throw ourselves into
the fray makes a joyful sound. When the meal is well under
way, he will say, 'Here you are, Mag,' handing over his
week's earnings. That's the signal for Mam to lay down her
knife and fork, take the envelope, and tip its contents on to
the table.

Our family life is, in many ways, democratic. Two one-
pound notes, eighteen shillings and four pence in loose
change lie on the table for all to see. Mam hands seven
shillings and sixpence back to Dad for pocket money; she
sets aside six shillings for rent; puts one penny for each
child in a separate pile for death insurance. The rest, less
two pence, goes into Mam's purse.

As though someone is waiting in the wings, listening for
the jingle of two pennies as a signal to enter, there comes a
knock at the door.

'Hello,' says Dad prophetically, 'poverty must get in.'

'See who it is, love,' says Mam to our brother Jack,
though she well knows who the caller will be.

'Stay where you are,' says Dad. 'I'll go.'

Getting up from his chair, he squeezes past Mam and
the hob to reach the passageway, then casually makes his
way to the front door.

'Ah, Mr Fulthorpe, 'tis a fine evening to be sure.'

'And a good evening to you, Father Bathbrick,' says Dad. 'Come in then. Don't stand on ceremony.'

'Sure 'tis not Father Bathbrick,' says the priest, sometimes mystified sometimes not. 'Father O'Connor it is that I am. I was just passing and thought I'd drop in.'

Father O'Connor is new. Before him it was Father O'Grady or O'Shaughnessy or Coughlin or Calhoun. Dad addresses them all as Father Bathbrick because, he says, he can't get his tongue around Irish names. Leading the visitor into the kitchen, he resumes his seat and goes on with his meal, leaving Mam to pay her respects.

Father O'Connor is young, pasty-faced with curly red hair and bushy eyebrows. His thin features are drawn out at the mouth and his beaky, swooping nose give him the predatory look of an eagle.

Beaming at us, he says, 'In the nick of time I am, my children, to give you my blessing.' He promptly launches into a Latin grace while we're attacking the meal with the frenzy of piranha fish. He ends by making the sign of the cross above our heads.

Mam is uncomfortable, a state of mind more sensed than seen. Priests collecting the parish 'dues' always catch her unprepared, no matter how predictable their visits. They arrive with clockwork regularity every Friday night.

'Will you be seated, Father?' Her tone of voice changes in the presence of priests and other important personages. I can never understand why. She sounds as though she has a mouthful of dry pie crust and is unable to speak in her normal voice, a deference she may have inherited from her Irish ancestors happy to touch their forelocks. 'Jack! Please get a chair from the front room for our visitor, there's a good boy.'

'No,' says the priest, putting a hand on our brother Jack's shoulder to keep him seated. 'Stand I will and grow to God.' Sometimes, the priest accepts a seat brought in from the front room. On one occasion a jolly priest ate Mam's stew and said it was the finest he'd ever tasted. He was the best.

Father O'Connor stands with his hand on the back of Jack's chair. 'And how is the family, Mrs Fulthorpe? In fine fettle, are they?'

'Very well, thank you, Father,' says Mam in a subdued voice.

As she can't eat and converse at the same time she usually puts down her knife and fork. To break the awkward silence that follows, she takes two pennies from her purse, saying, 'For the Poor Relief Fund, Father.'

'Ah, yes. Thank you.' He drops the pennies into the black collection bag he carries on his rounds, and continues without a pause, 'I was thinking, Mrs Fulthorpe, it would be a fine idea indeed to see these little faces at Sunday school. Would you be telling me now if they have been baptised?'

Two small red patches appear on Mam's cheeks. 'Er ... Jack? The Father's wanting the children to be baptised.'

Dad, showing not the slightest interest, goes on eating, not looking up to acknowledge Mam's unspoken query. Embarrassed, she gazes at her meal, growing cold, then looks in silence at Father O'Connor.

'Would it not be in the children's best interests to be brought into the faith?'

Mistaking Dad's preoccupation with his meal for indifference, and encouraged by Mam's humility, Father O'Connor is emboldened to press the issue. 'A good Catholic woman, Mother, should know her duty to the Church.' He sweeps our heads, bowed over our plates, with an expansive wave of his hand. 'Holy Mary Mother of God! 'Tis a travesty against our Lord's holy scriptures to keep these poor, gentle innocents in ignorance.'

We're taking our cue from Dad, who remains intent on his meal. Only Mam is suffering. We can tell her anguish is great because she repeatedly hitches her spectacles up, a sure sign of agitation. Her hooded eyes have taken on a look of patient misery.

Dad often says that priests making their Friday night visits are sent to the Fulthorpe house as a penance for sins committed during the week. Even priests, he says, commit sins, albeit only little ones, requiring atonement.

'Mrs Fulthorpe,' says Father O'Connor more sternly, 'do you not fear for your children? Will you deny them a good Catholic upbringing? These little heathens' – he encompasses us all in another sweep of his hand – 'will be consigned to purgatory to be sure.'

At the sound of the word purgatory our Dad raises his head. 'Ah, 'tis funny you should mention purgatory, Father,' he says, in Irish mimicry. 'I work in purgatory to be sure.'

'Do you indeed, Mr Fulthorpe? Tell me now where that might be.' He has provoked, and is now in turn to be provoked by, Dad. Provocation is part of his job and, from the indulgent smile on his face, he relishes the idea of a tussle.

'I'm a stoker in the gasworks, Father, and I make firebricks of fallen priests to line the furnace,' he pauses – 'but defrocked priests I lay gently on the coals.'

Though she's heard a variation of Dad's purgatory joke a hundred times, Mam sits open-mouthed. 'Oh, Jack, Jack! Please! I beg of you,' she whispers, utterly embarrassed.

Father O'Connor grips the backs of Jack and Harry's chairs till his knuckles show white. ''Tis a bold thing you say, Mr Fulthorpe, and understand you I do. 'Tis the finest training you will be having for the fiery furnace of hell for sure. Yet it is cold comfort if these poor creatures at your feet are to be denied the love and understanding of our Lady of mercy.'

Dad grins and flicks his knife to indicate us all ranged around the table. 'There's one thing for certain, Father. There was nothing immaculate about their conception.'

Mam gasps. 'Oh, Jack! Such blasphemy.'

I haven't the faintest idea what they're talking about.

'Don't be upsetting yourself, Mother,' says Father O'Connor with commendable calm. He speaks with the confidence of one well able to contend with an awkward customer. 'You must understand that there are no limits to the lengths our Holy Mother the Church will go to recover its own.'

'Is that a fact, Father?'

'It is indeed, Mr Fulthorpe, and welcome you would be too to come to the bosom of the Church of God.'

Dad wipes the last of the gravy from his plate with a piece of bread and puts it into his mouth meditatively, as though chewing over the priest's words. 'Well,' he says finally, 'I am a man of compromise, Father.'

Father O'Connor relaxes his grip on the chair backs. A shadow of a smile creeps into his eagle face. Persistence, he has no doubt been taught in the seminary, is the priest's most potent weapon.

'I am gratified to hear you say that, Mr Fulthorpe.'

'Jack!' comes Mam's whispered, but ignored, warning.

'And so, to avoid purgatory, you want these little heathens to be baptised,' says Dad in a quiet, mocking tone. How could an unworldly Irish priest understand the religious trials and tribulations our parents have been through for their marriage to survive?

'I do indeed, Mr Fulthorpe.'

'Jack! Please, Jack!'

'Here is my compromise,' says Dad with measured fairness. 'As they've been baptised in the Church of England, let us agree that we keep them till they're twenty-one. Then you can bloody well do what you like with them.'

Father O'Connor's face, suffused moments before in a pleased smile, becomes taut and grim. The colour drains from his cheeks and his body stiffens. I feel sorry for him. He has allowed himself to be bested by someone he probably considers to be an uneducated working man who should know his place. In his fury, he turns on Mam who, all this time, has said nothing beyond her whispered pleas to our Dad.

Mam is a devoted daughter of the Church who can stand any amount of abuse for her ungodly union. Yet she has remained faithful even if she has neglected her religious duties.

'Mother Fulthorpe, you will bring the wrath of just retribution on to the heads of these ... these ...'

'... heathens?' says Dad helpfully.

'... but more, to be sure, on your head,' says the priest in a tone of deep gravity. 'You, woman, are in grievous danger of public excommunication. See to it I will!'

Mam moans quietly. As the floodgates crack open, tears course down her flushed cheeks. Her appeal of 'Jack! Jack!' spurs Dad into action.

'Quiet yourself, Maggie,' he says, ominously setting down his knife and fork on his empty plate with a clatter.

Unmoved by her distress, Father O'Connor stands his ground, nodding his head solemnly to drive home the threat of excommunication. He is deceived by the casual way Dad, waggling a finger in his ear and looking at the ceiling, slowly rises from his chair and squeezes past Mam.

Being an old soldier, Dad takes his time. Once clear of the hearth, he moves with great suddenness. Seizing the priest by the collar with one hand, and by the seat of his trousers with the other, he wheels him into the corridor and along the passage. Our Dad is strong and the young priest is putty in his hands.

'Ah 'tis a grand gesture of compromise to be treating you this way, Father Bathbrick,' he says as he propels the priest towards the front door. 'An' proud it is I am to be giving our Maggie the comfort of a dutiful man. You understand my meaning?' Still with a firm grip on Father O'Connor's collar, our Dad opens the front door. 'And this, my son, is how I stoke the furnace in purgatory to be sure. I'll be seeing you next week when you call for your divvy.' So saying, he sends the priest flying into the street.

Coming back to his chair, Dad says, 'That's enough for this week, Mag. Turn off the waterworks, and as for you lot, take the grins off your faces. Now, what's for pudding?'

By the grace of God and Dad's intervention, our majestic Britannic mother has survived another skirmish. There are many in our precarious existence, some more difficult than others. Wiping her weepy eyes and pushing her glasses into place, Mam looks up. 'Blackberry pie and custard.'

'That's all right then. You'll like that, won't you? We don't get that every Friday night, do we?' says Dad to everyone. He then takes his seat and joins in the joyful struggle to polish off Mam's steak and kidney pie.

So passes another ritualistic day in the life of our family deep in The Boroughs, for the priest's visit is a weekly event. Poor Mam, a Roman Catholic thronged about by Protestants of her own making, must at times be in despair. We are her penance, her burden, a constant reminder of her transgression in entering into a mixed marriage. Does she long for redemption? If she does, from where will it come?

Yet we are children, innocent of any offence, safe in parental care from the evils of the world. The turbulence of our boisterous and rowdy lives is, in comparison, but the calm before the storm of the conflagration to come. The Second World War is about to burst upon us and, when it does, we will be swept away in its torrent up to our necks and our lives will change forever. Meanwhile we live our contented lives in the place we call Crane Hill.

2   Life in The Boroughs

THE BOROUGHS, where we live, was the original enclave of the once fortified town of Northampton. It lies adjacent to the site of the priory and the castle that once commanded the town and part of the area enclosed by the castle's outer fortified wall, now sown with rabbit warren alleyways and narrow, twisting lanes. The toffee-nosed residents of the new housing estates and more affluent areas derisively refer to it as the Burrows, implying that we breed like rabbits.

The Boroughs houses large families – and we Fulthorpes are no exception. On the other hand, our numbers are not out of the ordinary. We have something going for us of which those of upscale Northampton can't boast. This is a history packed beneath our feet, stretching back 1500 years or more to the fortified camps of the Celts, Saxons and Danes whose bones we help compress with every step we take. Indeed, we daily tread on the solid and undeniable foundation of our forebears.

How a single borough got its plural form, 'boroughs', is a mystery; its history is not. In medieval times, the wall of the castle built by Simon di Senlis, one of William the Conqueror's doughty knights, enclosed an abbey, priory, three churches, countless taverns, sheep market, stables, forges, ostlers, knacker's yard, shops and dwellings, all packed into a self-contained space. As there has been no record of battles or sieges in the castle's more than 400 years' existence it is no wonder that it fell into disuse, crumbled and decayed.

The Abbey of St. Andrew's didn't fare well either. It came to an ignominious end when those doing Henry VIII's bidding executed his edict for dissolution of the monasteries. Today, the only evidence of the castle and abbey is the arch of an ironstone postern gate removed from the castle proper and re-erected on Black Lion Hill, a short but convenient distance from where it once stood. Yet

the packed dwellings, alleyways and places of business bear
testimony to the district's ancient past: Monks Pond,
Scarletwell, Moat, Fort, Bath, Lower Cross Priory and
Castle are the street names; to these may be added Chalk
Lane, Bear Lane, Mare Fair, The Drapery and St.
Andrew's Road. As for public houses or taverns as they
once were, what imagination is there to be found in their
names: the Black Lion, White Lion, Red Lion, Golden
Lion (knights were obsessed with lions), Bear Tavern,
Moat Tavern and Gate Inn, to name a few. By the turn of
the century, 82 public houses flourished on the custom of
the leather workers and set the tone of the district. Most
have gone. Those that remain are reminders of the prolific
appetite workers and residents had for beer and ale.

Now in the 1930s leather workers are still in the
majority by a good margin. Other occupations include
carters, publicans, rag and bone men, bath attendants, gas
workers, plate layers, stokers, shopkeepers, eel catchers,
cockle and muscle vendors, fish and chip fryers, and
honeypot men who, with long-handled ladles, clean the
drains to prevent sewers from overflowing. Workers and
traders are the core of The Boroughs. They live in terraced
houses, row upon serried row, eat roast beef and Yorkshire
pudding, tripe and onions, sausages and mash, shepherd's
pie and kippers.

Housewives scrub and stone their front door steps daily
to a gleaming yellow. They know everything that goes on,
passing on news and scandal with the speed of fire in the
treetops. Wednesdays and Thursdays are market days,
maintaining a tradition from medieval times. There, on the
market square, women congregate in groups to gossip and
brush shoulders with the carriage trade coming to mingle
with the hoi polloi. The open air market is reputed to be
the largest in the world, but only because few know of the
souks of the Middle East and bazaars of India that would
make it seem Lilliputian by comparison.

In the centre of the market square stands a huge,
grotesque-looking cast-iron edifice of gargoyles spouting
water and winged lions, some say erected at the start of the

Iron Age. Each quarter of the monstrosity has steps and space to accommodate a speaker for haranguing anyone willing to listen on a Sunday night. One quadrant houses an evangelist and his supporters; another Blackshirt fascists; a communist gathering perhaps in the third quarter; and the Sally Anne in the fourth. The arrangement depends on who gets there first. Visitors on a Sunday night can take their pick of the entertainment. The town police frequently arrive to break up free-for-alls of rival followings. What with Saturday afternoon soccer and Sunday night meetings, modern-day hooligans have strong antecedents.

A few years ago in the mid 1930s, the town council began demolishing the row houses to make room for blocks of flats with a pebbledash finish and greener spaces. Change is not new. It has been going on since time immemorial. The last time it happened was during the Industrial Revolution. Red brick row houses replaced the iron stone dwellings of an earlier age, still evident from iron-stone buildings that survived earlier wreckage. Leather factories stinking of tanning operations replaced the cottage industries of a past age.

The new blocks of flats have well-lit walkways and balconies. Play areas for children have replaced dingy alleys. Green lawns and trees have brought light and colour where once the even drabness of red brick covered all. But with the spectre of war, all demolition work and rebuilding have ceased. The new look is small. Large tracts of row houses remain, but whether the old stays or the new appears, the familiar smells of the Boroughs hold fast.

Residents can navigate blindfolded from one end of The Boroughs to the other, guided entirely by the smells alone. Empty houses awaiting demolition have a pungent smell of their own; the burial ground of the old priory with its wall-to-wall mantle of gravestones, smooth-worn by generations of children, has its own sweet smell of death; the dingy vending shops that dot the lanes and alleyways offer the pervasive aromas of fish and chips, vinegar, cockles, mussels, winkles and fried eels. Some odours are enough to make a visitor gag; leather tanning operations for instance. All week thick, foamy, green streams of effluent ooze in the gutters to the municipal drains from tanning operations brazenly conducted on the pavement alongside the factory. God knows where it ends; in the once lovely River Nene, I suppose.

Our Dad has his own characteristic smell of coke, not unpleasant, yet he reeks of it as a habitual smoker reeks of nicotine. No matter how well he scrubs himself – and he is particular about his hygiene – that smell is always about his person.

Our house stands on the steep gradient of Crane Hill, sandwiched between a pub on one side, the Welcome Inn, and an off-licence shop on the other. As the only dwelling in a trio of buildings forming a block at the end of two rows of terrace houses, we occupy a prominent position. Nor can it be described as a terrace house, though its front door leads directly off the pavement. Looking from our backyard, the houses of the street uphill of us have been demolished. Those on the downhill side, Compton Street, are still occupied. From our back yard with its outdoor privy in one corner, you get a good view of the backs of the Compton Street houses. From our kitchen window, it is easy to see who is hanging out washing, going to the privy, having a blazing row. Ours is a private view of the private world that goes on behind other people's houses.

The traffic rumbles past our front door because, narrow as it is, Crane Hill with its dangerous incline immediately outside our house is one of the main thoroughfares in and out of town. It is a place of accidents galore. So much so that our front passageway serves as a regular casualty clearing station for the injured. Many a time in the dim light of the passage, I have seen our Mam give first aid, tea and comfort to the injured. Mother spends a lot of time on the front step, 'taking a spell from the hob', as she calls the kitchen fire, watching like a carrion bird for something to happen.

From the off licence, where Compton Street begins, Crane Hill falls less sharply to the traffic lights at the bottom where it intercepts St Andrews Road, where an open space called Paddy's Meadow begins. From our doorstep, Spencer Bridge may be seen crossing the River Nene as it meanders through Paddy's Meadow. Further on, Spencer Bridge crosses the railway tracks. That is as far as you can see. Spencer Bridge Road goes from Victoria Park to Jimmy's End, more properly known as St James' End with its inhabitants of middle-class pretensions. As far as we children are concerned, that is the end of the known world, the same for us as the Pillars of Hercules that marked the western end of the ancient Greek world. Why else would it be called Jimmy's End?

After the horror of trench warfare on the Western Front, our Dad stayed in the army and was posted with his battalion to India and returned to England seven years later when he left the army. That was the year our sister Mary was born. He could have signed on for another seven years, but our Mam, who had travelled to India to marry him against her parents' wishes, contracted recurrent malaria. His timing in leaving the army was unfortunate because it was the beginning of labour unrest and work was hard to find.

Despite the difficult employment situation, he became a coal miner with the help of friends with whom he'd worked before the war. This allowed the family to move into a newly built miner's house in Blidworth, Nottinghamshire, just in time for the birth of our sister Ada. I was born in 1929, and our Dad was out of work without benefit of strike pay because he hadn't been in the Miners' Union long enough. He'd been many things in his time, comedian, clerk, miner, soldier, so he could turn his hand to anything. He worked with a pick and shovel doing navvy work for a time. That put him at the bottom of the labour heap. When that job ended he took the family to Northampton, his home town, and moved in with our Grandfather Fulthorpe in the house on Crane Hill. Times were hard, so our Dad was grateful to his father for wangling him work as a stoker at the local gasworks which is where he now works. Dad will remain at the gasworks for the rest of his life and will even take over his father's job as foreman plate layer when the old man retires.

We were six Fulthorpe children when we moved to The Boroughs. By 1937, the year in which my story is set, there are seven of us – and another three, Margaret, Kathleen and Theresa, are to follow before the family is complete. In the years to come, Mam will tell me that she's had seven miscarriages, which means the poor woman has spent almost her entire life in a state of pregnancy. How she has kept order is beyond me. She is nonchalant about it except when dealing with her rebellious offspring.

'You little devil,' she'll shout across the table to anyone who might be playing up. 'Hold your tongue. I had five stitches for you.'

That would bring a chorus from the rest old enough to have developed the Fulthorpe cheek: 'How many did you have for me, Mam?' or 'I bet you had more for me, didn't you, Mam?' and 'Is that what you mean by "you put me in stitches", Mam?'

'Just shut up and eat, the lot of you.'

We haven't the faintest idea what she's talking about – our innocence is total. The procreation process is a profound mystery beyond our ken, even to the older children. Jack, the eldest, born in Bombay, has Dad's strong jaw and piercing eyes. Harry, born in Lahore, has Mam's hooded eyes and large forehead, but not her fiery temperament. Like Dad, he is easy-going but quick to anger when aroused. Mary, the next in line, has immense energy, good looks and a sharp tongue which leads the back-chatting at mealtimes. She's a natural leader, streetwise and protective where we younger ones are concerned. Ada May, hell-bent for perdition and the fires of hell if one is to believe Mam, couldn't tell the truth if it was beaten out of her, but she never gives in.

After me comes Fred, a chubby, introspective fellow who looks out for Fred. Malcolm, even as an infant, is the comedian, a laughing, happy-go-lucky fellow to whom life is a slice of bologna between two thick chunks of nothing. In the next few years Margaret, Kathleen and Theresa are to follow Malcolm, which nicely balances the sexes – except that the youngest is to die in infancy.

We moved in with our Grandfather whom we knew as the Gaffer. He got this name from his time working as a platelayer manager working on the Indian railways after he left the army. Back in England, he did the same work at the gasworks cutting and laying the intricate railway shunting lines that laced the works. His house was a modest one with three bedrooms, front living room, kitchen and back place with a gas stove and copper boiler, a cauldron-type pot like those seen in cartoons showing Africans boiling missionaries. Gaffer took the front room overlooking Crane Hill as his private abode while we took the rest of the house. He ate his meals with us and I remember him well, but he left abruptly following a monstrous row with our Dad, which began over our sister Ada and words of spite against our Mam.

Ada was fingered by Mam as a born troublemaker as early as I can remember. Even so, she enjoyed Mam's protection as well as the rest of us. Though guilty of many things, Ada was unfairly blamed for this rupture in our family life, being merely the catalyst for what happened and no more.

The Gaffer was sitting in his usual place by the back window when the incident occurred. We were at the time seated at the table waiting to indulge in our favourite occupation of feeding our meat holes – what else? On the wall alongside Gaffer's chair there hung a framed collection of faded family photographs going back to the turn of the century. One was of our paternal grandmother, Betsy Fulthorpe née Tobin, of Welsh Congregationalist persuasion or 'chapel' as its places of worship are known.

The photograph, taken when she was young, showed a striking woman with raven-black hair and dark, brooding eyes. She died on the night of the relief of Mafeking, besieged by the Boers during the Anglo–Boer War. She choked to death on beer and roast beef celebrating the relief of that city. Gaffer discovered her dead as cold mutton on the sofa the next morning. He turned teetotal after that. I'll not apologise for this diversion. It's important to the Fulthorpe heritage as you'll see.

Granny Fulthorpe having been Welsh, Gaffer English, Mam's parents Irish Roman Catholic and Highlander Catholic the blood of all four streams of the British Isles flows through our veins. Speaking the language of The Boroughs, however, our mixed heritage is known only to ourselves. But to get back to my story, Ada May took it into her head to inspect the photographs and stood on a chair to do so.

'You get down from there, my girl,' Gaffer commanded gruffly.

Mam serving out the food puckered her forehead. 'I'll thank you not to speak to my child in that tone of voice, Gaffer,' she said in a superior, hoity-toity voice.

'I'll tell her what I like, my girl,' said he sharply, adding under his breath while waiting for his food, 'B ... b ... bloody papist.'

'What did you say?'

'B ... b ... bloody papist!' he said in an outburst of anger. He stuttered alarmingly when upset.

Apples not falling far from trees, we know where Dad got his temper. He burst into the kitchen from the back place with a face black with anger. 'Papist! Papist? What the Christ are you on about upsetting my Maggie like that? And don't you dare tell my children what to do in this house.'

'Ah'll b ... b ... bloody well t ... tell 'em what I l ... l ... like,' Gaffer spat back in unabated fury.

Our Dad was all ablaze. 'Like hell, you will,' and he jabbed his forefinger threateningly. 'I'm the master in this house and don't you forget it.'

'D ... d ... don't you d ... damned w ... w ... well speak to me l ... like that, our Jack.'

'I'll speak to you how I damned well like.'

'N ... n ... not in m ... m ... my house, you won't.'

'Your house? Your house be damned. I pay the rent, not you. Giving Mag your share doesn't make it your house and leave her bloody Papism out of it, you damned bigot. What the hell d'you want to go upsetting her for? Who does the cleaning? Who does the cooking? Who does your washing? Who changes your sheets? I'll have none of your damned nonsense where Maggie's concerned and that's telling you straight.'

Mam had sat down. The spectacle of Dad and Gaffer going at it hammer and tongs was frightening. Having locked horns, neither would yield. They shook their fists, stamped their feet, face to face but inches apart, they bellowed at one another at the tops of their voices like sergeant majors on parade square. They must have been heard the length of Crane Hill to the far end of Compton Street.

'D ... d ... damn and b ... b ... blast it. A m ... man has to have s ... s ... standards and—' Gaffer was having such a difficult time getting his words out, which gave Dad the advantage and wouldn't let him finish a sentence.

'Bloody hell, man,' Dad shouted. 'This isn't Victorian England, damn and blast it. We're not living in the Dark Ages. You may be, but we're not, so give my children leeway.' He was in control and broke off to speak gently to our Ada May. 'Sit down, love.' Then he turned to face his father who used the breathing space to say his piece.

'Th ... there w ... won't be a next t ... t ... time,' he managed to spit out.

'Yes, yes, I know, Dad, but understand you're no longer the head of this house.'

So it went on. Going at it after that short break, they were like a pair of mountain rams and it was terrifying even if no blows were struck. Whatever faults the Fulthorpes might have, their rows were never physical.

Mam sat rooted to her chair with a white, drawn face, her lips quivering with agitation. Appalled by the quarrel and grossly offended by Gaffer's outburst of hostility to her religion, she gazed at us children with despair in her deeply hooded eyes, poor Mam.

Not letting up, Gaffer and Dad moved along the passageway – 'Don't you s ... speak to me l ... like that!' 'Damn and bugger it ...' and so on until they were out of the front door and on the street.

Mam, summoning courage, left the table and went to the front doorstep to plea for a truce, but too late. The quarrel had deteriorated beyond mending. Driven to distraction, and to the astonishment of neighbours who had come to their front doors to gawk, Gaffer by all later accounts flung his loose change down on the pavement. No one dared touch a hurled coin until a small boy plucked a penny from the roadway and ran. As though at a signal, other children scrambled like rats in the gutter to gather our Gaffer's scattered largesse.

The row ended as abruptly as it began. Dad hustled Mam into the house and banged the door shut. In an agitated state, he moved to the front of the fire, composed himself, then calmly sat in Gaffer's chair, which was from then on unmistakably his.

'Oh, Jack! Whatever shall we do?' Mam asked. 'The whole of Crane Hill is on their doorsteps gawping and gaping at us. I'm so ashamed.'

'Now don't you start!' he said. 'To hell with the neighbours, Mag. That's the trouble with you. You're always concerned with what other people think.'

Mam took the rebuke submissively and began serving the food, which had gone cold. Dad had leapt to her defence, which was a lesson in itself of sorts. We children were hushed. It was more than anyone dared, to provoke Dad in the mood he was in. We cast shifty looks at our Ada May and kept our thoughts to ourselves, each hoping by our utter silence to restore peace in the house.

We learned later that Gaffer, without a penny in his pocket, had stomped off to our Aunt Ada's house in Jimmy's End. Although St James End is less than a mile from our house on Crane Hill, Dad and Gaffer will never exchange another word except at the very end of Gaffer's life, for they are stubborn, cross-grained men who nurse an injury like a constant sore.

We are all sorry that this row has lost us our grandfather. He was good to us when we were destitute. The Gaffer is still the foreman platelayer in the gasworks – and by repute the best in the trade. I have to say this for him: with no more than a sketch, he can plan, cut and lay out railway crossing points with practised ease. Considering that he is illiterate and signs his name with an X – I once saw him with the newspaper, without a photograph, held upside down – his skill as a platelayer is remarkable. He has been a good grandfather to us children, generous, and with a great sense of humour.

Even Dad expressed regret afterwards for what had happened. The one good thing concerning our Gaffer's departure was an easement of our sleeping arrangements, especially with the family growing larger by the year. The house seemed big at the time, but like other workers' houses it is small and cramped, which is a case of Hobson's choice: in other words, we have to make do with what we've got.

The fireplace or hob, as we call it, is the centre of family life. It keeps the kitchen warm and cosy and is our refuge from the elements. Mam cooks all our food on its large, black range. It stands at waist height with horizontal bars in front to contain the fire, lit from first thing in the morning until last thing at night. It has ovens on both sides with a flat-top area for cooking pots. Using a steel H-frame to straddle the glowing coals, pots are brought to the boil, then set to one side to simmer.

We take our weekly baths in a galvanised tub on the hearth. When we were small it didn't matter in which order we were tubbed and scrubbed but, as we have got older, we have taken to going to the public baths at the foot of Crane Hill. We keep out of the kitchen when someone is having a bath there. Otherwise, in that same room we read, play, eat and endure our lot, packed like kippers in a box. In the evening, Dad cobbles the family shoes while Mam supervises darning or other domestic chores. We make Christmas decorations at the table, play card games, read, are sometimes read to, but not often, and listen to the wireless. The kitchen is the hub around which our lives revolve. And when from wind and rain and foul weather we step into the house, there's always that lovely warmth of the kitchen in which to thaw out.

During hot weather, Mam keeps the front door and kitchen window wide open to get cool air flowing through the house. On a Saturday morning the kitchen fire remains unlit, for the hob's cast doors, crossbars, grids and plates are blacked and polished with blacking until they shine like a soldier's toe caps. Saturday is the day Mam uses the gas stove in the back place to cook our porridge for breakfast.

The small room we call the 'back room' is part of the main thoroughfare for the passage of coal when the coal man calls, or of firewood, fruit and vegetables brought from the allotment, coke from the gas works, horse manure by the barrow load, the youngest sibling's pram, and anything that has to be moved from the front of the house to the backyard. The movement of anything through this thoroughfare is accompanied by much scraping and shuffling of chairs and furniture to make a negotiable passage.

We have a wheelbarrow, a large wooden box mounted on an old two-wheeled axle from a discarded baby carriage. Dad fashioned and nailed makeshift handles to the barrow. Most families in The Boroughs own a barrow, which is indispensable for collecting horse manure off the street, hauling home coke from the gasworks or carrying produce grown on the allotment that we rent from the town council.

Between the ages of eight and twelve boys and girls take their turn in collecting horse manure. It gives us a fine sense of understanding when we learn to sing:

Down in the sewer, shovelling up manure.
Working very hard at the bottom of the pit,
You can hear the shovel bang as they clang! clang! clang!
It's the working man who shovels up the coal.

Armed with a shovel and the barrow, we scour the town for manure. The coalyard at Castle Station is a good collecting place, for a constant stream of horse-drawn coal carts leave the yard for domestic and commercial deliveries about town. At Black Lion Hill, the horses begins an uphill climb from the coalyard. They drop their loads beginning the climb, but hardly ever coming downhill empty.

Collecting manure is a highly competitive activity. It needs agility to nip in, scoop up the steaming droppings and get out of the way before the next coal cart emerges or, more rarely, motor vehicles thunder over the railway bridge. On a good day you can get half a barrowful. The barrow is moved through the house to the backyard and not pushed to the allotment until it is full. Our rented garden allotment is at the edge of town, two miles beyond Spencer Road Bridge and alongside the railway to Mill Lane.

Because Dad works at the gasworks, we get our coke at a reduced price – threepence instead of the usual fourpence a bushel. We occasionally find one of Dad's former comrades on duty serving coke and he will throw an extra forkful into the barrow at no charge. When money is short, we gather coke that has been dropped or we knock off coke wagons leaving the gasworks.

Getting coke off the wagons can be dangerous. The gasworks supply coke merchants, who deliver it to the factories and commercial consumers. Leaving the yard, vehicles make a 180 degree turn to reach the main road. With coke piled high, wagons easily spill when making the turn, which gives those in wait ample opportunity for a free scramble to collect the fallen fuel. The bigger the children the easier the collection, naturally. Those with agility leap on to tailboards and hang on with one hand while sweeping the coke overboard with the other. They risk a cut from the carter's whip when others yell out, 'Whip! Whip behind!' And many a collector gets hurt doing the same thing with motor lorries, which are faster and trickier to plunder than horse-drawn wagons.

We also use the barrow to haul produce home from the allotment. Ours is a 20-pole or rod plot, about 100 metres in length. That's a small fraction of an acre taking the width, but hard when worked by hand. Dad took the allotment over from an old soldier. It includes four fruit trees – apple, plum, pear and cherry – along with current and gooseberry bushes, raspberry canes. Intensely cultivated and well-manured, the allotment keeps us in fresh produce all year round.

Clothing is a problem, though eased by a regular supply of secondhand clothes from Colonel Boldwell's wife, always spoken of respectfully as Lady Boldwell. Discarded clothes are stripped at the seams, pressed, cut and sewn back into garments for the younger children. Cutting and sewing are a repetitious process that continue until the last stitch of wear is extracted. Clothing too worn for further wear is cut into strips for making rag rugs or set aside for the rag and bone man. Buttons cut from garments go into a button box.

Our Mam's concern to turn waste into hard cash is constant. Nothing is thrown away. Rags are sorted into piles of woollens and cottons stored separately in the coalshed along with rabbit skins, beef bones and scrap metal scoured from wherever it can be found. Periodically, we load the barrow with rags, bones, rabbit skins and metals and cart them off to the rag and bone man. In his yard, the rag and bone man weighs each offering and calculates the amount owed, which rarely amounts to more than one shilling and sixpence. That's still a valuable contribution to the family finances. The stench of sour rags and old bones at that place is enough to make one gag; it constitutes one of the more dreadful of the countless odours of The Boroughs. No one likes the job of going there, but Mam needs every penny.

Saturday is housecleaning day. Everyone works. If Dad is not on shift, he takes one or more of us to work the allotment while the rest set to cleaning house, beginning with the bedrooms. Of the three, the largest, at the front of the house, takes two double-sized beds with peeling imitation brass grill work. The bedroom above the back kitchen has a double bed and nothing more. Our parents sleep in the room above the kitchen. Depending on the mix of children at any one time, the boys occupy the large front bedroom and the girls the small one. It's a tight squeeze all round.

Since Gaffer left, the front room with two sash windows overlooking Crane Hill has rarely been used. An odour of urine pervades the room, not from Gaffer's occupation, but rather from the public house next door. It isn't so bad when the fire's lit, but only then is it really habitable. I don't understand the reason for the smell until I am older. The up-street wall of the front room forms the opposite side of the public house's urinal, so eight inches of red brick are all that separate us from the men's urinals. Worse still, our front room floor stands a good few feet lower than that of the pub. There is no damp course in the wall, so urine has seeped through and stained the wallpaper, which means that our Dad has had to spend much time repapering. Mam acquired a working upright piano to stand against the wall to hide the inevitable stains that appeared. It has done nothing to rid the room of the smell, so Mam lights the front room fire well in advance of Lady Boldwell's weekly visit.

So that is our life in the house on Crane Hill. The atmosphere in which Mam rules nurtures us as surely as a branding iron marks a rancher's cattle. She is a benevolent dictator who tolerates a cranky and mutinous citizenry for form's sake, but brooks no nonsense in the management of her domain's interior economy. After all, hadn't she served on the frontier of India in the lower ranks of the British Raj? Hadn't she helped keep the boundaries of the empire secure? Hadn't she pacified squabbling neighbours who would encroach on her prerogatives? Not for nothing do I see her in an august and majestic Britannic light.

The pugnacity that so characterises her personality helps us survive and grow. We will need her spirit if the war ever begins. Only when we get older do we learn that wars are fought by the young, not the old.

3   Walking the Barratt Way

MAM BUTTERS and slices the bread while we watch in silence, captivated by her dexterity with the loaf, knife and butter. The squeak of the knife as it slices through the crust of freshly baked bread makes our mouths water. Mam bakes her bread the old way without baking pans. On top of a large round of well-pummelled dough smelling of yeast after it has risen she sets a smaller knob half the size of the larger one. She smears the top knob with butter and cuts the top two or three times with a sharp knife. She bakes the loaves, two at a time, one on each side of the upright grate fire, and what comes out of the oven is a delicious-smelling, golden brown crusty bread called a cottage loaf. The baker at the end of Harding Street, where we have our Sunday meal of roast beef and Yorkshire pudding cooked, bakes them by the dozen.

Placed on the sill of the open kitchen window to cool, they are under the protection of watchful eyes from birds flying about the neighbourhood. When ready, one loaf is put in the pantry for the next day, the other slated to be demolished at supper, the meal for which Mam is busy preparing. Having separated the two halves, she deals with the top half. Watching her in action is a sight to behold. She holds the round of crusty bread in one hand and, with a deft stroke of the knife towards her bosom, slices off the knob, which stays in place. She flicks it over with her knife, takes a dollop of butter and spreads the bread thinly with a couple of strokes, then uses her knife to place it on the plate.

The knob of the loaf is much prized, so everyone watches where it went on the plate, and works out how to get it. If you aren't used to the sight of buttering and slicing the bread you'd swear she's about to slice herself open each time she cuts, but she doesn't. In increments, she butters the open face, slices, cuts it in half and places the halves one at a time on the plate. There is no more mouthwatering sight than freshly baked bread being spread and cut and laid our for eating.

Mary uses her hand to waft to her nostrils the delicious aroma coming from the buttering and cutting.

'I'm watching,' says Mam, not looking up.

'I'm waiting,' says Mary.

'I'll have less of your lip, miss.'

'It's true, mam. Ain't we all?' She looks to Jack and Harry for confirmation.

Jack grins. 'P... p ... p'raps!' he says.

'You've spent too much time with your Gaffer,' says Mam, concentrating on her work.

Expert in this bread and buttering business, working there with us all seated at the table, waiting for our Dad's arrival, I believe she enjoys watching us watching her. Once seated, there is no coming or going. You stay where you are. That's not to say we're silent, far from it.

Mam pauses and lifts her head to survey those seated about her. 'Just look at him,' she says, laughing at Fred. 'Aren't his eyes popping out like organ stops?'

We laugh with her. Fred stiffens his jaw, letting the corners of his mouth dip in a smirk. 'If they are, I got them from you, our Mam,' he says. At seven, you know enough to be lippy, but you're not smart enough to hold your tongue.

'That's enough, Mr Smart Alec,' she says, going on with her buttering. 'If your eyes are bigger than your belly, you'll be in for a lot of belly-aching in this life.'

She speaks matter-of-factly, without resentment, merely offering a maxim from her vast store of aphorisms with which she peppers us daily.

'There ain't nothing wrong with having eyes as big as your belly, is there, m'duck?' says our Mary.

'There's no call for you to go piling on the agony,' says Mam.

'Agony? What agony? He's hungry, that's all.'

'All right, then, all right. Don't come the acid with me, my girl. You've got far too much to say for yourself.'

Who knows what she means by the 'acid'?

Behind her, the kettle is gently wheezing steam, ready for making tea the moment our Dad comes through the door. Mam times the meal and takes particular care to have it ready for serving the moment our Dad enters the house. This is not so much because our Dad expects special attention as from Mam's sense of order and domestic management. The smell of his smoked haddock supper wafts from the pan simmering next to the kettle. What threatens to become a storm because of Mary's intervention calms down the moment our Dad comes home.

Ada, looking through the back window, catches sight of our Dad walking along Upper Harding Street. 'He's 'ere,' she says. 'Our Dad's 'ere, Mam.'

'Orright! orright, missy!'

'Lovely to see you all looking so cheerful,' he says, removing his jacket to hang it on a peg in the corridor. Passing through to the back kitchen to wash his face and hands, he says, 'Be with you in a minute, Mag.'

His ablutions complete, he takes his seat, gives us a beaming smile, and rubs Malcolm's blond hair, saying, 'And how's the milkman's son, my son?' Like our Dad, we all, with the exception of Malcolm, have brown hair, though none has inherited Mam's jet-black hair.

'Jack!' says Mam, disapprovingly. I have no idea why she's admonishing him and I don't suppose anyone else does either.

She begins serving the meal, taking a plate hot from the oven and ladling a large segment of smoked haddock from the pan. This she sets before Dad, offering him servings of boiled potatoes, fresh green peas and steaming cauliflower straight from the pots. Only then does she permit us to start eating, wagging a finger and saying, 'Go easy with your trotters, you lot.'

We laugh and reach for a slice of bread from the pile, waiting our turn to dig a spoonful of damson jam from the stone jar set on the table and get on with eating. There's no time to be lost. Fred tucks into his slice of freshly baked bread without awaiting his turn for the jam jar. If he gets a head start he'll be the first to reach for another slice and will also have free access to the jam pot.

Pouring out the tea, Mam says, 'Don't you be so liberal with the jam, our Ada.'

'Oh, let them get on with it, Mag.' Dad raises the cup of scalding hot tea to his lips and slurps it into his mouth. He breaks off a flake of fish with his fork and blows it cool, then offers it to Malcolm, who opens his mouth like a cuckoo.

We eat with deep concentration and no one speaks for fear of missing a bite. Dad is enjoying his haddock; Mam is savouring a smaller portion she saves for herself; the rest of us make short work of that buttered bread, the fire casting a warm glow in the room as heavy rain begins clattering against the kitchen window.

'Looks as though I got home in the nick of time,' Dad says, turning to look into the back yard. Silence. 'A nice bit of haddock, Mag.'

'I'm glad you like it, Jack.' She gives her vegetables a liberal sprinkling of salt, all the time casting uncertain looks at Dad. Then, after a while, she says in a subdued voice, 'Jack!'

'Yes. What is it, Mag?'

'I think you should know I'm walking the Barratt way.'

As Mam has varicose veins and swollen ankles that make walking difficult for her when her legs are playing her up, I wonder if that's what she's on about. With so many children to fetch and carry for her, it's not her habit to walk anybody's way.

Dad lays his knife and fork down on his plate and stares at her for some moments. 'Good God! Not again, Mag?' His countenance expresses disbelief.

'I am, I tell you,' she says, crossing herself Roman Catholic fashion.

What is she talking about? Our parents so often speak to one another in riddles their conversations can at times be utterly puzzling.

'Well, I'll be damned.'

'Jack!' she rebukes him. She raises her eyes to the ceiling and mutters, 'Holy Mary, Mother of God,' puckering her forehead as much as to say, 'not in front of the children', though she is no model herself when it comes to strong language.

'Can I walk the Barratt way, Mam?' Mary asks, flicking her short, cropped hair with a sharp cock of her head.

'That's enough from you. Just hold your tongue,' says Dad reprimanding her.

Mary hunches her shoulders and goes on eating. Perhaps she knows something I don't because she looks sheepish under the rebuke. Mam often calls her Miss Know-It-All.

Harry gives Jack a knowing look; they may have an inkling of what walking the Barratt way means, but if they do their understanding is unspoken.

'What's the Barratt way, Mam?' I ask.

'That's none of your business, Mister Inquisitive,' she replies. 'You know what curiosity did, don't you?'

'What, Mam?'

'It killed the cat.'

If she thinks our Mary is a know-it-all, she considers me too cocky for my own good and she often says as much, which didn't go down well with me because I was only asking a question.

'The sweet mystery of life, my son,' says Dad more kindly. His words leave me no wiser.

'Are you all right, Mam?' Harry asks.

He is the quiet one of the family. Being more like our Dad than any of us, he is close to Mam in spirit, always concerned for her well-being. I believe his concern stems from the time he was at death's door with scarlet fever and the ambulancemen came and laid him on a stretcher bundled in red blankets and took him to the isolation hospital. I've never known Mam to be so white-faced and distraught, but from that time on, Harry has developed an especially close relationship with her. After he got better, he favoured her with little presents of chocolate and sweets that he'd paid for himself from his meagre earnings working at the market.

'Yes,' she says, giving him one of her martyred looks, 'I'm all right, son.'

Mary begins saying something about Mr Barratt, but Dad cuts her short.

'That's enough,' he says. 'The less said on that subject the better, my girl.'

Mr Barratt owns a number of leather factories working in the boot and shoe trade. He employs hundreds, probably thousands, of workers who do everything from curing the hides to boxing finished footwear. The Barratt leather tanning factory at the bottom of Crane Hill stinks to high heaven when they are washing and treating the hides, causing a green effluent to run in the gutters of Monks Pond Street and into the corporation drains. Mr Barratt, a pillar of society, is depicted on posters plastered on billboards striding out with confident step, dressed in pin-striped trousers, a black jacket, starched wing collar shirt and bow tie, bowler hat, rolled umbrella and briefcase. Most prominent are his gleaming black shoes stepping over a bold statement at the foot of the poster reading 'Walk the Barratt Way'.

A few years earlier in the mid 1930s, the town's benefactor has endowed the community with a maternity hospital known as the Barratt Maternity Home. Its ultra-modern facilities are a boon to expectant mothers, for it has meant the end of home deliveries. Naturally, to 'walk the Barratt way' has become a popular euphemism for anyone pregnant and in the family way. Of course we are not aware of this at the time, even the older siblings, Jack and Harry, who are in their teens. They may have some knowledge of the situation, but I doubt it. Ours is about the last generation to have reached adulthood ignorant of the laws of procreation. Sex is simply not a subject discussed in or out of the family.

Nevertheless, another child in the offing means another mouth to feed, another sleeping place to find, more clothes to provide. Our parents care for us as best they can, but something has to be done to relieve pressure on the available space and family finances. Although we children are unaware of the true state of affairs, Colonel and Lady Boldwell offer Mam and Dad a plan to ease the burden, for we are a military family in need of the army's charity and benevolence.

In the same way that Mr Barratt is a philanthropist to the town, the Boldwells are our benefactors. Colonel Boldwell was Dad's company officer and has since risen to become the commanding officer of the regiment. Dad reached the rank of lance sergeant, which is not quite a sergeant, but rather like a lance corporal not being a full corporal. Still, it gave him entry as a civilian to the sergeant's mess and all the privileges that went with it. He maintains close ties with his former comrades and often takes us to the regimental depot on a Sunday morning to watch the church parade. He is respectful of the commanding officer and touches his hat when the colonel recognises and exchanges words with him.

Then there's Lady Boldwell, who takes close interest in our welfare. She regularly visits the house to bring Mam her children's cast-off clothes as well as some of her own. She and Mam being the same shape and size, her clothes fit Mam to perfection.

*

One Sunday morning in the height of summer, soon after Mam's 'walking the Barratt way' news, our Dad has me go with him to the regimental depot. It is the regiment's annual Talavera Day to mark the anniversary of the regiment's battle honour won at Talavera one hot day in July 1809. On this important occasion, the Duchess of Gloucester, Colonel-in-Chief of the Regiment, Colonel Sir Harry Knox, Major Allan Hill-Walker, senior VC of the Army, and the film star Winifred Shotter, married to a Colonel Green, are present to inspect the battalion and to take the march past in 'review order'.

The entire battalion dressed in its World War I khaki uniforms, complete with calf-high putties, peaked caps, rifles and full web equipment, have waited for the General's arrival in the sweltering sun. On this parade the officers wearing their ceremonial silver swords present a splendid sight for all to admire. Dad, too, looks trim in his Sunday best and bowler hat with his medals on his chest.

Mam is giving me a lot of attention this Sunday morning. We children wash and dress ourselves for outings, but today, Mam satisfies herself that I am in a fit state to accompany my Dad. Tying the laces of my new shoes, rather too tightly for my comfort, she issues her instructions. 'You watch your Ps and Qs, our Arthur,' she says. 'D'you hear what I'm saying? No playing around either. Be on your best behaviour and speak properly to anyone who speaks to you. And mind you keep your socks up.'

'The laces are too tight, Mam.'

'Nonsense! New shoes always seem tight and stiff. You have to wear them in.'

She inspects my ears, combs a straight parting in my hair, and brushes imaginary dust from my jacket and grey short trousers with the clothes brush.

'There you are, Jack,' she says when she is satisfied with my appearance. He'll do.' Mam's close attention is unusual because we've been taught from infancy to take care or ourselves or one another. Mam has enough on her hands to cope with the latest addition to the family. The attention miffs the others, but especially Fred who is closest to me. It is settled. I am to accompany Dad alone.

The asphalt of the parade square shimmers like liquid tar in the summer sun. No whisper of wind disturbs the limp Union Jack on the parade flagstaff. I stand alongside Dad behind a roped-off area at the edge of the parade ground. All is quiet, all is still. The pigeons perched on the window ledges of the ironstone barrack buildings take flight at every resounding crash of the rifle butts, flying in alarm before settling once more on to their perches.

Formed up by companies in the pre-war formation of four ranks deep, the battalion stand immobile in solid blocks of khaki, brass buttons on the throat-choker jackets gleaming in the sun. Puttees tightly wound from ankle to calf give the soldiers the appearance of military golfers in khaki plus fours; the red sashes of the company sergeants and sergeant majors add a dash of colour to the solid walls of khaki; black boots shine and brass buckles glint. The regiment is a splendid sight to behold. To think that he had once been a sergeant wearing a red sash on parade makes me proud to be standing there with him and I bet he's sorry he ever left the army.

The snap and crack of rifles being moved to the present, shoulder and order arms positions at the Regimental Sergeant Major's command is thrilling to behold. During the Colonel-in-Chief's inspection, the band play a slow march with the bass drummer thumping out loud, measured beats. I find it impressive that not a single man moves a muscle through the entire inspection. How can soldiers be so disciplined?

Then, at last, the inspection party completes its round and return to the reviewing stand to await the march-past by companies in line abreast. We are standing so the companies come by us in line and I marvel that they pass by in perfectly straight lines. I certainly want to be a soldier when I grow up.

The spectators behind the roped perimeter of the square are the wives and families of soldiers on parade. The children are in their Sunday best; their mothers and older siblings and relatives are all dressed in best bibs and tuckers and look a grand sight, as impressive in their own way as the soldiers on parade.

'Do you miss the life, Snappo?' asks a matronly woman standing next to Dad.

'It's a grand life, Madge,' he says, 'but it's a young man's game, like him for instance if he's lucky. As for me, I'm past it. No regrets, no. I've had my dibs, but I like to see a parade, don't you?'

'I do, Snappo,' she says, leaning to the front of my Dad to take a closer look at me. She smiles, showing nicotine-stained teeth. 'Are you going to take after your Dad, sonny, and follow in his footsteps?'

I'm shy. I don't know what to say, so I lower my head and give no answer.

Holding my hand, my Dad gives me a gentle squeeze and looks down at me. 'Well, what do you think, my son?' he says. 'Would you like to be a soldier?'

'I don't know, Dad.'

'You don't know? What would you like to be when you grow up then?'

I haven't the faintest idea, but I think for a moment and say the first thing that comes into my head. 'A stoker like you, Dad.'

'No, not a stoker, son. That's a dirty job.'

'But it's always warm near the furnace, innit? Besides, I like it when you put your billycan on your shovel and stick it in the fire. I like that; it boils in no time, don't it?'

'He's got a tongue in his head, hasn't he?'

'I should hope you'd aspire to something more than a stoker, son. Think of something else.'

'A writer then. What about a writer?'

There is no precedence in our family for so useless an occupation as writing. We don't have more than two books in the house at the same time and they are from the town library, so why I say that I'll never know. I like reading and have the reputation in the family for bookish ways. Mam doesn't discourage reading, but she is not above making caustic comments about my getting big-headed from all my reading. The thing is, all our forebears were manual workers: stokers, platelayers, labourers, leather workers, and soldiers most of all. We've had a long tradition of soldiering going back to the Napoleonic Wars. Having reached the rank of sergeant in his nine years of military service, Dad could have done well in his military career.

Dad laughs, not unkindly. 'A writer?' he asks. 'Well, son, you can't write until you have something to write about, can you?'

'I suppose not.'

'That means you'll have to be at least forty, son. Meanwhile, you best learn a trade. That's important, don't you think.'

As I haven't given the least thought to the future, I don't think in terms of learning a trade or anything else for that matter.

'It certainly is a grand life, my son,' my Dad repeats. 'Three square meals a day, all found, money in your pocket, and nothing in the world to worry about. What's more, it's a family tradition to be a soldier.'

What eight-year-old boy wouldn't want to go to war? We Fulthorpe children have been raised on the stories of garrison life in India. Military metaphor is woven into the fabric of our lives. Mam's platoon system of management means that everyone has a daily cleaning chore about the house and conforms to the discipline Mam exercises at the table.

The Northamptonshire Regiment has battle honours enough to fill its regimental colour twice over. I'm sure now that those who glory in its deeds do so totally detached from the carnage that goes with conflict. Old soldiers visiting our house talk with nostalgia of battles, advances, retreats, garrison duty on the Rock of Gibraltar, in Ireland, of Talavera (the Regiment's shining hour in battle under Wellington), and life on the North West Frontier (present day Pakistan), but no subject is more chewed over than that of life in the trenches during the Great War.

I once heard our Dad tell of standing guard up to his waist in mud during a retreat and being so cold he couldn't have fired his rifle even if he'd wanted to. His rare but matter of fact accounts of gas attacks, squalid living conditions in the trenches and of the rats that grew fat on the dead in no-man's-land impress me as the very worst kind of hell. And so vivid are his accounts of trench life during the war it is as though it all happened only yesterday.

It is hard to reconcile these appalling reports of soldiering with my Dad's nostalgia for the comradeship of

military service; I am too young to fathom the
contradiction. Still, when you are a child bathing in the
warm sunshine of a Sunday church parade watching a
regiment respond as one man to commands, the effect is to
mesmerise. So it is in this atmosphere of soldiering that I
think it might not be so bad to be a soldier after all.

'How would you like to play in the band, Arthur?'

'D'you think I can when I'm older, Dad?'

'Of course you can, be a musician, my son, learn a
trade.'

My heart swells with pride watching the battalion
march past the saluting base with the band playing the
regimental march past. I can imagine myself as being of
their number as they march through the depot gates and
along the road to the garrison church. I am thrilled to
imagine a thousand men responding to the beat of the
drum and a stirring march. A separate column of old
soldiers wearing their campaign medals fall into step behind
the last company and disappear through the barrack gates.
The muffled sound of the music gradually fades as the
battalion makes its way along Barrack Road.

'Come along, my son,' Dad says, taking me by the
hand. 'The Colonel wants to meet you.'

'What? *Me*, Dad?'

'Yes, you.'

'What for?'

'You'll see.'

Ducking under the rope that separates the spectators
from the parade square, Dad walks, or, rather, marches
towards the reviewing stand where a knot of officers and
their wives are congregated. A number of spectators have
followed the marching column. Others are beginning to
leave too, so the spectacle of another, rather special Sunday
parade has come to an end.

Lieutenant-Colonel Boldwell stands in conversation
with Major General Knox. The Adjutant and Second-in-
Command are a little way off, forming a separate party with
their wives and guests including the delectable film star
Miss Winifred Shotter who is the centre of attention.

General Knox wears a khaki twill uniform with red tabs on his uniform collar, a red band around his peaked hat, cavalry trousers and highly polished riding boots, a most impressive figure. A polished to shining Sam Browne belt, sword attached, and shoulder strap contain his corpulence like the iron band of a wood-stave barrel. A large walrus moustache gives his countenance a stern look.

Dad halts at a respectful distance, waiting to be noticed, and I stand by his side with a certain feeling of wonder and apprehension. I'm glad to see a face I know in Lady Boldwell, dressed in a bright red and grey suit; she stands talking to Lady Knox whom I've seen arrive with the General. Lady Boldwell acknowledges Dad with a slight nod of the head and must have caught her husband's eye because, though standing with his back to us, he turns abruptly and nods to Dad to approach, which he does promptly. Coming to a smart halt, he touches his hat in a sign of respect before removing it, then turns and beckons me to join him.

'Ah! Sergeant Fulthorpe,' says Colonel Boldwell, giving Dad a pleasant smile. Next he addresses the General, saying, 'Sir! Lance-Sergeant Fulthorpe – served with the regiment on the North West Frontier. A good soldier, sir. Sober, industrious, a credit to the battalion.'

General Knox nods his head gravely. 'Very good,' he says. He next turns his attention on me with a penetrating gaze. 'And is this the fine young fellow who's going carry on a family tradition, eh Sergeant?'

Dad, standing rigidly to attention with his mouth tightly closed, grips his bowler hat by his side. I can hear him breathing hard through his nostrils. He's taking in such large amounts of air that his chest expands and contracts in a most unusual way. He isn't normally a nervous man.

'It is, sir,' he says and eases me forward by the shoulder without looking down.

The General's face breaks into a benign smile. 'So you want to be a soldier, do you, lad?'

I stare back at him and maintain my silence.

The grey-haired General is nonplussed. He addresses Colonel Boldwell. 'I like a man to look you straight in the eye.' To me he adds, 'I'm sure you'll make a fine soldier. Am I right?'

'Yes, sir.'

'That's the stuff. I like the cut of his jib, Boldwell. Might even make an officer of you, eh! Wear a sword, command men. That's the spirit. How old are you?'

'Eight, sir.'

'Lots of time yet. All right, Colonel. Send his papers in. I'll sign them in the morning.'

'Very good, sir. Have you filled out the application, Sergeant Fulthorpe?'

'I have, sir.'

'Very well. Then we'd better have the boy examined. He'll have to pass a medical.'

'He will, sir.'

'It's settled then. I'll have the Adjutant send a note to the medical officer and arrange an appointment.'

'Very good, Sergeant. Young fellow will do well,' says General Knox and, with this observation on my future prospects, he brings the meeting to an end.

'Thank you, sir.' Dad raises his hat once more, says, 'Thank you, sir' to his old company commander, and we take our leave.

This meeting is my baptism into military life, but because nothing happens for a long time after, I forget about it. Three weeks later, it comes back to me when Mam takes me to the depot for a medical examination.

The medical officer, another grey-haired gentleman with a large red nose and bushy eyebrows, gives me a thorough medical examination. I must be the youngest recruit he has inspected in his career, for he carries on a monologue of amazed tut-tut-ting as though I were at the end of his stethoscope, and the rarest of specimens.

'Why, boy! Tut-tut! Sound chest, firm cavity! Tut-tut! Breathe in. Breathe out. Fine.' He notes my chest expansion, measures my limbs, shoulders, head, neck and feet, noting every measurement on the sheaf of forms on his rolltop desk. Half an hour later he tells me to get dressed, then calls Mam in for consultation.

'Tut-tut! A fine young chap, Madam,' he says. 'Well-nourished, good frame. Nothing wrong there. Weak in the right eye. A good left. Nothing a monocle won't put right.' He laughs at his own joke.

'It's heredity, doctor,' says Mam, indicating her own thick lens in her spectacle frame. She speaks in her Lady Boldwell voice. 'But he's in fine fettle even if I say so myself.'

'Exactly, Madam. He'll come to no harm with that eye till he's in the army's care. A pair of glasses will soon put him right. Save on the expense, what! Otherwise the little chap is A-one, fit as a fiddle.'

So it's settled. I am found fit to lead a military life, though at this time I have no way of knowing what form it will take. My parents don't consider it necessary to discuss the matter. Only in retrospect do I realise that Dad's talk about the need to learn a trade and be a musician is his way of conditioning me to accept the inevitable.

During the months that follow, I do begin to ask myself, *Why me? Why not Jack or Harry? Are they going into the Army? And do they know anything about it?* I ask them.

'Why me?'

'Search me,' Jack says. 'You're more in need of it than I am. Knock some of the cockiness out of you though, won't it?' He laughs.

He thinks I'm cocky, too, does he? I suppose our Mam thinks the same way or she wouldn't have dressed me up and combed my hair and sent me packing to see Dad's company officer. Strange as it may seem, I don't associate Dad with the decision to send me away. If anyone is to blame, I reason, Mam is. She is the one who got me ready to meet the General, took me to the medical officer, assured me that I'd be all right and would be well looked after. How can she not be the one, the only one responsible for my leaving home? I can like it or not. The choice is not mine but, as things turn out, I just happen to be our parents' first sacrifice to the Fulthorpe war. In a way, I am soon to be treading in Mam's footsteps as she walks the Barratt way.

What I learn later is that we are sufficiently poor to be in need of the army's charity and connections assure that we get it. (I haven't intended writing about myself at this time, but I need to give an account of the events leading up to my departure from the bosom of the family.)

As it turns out, technically, I'm not the first to leave home. That distinction goes to our sister Mary, who is admitted in 1938 to the Royal Soldiers Daughters Home. Suddenly, and without explanation four months later, she comes back home. No one knows why until many years later.

Mary has been expelled for being caught stealing.

4 Ada May, but Ada May Not

OUR MAM loves a play on words when one occurs to her. 'Ada May, but Ada may not,' she says with barbed meaning. 'Ada may not' is, much to her pleasure, simple enough for everyone to understand. On an occasion that firmly establishes character, our Mam continues her tirade with 'You can lock a door against a thief, but not a liar and, by Jiminy, I'll have you behind bars yet.'

Ada May is without doubt destined for a life of crime according to Mam. Still, I wish she wouldn't get on to us the way she does because, once she gets going, there is no stopping her. She fires her broadsides at the least provocation and God help anyone who is in her line of fire.

The trouble this time stems from the errand Ada has run. She's been sent to Downes, the off-licence-cum-grocery shop next door, for a quart of milk in the large ironstone jug kept for the purpose. (Milk is ladled from the urn, so customers have to bring their own containers.) When Ada returns, Mam takes one look at her and says, 'You little bugger! You've been drinking the milk.'

'No I haven't.'

'Yes, you have. Come here! Get on that chair,' and, grabbing her by the arm, Mam forces her to stand on Dad's chair and face the mirror above the mantelpiece. She has Ada's chin in an iron grip as she thrusts her face into the mirror. 'Look! Look! Just look at that,' she says, 'There's milk all over your lips, you little liar.'

Ada wriggles like the slippery eel she is and breaks free. 'No it's not,' she says, quick as a whip. 'It's chalk, our Mam. I wanted to see what I looked like with a moustache.' Her boldness distracts Mam long enough for her to break free and flee to the back door ready to do a bunk. She cuffs the evidence away with her coat sleeve and turns back. 'See! I've got the chalk in me pocket.' She plunges a hand into her ragged coat pocket and, with a hurtful expression, stares our Mam out. 'Just look here' – pause – 'Oooh! Would you believe it? I must have dropped it on my way home' and, quick as a wink, she makes her escape with our Mam screaming for at her to return.

'Come back here, you little villain, and I'll tan your bloody hide for you,' she hollers, but it's no use. Ada knows when to make herself scarce.

I think our Mam is about to deputise me to capture Ada and bring her back because she turns to me with her eyes ablaze with fury. 'And you can wipe that grin off your face, you cheeky, brazen chump.'

'I haven't done nothing, Mam,' I protest.

'It's not what you haven't done. It's what you'd do if you had half a chance. Go on. Get to the table and sit down.'

The following Sunday, the milk theft incident past but not forgotten, Ada is sent to the baker for the family pan of roast beef and Yorkshire pudding. The pan is too large for the kitchen oven, so it is taken to the baker on Upper Harding Street. He keeps his bake oven going to cook family roasts at a penny or tuppence a roast on a Sunday. We think Ada is taking a long time, but she returns staggering under the weight of the Sunday roast held in a thick towel on account of the heat being given off. When placed on the table, a large chunk of the Yorkshire pudding is found to be missing.

The rest of us are seated, eagerly waiting for our Mam to serve the meal. Dad is due to arrive at any moment from the sergeant's mess where, as an honorary member, he sometimes goes on a Sunday. Nothing can start without him for he does the carving. Protocol and ceremony of this kind form the bedrock of our existence, as important to us as the pomp and circumstance of the changing of the guard at Buckingham Palace.

'Well, I'll be damned! She's pinched the Yorkshire pudding, Jack,' says Mam to our eldest brother. In Dad's absence, Jack stands in as the male head of the house.

Ada protests. 'No, Mam. That's not true. Let me tell you an' God strike me dead if I tell a lie. I was walking along Harding Street proud as in Indian rajah an' who should set upon me but the Spragg boys. "Give us a bite," says Bert Spragg. "Not on your life," I says. "Clear off or our Mam's going to kill me!" Then all of a sudden George Spragg grabs me from behind and says, "Go on, Bert! Have a go," an' he did and they both ran off laughing.'

'You bloody liar,' says Mam, hitching her glasses farther up her nose. 'I swear you'll be the death of me before you're through. Get sat down. I'll let your Dad deal with you when he comes in, just you see if I don't. And I won't half laugh when he thrashes you from here to kingdom come.' The rattle of the front door opening announces the arrival of our Dad. 'He's here now, you little bugger. You're going to be in for it.'

Ada sits next to me and kicks me under the table when she realises she's got off scot-free. Our Mam doesn't tell. She has to be provoked beyond endurance before she reveals to Dad the criminal charges accumulated in his absence. The threat of disclosure hangs over our heads like the Sword of Damocles, for we can never tell how he will react when Mam lays charges, which on rare occasions she does. I swear to God she is like a platoon sergeant at times, our never knowing how she'll react. Sometimes Dad lets fly, like the time he chases Jack up the street with a knotted scarf because Jack has been doing the same thing to girls on the way home from school. The experience terrifies Jack and he never chases girls again; not with a knotted scarf anyway. Yet Dad has a soft spot for his little 'heathens' as he calls us in deference to Father O'Connor or some other priest sent to visit us every Friday night.

It often happens that the more heinous the offence the more our Dad gives comfort. As our Ada seems more bent on a life of felonious activity than any of us, she comes in for an extra measure of his attention. 'Come here, you little devil,' he'll say to her after she's been charged with yet more wrongdoing by our Mam. 'I don't know what the hell I'm going to do with you.'

She'll climb on to his knee by the glowing fire and fling her skinny arms about his neck and bury her head in his shoulder. I know what she loves about him. He has that delicious smell of coke and the fiery furnaces of the gasworks. He never tells Ada to be a better girl or to mend her ways, nor does he exact promises that she'll not tell any more lies. That would be like extracting a promise from Napoleon not to make war and he knows it.

'She's Annie Hopwood to a T,' Mam says. Annie Hopwood is a great aunt on our Dad's side, renowned for her improprieties and, therefore, the most interesting of our relatives.

'Hold your tongue, Maggie,' says our Dad. 'Annie's been a good friend to us.'

'That girl will be the death of me yet,' says Mam, and she gives Ada May a withering look. 'I knew the day she was born she spelled trouble. Didn't I get ten stitches for her? She's been nothing but a bloody troublemaker from the word go.' She is always on about her stitches.

'How many stitches did you get for me, Mam?' Fred asks.

'Is that what you mean by "you 'ave me in stitches", Mam?' Mary asks.

'Don't be so bloody cheeky,' says Dad at the same time that Mam snaps back at Fred.

'Seven, Mister Know-It-All.'

Fred is not much of a model to go by when it comes to telling the truth. As for Mam's stitches, neither he nor any of us have the faintest idea what she is referring to. As far as sex and procreation are concerned, we live in a world of innuendo and allusions.

'That's enough of that, Maggie,' says Dad. 'They'll learn soon enough without your instruction.'

'W ... what's Mum on about, Dad?' asks Jack with a touch of Gaffer's stutter.

'Never you mind, Mr Nosey Parker. It's the sweet mystery of life that will come to you quicker than you think,' says Dad.

We get on with the meal of roast beef cut from the bone, Yorkshire pudding, potatoes, Brussels sprouts and thick brown gravy, with Ada's theft of pudding not mentioned, but not forgotten either. The deed is, in Mam's mind, added to Ada's crime sheet. A few days later, she puts herself firmly in the rogue's gallery alongside our great aunt Annie Hopwood.

She goes to play with friends in Paddy's Meadow and public park at the foot of Crane Hill. The River Nene flows through the meadow. At one end stands an iron railing enclosing a children's playground with swings, a roundabout, two ancient slides and a couple of seesaws. The river, dammed to create an open-air swimming pool, forms one boundary to the park. St Andrews Road leading to and from Castle Station on the main railway line to London forms the other. Footpaths thread among a grove of willow, elm and plane trees lining the river bank. The meadow separates the trees and the road. In the spring, lush grass springs to life, but public use the summer long has worn it thin and brown. Residents of the area walk their dogs, which foul the grass with their droppings, so those using the park need to be careful where they tread.

With the girls she hangs around with – Doreen and Iris Dicker, Flora Colby, Betty Bills, and Joyce Scroggs – Ada May is set for an evening of fun.

'Let's play tip-the-wicket,' says Doreen.

'We're always tipping the wicket,' says Joyce Scroggs. 'Why do we always have to play stupid boys' games?'

'What about hide and seek?'

'That's a sissy's game. Besides, we always play that at home,' says Joyce whose father owns the Welcome Inn Public House across the road from our house. With her higher social position, Joyce assumes she has leave to turn up her nose at whatever lacks appeal.

'I know. Why don't we play taste?' says Ada.

Taste involves sampling sweets with eyes closed and guessing what has been put in the taster's mouth: Bridy's homemade toffee, aniseed balls, liquorice nibbles, mints, and gob stoppers. Ada needs money to buy sweets to play taste, but lack of funds never deters her from suggesting games that only the rich can afford. She gets her way and everyone agrees to buy sweets.

'Can you lend me tuppence, Joyce?' Ada asks.

'Who d'you take me for? Lady Muck or something? Get your own.'

'Go on. You can lend me a measly tuppence.'

'No I can't and shan't,' says Joyce, who runs off laughing and jingling her pocket money to annoy.

'I'll get you for that,' Ada shouts. She nurses a grudge easily and is particular about repaying any considered slight.

Neither Flora Colby nor Betty Bills has money to spare and Ada knows it. Florry's father is out of work; Betty's mother has three children to look after and no husband. Joyce Scroggs returns to the group, her meanness forgotten.

'Come with me, Ada. I'll give you some of mine,' says Doreen.

'You're ever such a good friend, Doreen. Thanks. I won't forget you.'

A short time later they move under a willow tree and the play begins.

'Open your mouth and close your eyes, then you'll be in for a big surprise,' says Betty Bills to Florry Colby. Florry obeys. Something is placed on her tongue and she tries to guess what it is without closing her mouth.

'Mint!' she says. Because she's guessed correctly there is no forfeit to pay. 'I smelt it,' she says, opening her eyes.

The trick is to guess what's there without first tasting. The game carries on until it is Ada's turn to close her eyes and stick out her tongue. She feels something placed there, near the back, but can't tell what it is by feel or smell.

'I give up,' she says through her open mouth.

'Taste, then,' says Joyce Scroggs.

With a flick of her tongue, she gets the lump between her back teeth and crunches a piece of coke.

Coughing and spitting the grit from her mouth, she is furious that the others should think it funny enough to laugh themselves silly. 'You filthy pig!' she yells through tears of anger.

'That's what you get for saying you'll get me,' Joyce says and she hoots with laughter.

But Ada May never suffers humiliation easily. It is bad enough that Doreen and Iris have laughed, but they at least deserve forgiveness for sharing their money. Joyce Scroggs is the one to be dealt with or Ada will never hear the last of it. She wanders away on her own, searching for a way to get even. She finds what she's looking for and returns to the group, her face wreathed in smiles and forgiveness.

The sun is going down. It's time to go home, but being late is not something Ada loses sleep over.

'You orright, Ada?' says Doreen.

'Course I'm orright,' she says. 'I don't let little things like that worry me. Joyce didn't mean no harm, did you, Joyce?'

Joyce smirks. 'Course not, silly. It's all in good fun.'

Joyce then obeys the summons to 'Open your mouth and close your eyes, then you'll be in for a nice surprise.'

Holding a stick, Ada gives it a sharp flick and sends a lump of dog shit flying to the back of her victim's throat. Not waiting to see the result of her handiwork, she turns on her heels and takes flight. Dodging among the trees and into the open meadow, she speeds homeward, crosses at the traffic lights and all the way up Crane Hill to the house. She heard the howl the moment she took off at a stretch gallop and stops only when she reaches the house.

Gasping for breath and trying to calm a thumping heart, she waits before going indoors, looking downhill to check if there's anyone in sight. No, the coast is clear. She takes a couple of deep breaths and gingerly opens the front door. She knows that if she goes into the kitchen panting Mam will know that she's been up to no good.

Ada's next aim is to get to bed without being seen so she can deny that she was ever in Paddy's Meadow with Doreen, Betty Bills and the rest. She can imagine Joyce Scroggs by the river, doubled over, gagging and coughing and spluttering. Serves her jolly well right.

'Hello! Who's that?' says Mam. No move in the house escapes her notice. She's sitting by the fire darning socks, and she leans over to peer up the passageway.

'It's all right, Mam. It's only me,' says Ada.

'It is, is it? Come here. Let's have a look at you.' She can tell by the way Ada speaks that she has been running.

I'm at the table sorting my stamps. Abandoning pretence and stealth, she hangs her coat on a peg in the passageway, and pops her head around the door frame.

'I'm just going up to bed, Mam,' she says.

'Oh! are you? And what have you been up to?'

'Nothing, Mam. I've been playing along Upper Harding Street. I knew it was getting late so I though I'd better come home.'

Mother looks up at her. 'That's a likely tale. Come on out with it, my girl. You've got a guilty look on your face. I know you've been up to something.'

'I haven't, Mam, honest I haven't.'

'Honest? You don't know the meaning of the word.' From the way she peers over her glasses I know she doesn't believe a word of what Ada has just said. She has this uncanny sense of understanding when one of us has been up to something and has no difficulty seeing guilt on a face.

'Yes I do, our Mam. It's what you are, isn't it? I got mine from you.'

'Don't give me your lip, my girl. Get up them stairs to Bedfordshire or I'll tan your hide for you.' With that, Mam goes back to her darning.

With a grimace and cheeky wink to me, Ada ducks her head away from the door and goes upstairs to undress and climb into the bed. I think no more of it and carry on sorting my stamps under the gaslight while Mam pokes the fire and settles back to her work. Dad's on late shift, the youngest ones are in bed. We two are alone.

Half an hour or more later a sharp knock on the front door brings us both alert. A caller at that time of night is unusual. It can't be one of the family because the door is unlocked and they would come straight in. Our front door is never locked, even when everyone is asleep.

'Who's that come knocking this time of night?' says our Mam, peering at me over her spectacles. 'Go and see who it is, lovey.'

I open the door to be confronted by a huge policeman with a bushy moustache and beet-red cheeks.

''Ello, sonny. Anyone at 'ome?' the constable asks in a strong Northampton accent.

'Mam!' I call. 'It's the police.'

'Oh, my God!' I hear Mam say. Moments later, she's at the front door, her face creased in alarm.

'Are you Mrs Fulthorpe, madam?'

'Yes! Yes, I am. Is there something wrong, Constable?'

She is flustered. The police only call in The Boroughs when there's trouble and this could be serious: one of the siblings in emergency, an accident at the gasworks; a complaining neighbour.

'Can I come in a moment, madam?'

'By all means, Constable. Do come in. My son is just going to bed, aren't you, son?' It's an obvious hint to leave her alone with the constable. Leaning heavily against the wall, staging her best Lady Macbeth appearance by clutching a hand to her thumping heart, she adds, 'Have you come to tell me my husband's had an accident?'

'No, madam. Just an enquiry, madam.' He detaches the chin strap of his helmet from his chin and pushes his helmet from his forehead to balance on his head before reaching into his breast pocket for his notebook.

'That's all right, then,' says Mam, making a remarkable recovery. Knowing that the constable isn't the bearer of bad tidings about Dad makes her feel much better. 'What can I do for you?'

'Is this the residence of a Miss Ada May Fulthorpe, madam?'

'It is.'

'Then I should like to ask her a few questions in pursuit of certain enquiries.'

'Why? What's wrong? Has something happened? Has there been an accident?'

I now have a gut feeling that Mam knows for certain, contrary to Ada's assurance, that she has been up to something. That and the mischievous grimace Ada threw me are proof she's been up to some mischief. Dealing with

Ada May in the family is one thing; 'certain enquiries' from the police are another altogether.

Mam has the instinct of a border collie at times like this: face, eyes and ears alert for the slightest indication of what is to come.

Her face relaxes, becoming more neutral. 'Won't you come into the kitchen?' she asks in her Lady Boldwell voice. 'There's more light there.'

'I will, madam,' says the constable. He removes his helmet and follows Mam into the living room where he places his helmet on an empty chair and his notepad and pencil on the table.

'I thought I said it was time for your bed, son,' Mam repeats. 'Say goodnight and run along like a good boy.'

I want to stay, but this is adult business and Mam will have none of my inquisitiveness.

'Off you go,' she says. 'It's past your bedtime.'

'Yes, Mam. Good night!'

'Goodnight, son,' says the constable as I leave the room, but once in the darkened passage with the door only slightly ajar, I crouch at the bottom of the stairs and listen.

'One of my sons. He's a good boy. They're all good children,' Mam explains, laying it on thick.

'Yes, missus, I'm sure they are. I've got two of my own.'

'Is that so, Constable? And where do you live if I may ask?'

'Weston Favell.'

'Oh my. That is a posh district. Well, now, what can I do for you, Constable?'

'I should like to speak to Miss Ada May Fulthorpe, madam,' he says, consulting his notebook.

'I'm afraid that is out of the question,' Mam replies promptly. 'The child has been in bed for the past two hours and is fast asleep by now. Has something happened? Can I help?'

Through the crack of the partly open door, I can see the constable rubbing his chin thoughtfully. He gazes calmly at Mam, his expression neutral as though summing up Mam, just as she I'm sure is taking his measure. He says nothing for a while. A long silence follows.

'There's been a complaint, madam. A little girl ...' he consults his notes '... Joyce Scroggs, aged nine, has been admitted to the General.' He means the General Hospital.

I can't see Mam's face, but I can imagine her cocking her head quizzically as she says, 'What on earth has happened?'

'A child in Paddy's Meadow forced her to eat dirt,' he says. 'So I'd like to ask your daughter what she knows about it.'

'Dirt?' exclaims Mam, her voice rising.

'Muck! Dirt, ma'am,' he explains, as though dealing with a halfwit.

'Muck? Dirt?' Mam repeats the words. I know she is on her mettle, playing for time. She can be as quick-witted as a ferret when the occasion calls for it.

'Dog shit to be blunt. It seems that Ada May might be able to help in our enquiries—'

I don't catch the rest of what he says because Mam is suddenly convulsed in a loud choking and coughing fit, which I strongly suspect is suppressed laughter, though I can't be sure, of course. Her coughing and spluttering are awfully loud as she tries to control herself. That much would be obvious to anyone who knew her.

'Well, I'll be jiggered,' she says with great seriousness when she has regained control of herself.

'I beg your pardon, missus.'

'It's nothing. Just a thought that occurred to me.' Mam coughs again to collect herself. 'I'm very sorry,' she says, 'but the child is fast asleep and should not be disturbed at this time of night. It's past ten o'clock, Constable,' and, before he can object, she asks, 'Is the little girl all right?'

'The doctor was pumping her stomach out when I left the hospital. I think she is in good hands.'

'I'm very pleased to hear that,' says Mam emphatically. 'But what on earth induced her to take it in the first place? It seems foolish and infantile to me.'

'It was, missus, but it seems they were playing a game, a childish game of taste.'

That Mam doesn't immediately dissolve into a fit of screeching laughter tells me she is exercising the strictest self-control. She enjoys a joke when it is at someone else's expense.

'I understand your concern, Constable. First thing in the morning I will ask my little girl –and I can't for a moment imagine that she would indulge in such gross behaviour – Ada May is such a gentle child. There must be some mistake, I can only think she has been unjustly accused. I remember asking her when she came home, "Where have you been, darling?" and she said, "I've been playing in Harding Street, Mummy, and came home because it was getting dark." Those were her very words, and a more truthful child I've yet to find.'

The burly constable cocks an eyebrow and looks searchingly at Mam.

'Look, Constable, it's very late. I'll question her in the morning and bring her to the station if you think she can help.' In the same breath, she changes the subject, saying, 'Have you just come on duty? Can I get you a cup of tea?'

She certainly knows how to deal with the law.

The constable's face is one of concentration, wondering perhaps what to make of Mam. He makes a note in his notepad, then slowly raises his eyes and never, I think, have I seen an expression of such calm disbelief.

He rubs his chin ruminatively in his massive fist wondering, perhaps, how to deal with the situation. The police of our town uphold the law in their own way. Children they catch doing what they ought not to be doing get a clout across the ear or a heavy crack of the policeman's hand on the backside. The punishment administered keeps order on the streets and the people of The Boroughs accept that discipline as just and right.

'No, missus,' he says at last. 'I think I'd be getting along. I'd speak to her all the same if I were you, madam. We can't go having that sort of thing going on, can we?'

There is no answer. I suppose at this point Mam follows her own dictum of least said soonest mended, and it's not in her interest to provoke the law.

The moment he pushes his chair back, I scoot up the stairs and disturb someone on the darkened landing. I hear a fluttering, flitting movement as the shadow disappears into the girls' room. Ada May, the most truthful of sisters, must have scurried back into the bed.

I go into the darkened room and feel my way along the bed. At the head, I whisper, 'You awake, our Ada?'

There's no reply. I'm on my knees, elbows leaning on the bed. Together with the sound of breathing from Mary or Margaret further over perhaps, I feel the bed rocking as of someone convulsed in repressed sobbing.

Feeling in the darkness, I touch Ada's shoulder, which is rocking.

'Ada!' I whisper. 'Are you all right?'

The shaking gets worse and I lean over. Then I realise she isn't weeping at all – she is doubled up with laughter.

'You aren't half going to catch it in the morning, our Ada,' I say.

Her hand shoots from under the bedclothes and grips my wrist, holding it tight. 'I will if our Mam catches me,' she says with laughter.

5   No Time for Losers

IN THE SMALL hours of a cold, dark, frosty night in January 1939 Mam shakes me awake and whispers for me to get up and dress, and not to wake the others.

How she can tell in the dark which of us is which is a complete mystery, but it's just as well she can because there's no lighting upstairs. We boys have two double beds in the large room; the girls in the smaller. If we need light we use a candle stuck in its own wax in a saucer; the family plate does not include candlesticks. I sleep with Malcolm and Fred in one bed, Jack and Harry share the other.

Awake, but drugged with sleep, I slide from the warmth and grope about in the dark for my clothes at the foot of the bed where Mam set them in a neat pile last night. I dress in silence while my brothers sleep on, breathing in heavy sleep. Jack has an unmistakable snore; Harry is silent; Fred breathes solidly through his mouth; Malcolm is dreaming and mumbling to the world about it. Holding on to the bottom bed rail and feeling my way, I reach the bedroom door, step on to the landing, take hold of the handrail, and descend to the dim light coming from the living room.

In the back kitchen, I wash in the near freezing water of the cold tap by the light of a candle (we have no gaslight there either) and dry on the roller towel hanging behind the back door. Then I go into the kitchen where Mam sits waiting for me with a steaming bowl of porridge.

'You can sit in your dad's chair,' she says. 'You'll like that, won't you? Have a good helping of jam. It's damson, your favourite.' We are normally only allowed one spoonful of jam to mix with our porridge, so the invitation to help myself to the jam jar is unusual. Mam makes preserves every summer, great stone jars of them, which have to last until the following spring. That means they are doled out sparingly, so I'm not piggish at her invitation to help myself. I take a moderate spoonful and work it round and round into the bowl of porridge.

PETERBOROUGH PUBLIC LIBRARY

The mantle of the gaslight has become brittle – it is easily damaged when lighting the gas with a match. The gas mantle emits a fierce bright light, but a flake of loose material gives off a rippling sound, the only noise in the room as I eat my porridge in silence.

I have a good feeling seated in Dad's chair eating my breakfast. I catch Mam looking at me over the rim of her teacup and, seeing me looking at her, she gives me a conspiratorial wink as though what we're doing is something that we share between us. Neither of us speak. I think she looks tired and worn. Her eyes have a weary, drained look about them. But the next moment, she perks up and gives me a lovely smile.

'Eat up, my son,' she urges. 'We've got the six o'clock train to catch.'

The significance of this journey hasn't yet dawned on me. I am leaving home, but have given it little or no thought. The inattention to my situation helps me when I do remember and well enough too that I commit the detail of this last morning to remain forever indelibly etched in my memory: the chipped door frames from axles of the wheelbarrow being trundled through the house; the worn and twisted implements with which we stoke the fire; the threadbare linoleum of the passageway connected to the back kitchen; the gaslight and throb of the loose gas mantle; the rag rug on the hearth. Making rag rugs is a winter industry in our house with hours spent cutting old clothes into strips and fitting them strip by strip into washed hessian sacking. A home-made rag rug will last us about two years.

Mam startles me when she suddenly leaves the table and goes into the back kitchen. I hear her retching at the stone sink. She comes back, sits down and then goes back to the sink to retch again. Alarmed, I follow her.

'You orright, Mam?'

She waves me away. 'Yes, of course I'm all right, son. Something must've upset me. I'll be fine in a minute. Go and finish your breakfast. There's a good un.'

I do as she bids. A short time later she comes into the room rubbing her face with a towel and smiling, but she doesn't look at all well to me. With forced cheerfulness, she says she's feeling much better – it was just a funny turn, she says. She asks if I'd like any more to eat.

No, I'm full, I tell her.

'In that case I think we'd best be getting along or we'll miss the train. Good gracious!' she says, looking at the clock. 'We are going to be late. Come along. Don't forget your parcel.'

She has baked a cake and made up a parcel of things she knows I like. She hurries into the passage to put on her hat and coat, then comes back into the kitchen to extinguish the gaslight after picking up her handbag and gloves from the kitchen table. Speaking to herself, she says, 'Now, I haven't forgotten anything, have I? Come along then.'

We leave the house and take the Lower Harding Street route to Castle Station, the same route Dad takes to go to the gasworks. There's not a soul in sight. The Boroughs could well be deserted. It's a cold walk and although I have no topcoat, Jack has loaned me his scarf on condition Mam returns it to him. We walk slowly on account of Mam's varicose veins. Crossing Scarletwell Street, a dark figure steps from the shadows of the Crispin's Arms pub and startles the life out of me. The figure shines a light. He's a policeman.

'It's all right, missus,' he says. 'My mate's near the Jolly Tanner. He'll be expecting you.' Mam thanks him and we go on our way.

That's the thing about The Boroughs. You are as safe as houses walking through its dingy ill-lit streets, especially if you tell the constable on the beat the night before to expect you. He will pass the word on, which means the next constable will look out for you. Mam has spoken to the constable on the evening beat, which explains the appearance of the policemen along the way. The system works well throughout the town with constables on their beats. We make slow progress along Scarletwell to Lower

Cross Street, then turn left at Chalk Lane to get to Black
Lion Hill, our passage marked by the public houses en
route: the Riveter's Arms, Sportsman's Arms, Baker's
Arms. At last we reached the Jolly Tanner.

'Good morning, missus,' says the next constable who is
standing in the doorway of the pub, his thumbs hooked into
his breast pockets with his battery lantern clipped to his
belt. 'It's a cold night.'

'It is an' all, Constable,' says Mam.

'You'll be all right to the station, missus.'

'Thank you, Constable. It's a comfort to know there's
someone around.'

'Ah! There's not much happens around here that
escapes us, missus.'

Mam holds my hand while we wait on the platform for
the early morning 'workman's train' to London. Her hands
are always warm and soft.

'Look after your money,' she says, 'and make sure you
write every week, d'you hear?'

I have two shillings, a sixpence and tuppence halfpenny
in my pocket. Humming to herself, she walks me up and
down the platform until the train stops at the platform,
waiting for its six o'clock departure. Steam billowing from
the engine hangs low on the platform, forming a patch of
fog beyond the subdued lights of the platform.

We find an empty compartment in the carriage next to
the engine and settle on opposite sides with window seats.
As soon as the train begins pulling out of the station Mam
stands up and fiddles with the leather strap of the window
to lower it to its full extent. 'Here! Let's see if your Dad's
come to see us off,' she says, peering into the gloom. A
short distance from the station, a spur line connects the
main train with the gasworks. As we near the spur line,
Mam says, 'Here! Be quick. Your Dad's here. Change
places or you'll miss him.'

We change places and I catch sight of Dad close to the
track. He waves his hat at me and shouts something that
may be: 'Good luck, my son. Good luck.' He shouts
something else, but the noise of the wheels grinding over

the points drown out his voice. The sight of Dad, lit by the lights of the passing carriages flashing on his head and body is another image that remains with me. I wave back long after he's disappeared from view.

I have a strange feeling of longing; not sadness or pining at leaving home, simply a wistfulness as it dawns on me I am leaving. I sit down again and Mam closes the window. My parents must have arranged the meeting before Dad went to work on the graveyard shift last night. He finishes the night shift about six o'clock in the morning, so he must have gone through the spur gate to catch the London train leaving the station.

The journey to London is long because the train stops at every station as far as Watford Junction to pick up workmen carrying their enamel teapots and packed lunches. By the time we pull into Euston Station, the carriage is filled to capacity, the air thick with tobacco smoke. Mam drops the window part way to get fresh air into the carriage and a stroppy workman closes it again, but Mam wouldn't have any of that nonsense. She promptly opens the window again, saying to the full carriage in her Lady Boldwell voice, 'We'll have some fresh air if you please. My little boy needs it.'

'Quite right, too, madam,' says one worker who is not a smoker.

We cross London on the Circle Line of the Underground to Victoria Station and there have an hour's wait for the Dover train. Arriving at Priory Station just after noon, we step into brilliant sunshine. The air has a salty sea tang like the one time we went to Skegness. As compared with that one day trip to the seaside, the journey across London to Dover is the longest in my life.

I look around and ask, 'When will we be going home, Mam?'

'Don't be silly. We've only just arrived. I haven't come all this way for nothing, so I hope you're not going to play me up.'

'I'm not playing you up.'

'Let's get on the bus, then.'

Mam is in a strange mood, alternating between mildness and severity. One moment she's chastising me for playing her up as she calls it and the next she's clasping my hand in hers to urge me to be a good boy and write often. Her mood changes don't make sense to me.

The East Kent bus drops us at the main gate of the school. Mam stands still for a while after we alight, taking her bearings and deciding what to do next, I suppose. She hums quietly to herself and spends silent moments gazing through the black iron gates to the cenotaph at a fork in the gravel road. The lush green grass of manicured lawns contrasts vividly with the red brick buildings in the distance. Behind us, on the opposite side of the road, the gorse-covered downs swoop gently away into the far distance to the white cliffs. Everywhere is fresh and green despite the cold.

After that pause to get her bearings, Mam says, 'Come along, then. We might as well get it over and done with.'

We go in through the open pedestrian gate next, crunching the gravel alongside the gatekeeper's house. We haven't gone more than a few steps on to the property before the porter pops his head out and says, 'Hello, there! Can I help you, madam?'

'How do you do?' Mam replies in her best voice. 'I've brought my son.' She searches her handbag and extracts a letter.

'Aye! I can see that,' he says pleasantly. You can tell by his bearing and manner that he's an old soldier. He reads the letter and, having satisfied himself, points to a redbrick building in the distance opposite the church. 'You see that building, ma'am? The first on the right? That's the headquarters block. Walk right in, there'll be someone there to attend you.'

Mam thanks him and we crunch our way along the road, passing the cenotaph on our right. This massive structure of grey stone marking a fork in the road is a huge cross on which is embossed a giant black sword, its blade pointing down. We take the left hand road as directed. It stretches straight as a pikestaff into the distance, with a vast

expanse of playing fields on the left dotted with rugby and
soccer posts. The second gravel road takes a wide curve
alongside a line of red-brick and pebbledash buildings.

We tramp along – left, right, left, right – in slow time to
spare Mam's legs, which are acting up, she says. The place
is deserted with neither vehicle nor human being in sight.
Overhead, squabbling seagulls wheel and dip and screech.

'It looks ever so nice,' says Mam as we near the
building we are to enter. 'I'm sure you'll like it here.'

'I wish you wouldn't keep saying "I'm sure you'll like
it," our Mam.'

'Well, I'm sure you will. It gives me a good feeling.'

'I don't like it much.'

'Oh for goodness sake, don't be so difficult, there's a
good 'un. You don't understand.'

'Oh yes I do,' I say, 'an' I don't like it. Why can't I stay
at home like the rest? Why does it have to be me? Look
around. There's no one here, Mam. Do I get this place to
myself?'

She takes hold of my hand. 'That's enough of the
sarcasm from you, Mr Know-It-All. That always was your
failing. It'll get you into trouble one day, mark my words.
Here we are then, let's go in, and don't speak unless you're
spoken to, d'you hear?'

'Yes! I hear.'

'Very well then.'

A towering figure in khaki with a waxed moustache
with pointed ends emerges as we are about to enter and
turns to escort us inside. He tells me to wait in the foyer
area while he takes Mam along the corridor and disappears
into an office. After what seems an age, he returns with her
and escorts us down a side road, across a parade square and
into a large building with a clock tower soaring above it. We
have entered a baronial dining hall.

'You'll be all right here, our Arthur,' Mam says, giving
me a hug. 'I have to run an errand, so you can give us a
kiss.'

I do as she bids. She smiles, crosses herself, whispering as she does so, 'Holy mother, take care of ...' I don't catch the rest.

Mam doesn't say she's leaving and not coming back or anything so deceitful. Oh no! Instead it's 'I have to run an errand, so you can give us a kiss.' After crossing herself and whispering a prayer, she leaves humming a popular song with words that go something like, 'It's love makes the world go round.'

There are no histrionics at our parting, no tears, no sloppy or mushy or endearing words. She has pressed a half-a-crown into my hand and given me the parcel of cake and other things she said I would like. With the money already in my pocket, the half crown is more money than I've had in my life.

I should have remembered that Mam only hums when she's agitated, but I don't. I might even have believed that she really is running an errand and will be back, but I'm not anxious at her departure. She leaves and that's that. I am now on my own.

The hall in which I now found myself has flying arches of black timber like those sometimes seen in old wooden churches. Polished oak panels on the walls bear the names in gilt letters of those who have distinguished themselves in sports or won trophies for positions of prestige in one skill or another. A large oil painting of boys in red serge hangs above the double doors at one end of the building. On another wall there's an equally large painting of an imposing figure resplendent in the red uniform of a general. Halfway along one side of the hall, a gleaming eagle lectern flanked by two First World War Lewis guns stands on a red-carpeted dais. I wander along to inspect the guns and am busy holding the trigger guards and peering along the barrel of one when a deep voice startles me from my reverie.

'Come along there, boy. Let's see if we can make a soldier of you.' The owner of the voice, an overweight sergeant major, has appeared from nowhere and is bearing down on me.

He leads me from the hall and on to the road. He seems very old for a serving soldier. He has short, grey hair under a peaked khaki cap with a highly polished chin strap; his cheeks are ruddy, his nose red and bulbous; he too, like the first soldier we met earlier, has a waxed moustache – completely grey with the ends twisted into spikes.

'I'm Sergeant Major Johnson, son,' he says as we walk side by side along the road. 'Here's my advice to you. Keep your nose clean. It's the best way to get on, here or in the army!'

I rub my nose, thinking he means that it's running.

'I don't mean that. Just keep out of trouble and you'll make old bones, boy. What's your Father's regiment?'

'The Northamptonshire Regiment, sir.'

'Ah! The Steelbacks, the 48th of foot. Do you know how they got that name?'

'No, sir. I don't.'

'They had a colonel who had them lashed with the cat o' nine tails as soon as look at them, he did. They say you needed a steel back to serve in the 48th and take that sort of punishment. The name Steelbacks has stuck like blood and mud from that day to this.'

'Yes sir,' I say and walk alongside him in silence. We pass a number of red-brick buildings, each with a board above its entrance: Roberts, Wolseley, Kitchener, Haig; generals famous in their day, some not so famous in history as I will later discover.

At the stores, a taciturn quartermaster tosses a kitbag over the counter and tells me to hold it open. He roves along the storeroom shelves drawing articles and tossing them into the kitbag like someone at a fair aiming balls at a coconut stand: there are knee-length stockings, underwear, two flannel nightshirts, buckles, brushes, white belt, handkerchiefs, face flannel, towels, toothbrush, khaki shirts, an oddly shaped iron for cleaning brass buttons, a 'housewife' of cotton and needless for repairing clothes – the list seems endless. Items too big to get in the canvas bag he stacks on the counter. Then, taking my measurements, the quartermaster issues me with five uniforms: three of red, two of khaki, along with a greatcoat, peaked cap, forage cap, two pairs of boots, all far more than I'm capable of carrying. And to think that when I passed through the main gate an hour ago the only things I possessed were the clothes I was wearing.

Sergeant Major Johnson helps me carry the load from the stores and across the road to one of the red-brick H-blocks. Bearing my share of this enormous weight of new possessions, I follow in his wake. He leads me into one of dormitories where I dump my kit on to the bed to which I've been assigned.

'You can begin by putting on this and this and this,' he says, sorting out a uniform, shirt, pants and socks. Leaving me to sort things out as best I can, he leaves the room. Discarding my clothes and getting dressed in the suit of rough khaki is a new experience for me, for nothing fits. Everything is too big: underpants, short khaki trousers that fall below the knee, a collarless khaki shirt that comes to my knees, knee socks too loose, khaki jacket with its brass buttons more like a coat. While I am thus occupied sorting myself out, two boys helped by another sergeant major enter the room carrying mountainous loads of equipment.

They too are newcomers, ill at ease and awkward with one another as well as with me. We say hello after a while and exchange names. We sort out our new possessions in silence, consumed with our own thoughts. Then the same sergeant major who brought the newcomers returns to escort us to the dining hall for supper.

The newcomer assigned to the next bed to me gets talking when we are eating our meal. His name is Witney, a podgy boy. He asks me where I am from.

'Northampton,' I say, 'an' you?'

'Coventry.'

'The Leicestershires?' asks the other new boy, Podger Witney's next door neighbour.

I don't like his tone of voice; nor does Witney who says, 'So what?'

'Bloody infantry. And you, I suppose, are the Northants?'

'That's right. Another infantry regiment. And what's your dad's regiment?'

'The Blues,' he replies with a superior smirk. He means the Household Cavalry.

'Don't they clear out the stables for the infantry?' I ask.

He lunges across the table to punch me, but I move out of his reach in time. Witney laughs.

'You'll pay for that,' says Wright.

It's not an auspicious start to my first day at school: I know from that first brush that I'll have trouble with Wright. He is arrogant and, as I later gather, I am too sharp-tongued for him. He speaks with that southern English accent I have come to associate with the haughty and snobbish.

With the return of hundreds of boys from their Christmas holidays the next day my embryonic military life begins. The first month is a difficult period of adjustment. I am still mystified about the nature of this school to which Mam and Dad have sent me. Is it in fact a school at all or am I now in the army? Mam told me nothing about it on the train journey to Dover, nor have my parents prepared me for this apocalyptic change in my life.

Not surprisingly, in the first few weeks I am intensely homesick. As the days wear on, I begin to grasp that this is no ordinary school but a military school originally intended for the orphaned and needy children of rank and file soldiers, introduced as an incentive to militia soldiers to enlist in the regular army. Its full name is the Duke of York's Royal Military School, though everyone just calls it Duke of York's. Apparently at one time, back in the 1870s, children as young as six were admitted and earlier still in the 1830s the Army even ran an Infant Branch in which the youngest was six months old. So it isn't so surprising that a lad of my age – I'm just a few months away from my tenth birthday in April – would be sent here.

Even so, I feel intensely lonely and miss my home and my family. Being a new boy and a junior, I feel alienated from all but Witney with whom I have struck up a friendship. The antipathy between Wright and myself is mutual and it grows. We learn to keep our distance from one another, he drawing strength from the presence of his older brother in the next dormitory.

For the first few weeks, we of the new intake are taught how to march and dress and salute before being permitted to take our places in the ranks of our companies. Gradually, we assimilate with the crowd.

Daily, the more than six hundred boys who make up the school population parade, drill, practise saluting and follow their trades. We are assigned to trades and occupations according to our companies: tailoring, cobbling, signalling, gunnery or, in the case of my company, are given a musical instrument to learn. When not in the classroom, we clean our equipment, play sports, run a weekly marathon, box and practise for the annual trooping of the colours, which is the highlight of the school year. Life is full and we are rarely idle. The sergeant majors, schoolteachers and sergeant prefects keep us occupied from early morning until the final 'prayer' parade before we tumble into bed, when we kneel by our beds to pray at the command of a boy corporal. Our lives are ordered if not orderly. Only on a Saturday and Sunday afternoon are we given walking-out passes. For this privilege we have to pass the duty prefect sergeant's inspection.

A month after I arrive, Boy Wright moves to another dormitory of which his elder brother is a sergeant prefect. But two days before the Easter break the animosity between us comes to a head. I am one of a dozen boys talking, playing draughts, polishing boots and darning socks in the common room. In Podger Witney's company I concentrate on boning my boots, as we call it, to a high shine. Wright rushes into the day room, chased by someone and, not watching where he is going, collides into me, which sends me flying for six across the floor.

'Idiot!' he yells. 'Why don't you watch yourself?'

'That's why,' I shout, and fling my boot at him which strikes him on the head. He staggers back, shaking his head and looking at me in astonishment. The room has gone deathly quiet. Then, with a roar of fury, Wright comes at me like a bull.

It is an unequal contest from the start. He is heavier than me and taller. Even so, I play by my rules by thumping him with my other boot. Our Dad says that if you have to fight, make sure you strike the first blow.

'Foul!' some onlookers shout. 'Foul! Foul!'

I don't care. I have had a good instructor in my sister Mary and I lash out for all I'm worth.

The uproar brings a crowd running. Within seconds, a ring forms and shouts of encouragement to fight to the finish ring out. My opponent circles, comes in punching with his head down, and ducks out of the way. Inspired, perhaps, by my tactic of using a weapon instead of fighting cleanly with my fists, Wright uses his superior weight and a leg hooked behind mine to topple me on to the floor. Having got me down, he sits astride my stomach and pummels away. I'm getting the worst of it, no doubt about that: face, chest, shoulders. The blows rain down and I strike back wildly. Then stronger hands pull us apart and yank us to our feet.

'If you want to fight, you devils, it'll be in the boxing ring, not here. The rest of you, clear off! Go on. Clear off I tell you.'

Sergeant Major Johnson, who lives with his family in the wing of the H-block, has been attracted from his quarters by the noise and promptly pushes through the crowd gathered about and pulls us apart.

Cut by my own teeth from a blow on the mouth, I have lots of blood. My ears ring, my head pounds. I am breathing heavily. So is Wright, who has a large bump on the side of his head from my boot, so he hasn't had it all his own way.

'I don't want to know what you're fighting about and I don't care,' says the Sergeant Major. 'Now you'll shake hands, d'you hear? Go back to your rooms and report to the gym tomorrow at three o'clock and settle this in the ring with boxing gloves. That's an order. Now be off with you.' He clouts first Wright about the head and then me to help us on our way. We glower at one another, but dare not renew the fight.

Two days later, the school breaks up for Easter leave, so I still have the remnants of a cut lip and black eye. I get a good reception, but Mam has to hold my face to inspect my bruised eye.

'You've been in the wars, I see,' she says.

'Yes, I have a bit.'

'Got the worst of it, did you?'

'Perhaps. Maybe. I don't know.'

'Serves you bloody well right,' she says, taking it from my answer that I've come off second best. 'Next time make sure you come out on top.'

Our Mam has no sympathy for losers.

6   The Sour Taste of Mystery

WRIGHT AND I have our bout in the ring some time
after we return from Easter leave. There's nothing
unusual about the delay. We head to the gym the
day after our fight, but the match is postponed because the
physical training sergeant major has lots of differences like
ours to arrange. He holds boxing matches monthly with the
whole school in attendance, which means that bouts such
as ours take on the mantle of gladiatorial combat before a
roaring crowd in the Roman Coliseum. The use of boxing
gloves means there's little chance of anyone suffering
serious injury from an opponent, so boxing is counted a
spectacular sport for the spectators to see differences settled
in the ring.

Our fight is inconclusive, but it means we both come
out of the ring unscathed. I don't mention the scrap in my
weekly letters home, as I could do without Mum's
reproach. (I no longer called her Mam – something I've
learned at school is that Mam is not a good word among
the more well-spoken boys of Wright's upbringing.)
Besides, battling with my foe is the least onerous of the
trials to be endured. We new boys have to endure more
serious tribulations, and to suffer them in silence.

The practice of humiliating new boys is common
throughout the school. Ours being an institution with a
strong military ethos, new boys are subjected to a military
trial that takes place late at night under the glare of a single
electric light shone in the victim's face. Strange voices
behind the blinding light demand to be given details of the
boy's father's military career – his regiment, rank, service,
campaigns fought, the regiment's history, battle honours,
overseas service. The questions are endless, the punishment
awarded both inevitable and inescapable.

Podger Witney, seated on an upturned laundry basket
and condemned to the 'electric chair', has a darning needle
thrust up his backside by a boy concealed underneath. The

shock and howl of pain he suffers gives those hidden by the light and witnesses about the room vast amusement, but they have reckoned without Podger's fury. Screaming bloody murder, he lashes out at his hidden tormentors with a buckled belt wrapped around his fist and cracks a couple of heads, which no one considers sporting. His reaction, all the same, is enough to make the rest of the dormitory steer clear of him from this time on.

He also endears himself to me for I have undergone my third degree and punishment without fierce reaction. I am merely 'condemned to the dungeons', which means having the blanket on which I stand for questioning whipped from under my feet by unseen hands. Tumbling over backwards, I bump my head on the floor, which knocks me senseless for a while. Later, on leave, describing the experience to Jack and Harry, they say that explains why I appear weird to them. Still, I know it wouldn't have happened had they been there.

Life in the dormitory can be hell at times and as noisy as Bedlam when boys, NCOs and more senior boys are at night school. As noisy as it is, order is restored at our last parade of the day when, for evening prayers, we stand in our nightshirts at the foot of our beds and, at the sergeant prefect's command, fall to our knees and pray. During this obligatory two minutes of silence, we – if the others are like me – vanquish our enemies, win the next marathon, speculate on how we'd conduct ourselves from promotion to promotion when we join our father's regiment to become its commanding officer, our having been taught nothing is beyond us. Other than this compulsory two minutes of silence, the noise is unceasing. Even after the duty bugler plays The Last Post, which is our signal for 'lights out', the noise continues unabated until the last mouthy boy has laughed himself to sleep from the wit of his own jokes.

It is the brooding silence of the night that brings the more sinister trial of endurance of which, in the light of day, we either may not or dare not speak. My own Satan, for I regard him as the cause of my despair, comes in the shape of Corporal Miles, a tough, blond-haired fifteen-year-old, who has the next bed on my left and many a night slips into my bed to lie with me.

The first time he does this he puts his finger to my lips in the dark to signify absolute silence and I obey, for I am terrified beyond belief. I have spent my whole life sleeping alongside my brothers and sometimes my sisters when we were young, but having another boy in bed with me is an odd, uncomfortable and bewildering experience.

But it gets worse, and from this night onwards Corporal Miles comes to represent the epitome of evil for me. This time, when he climbs into my bed, he begins to run his hands slowly over my body until I can feel his penis hardening. I am frozen in terror, sweating clammily, but unable to move as he is now clutching my body in a vicelike grip. Then, to my horror and undying shame, I stifle a scream as he roughly penetrates me from behind, thrusting into me again and again. Finally I hear a muffled sigh. I lie inert, not daring to move or make a sound, although I am now suffering waves of intense pain.

Who can I tell? Miles is years my senior, a corporal as well, so who will believe me? I lie awake for hours after he leaves my bed, getting angrier and angrier. I listen to the quarter hour chimes of the tower clock announcing the mournful passing of the night. Damn that clock, I tell myself, lying there in the dark. Why can't they shut it up and let us get to sleep?

Somehow I manage to put this terrible experience to the back of my mind – maybe for the sake of my sanity. Instead I focus my rage on the chiming of the tower clock. The idea of stopping the chiming comes as a revelation one Saturday afternoon walking back to school with Witney. We have been to Dover Castle where we've rolled a couple of cannon balls over the cliff for a lark. Our behaviour is downright dangerous considering that people are wandering along the beach below. A kick in the backside would have done us the world of good, but as we aren't caught the possibility of hurting someone below doesn't occur to us. We amble back to school over the Downs; the gorse is in full bloom, a mass of yellow. With sticks, we swipe at bees sucking the nectar and running and yelping like fools in fear of being stung, for the gorse is alive with bees.

The clock strikes five, which means we have half an hour to get back for supper. That's when a thought occurs to me.

'D'you hear the clock strike, Witney?'

'Of course I hear it. D'you think I'm deaf?'

'Well, I'm going to stop it.'

'Stop it what?' he says.

'Stop it chiming?'

'Why do you want to do that? It's done you no harm.'

'It keeps me awake at night.' I don't dare discuss my reason yet, although the possibility of a companion in bed barely four feet away not hearing suspicious movements and noises in the next bed never occurs to me.

'You're daft,' he says, 'just daft. You wouldn't know how anyway. What d'you know about clocks? Go on, tell me, what d'you know?'

'Course I do. I was in the choir back home. The choirmaster used to take us up the clock tower. He looked after the clock and told us how it worked. It's ever so easy and simple when you know how.'

'Go on with you,' says Witney. 'You wouldn't have the nerve.'

'I would. Just wait and see.'

See he does, or rather he guesses before anyone else knows because, a few nights later, I slip out of bed, tuck my nightshirt into my blue gym shorts and put on my running shoes. Corporal Miles has left me alone tonight but I still can't sleep. I'm too wound up. Witney is asleep, I am sure because I tap him on the shoulder to let him know I'm going as promised. He doesn't move. The 11.30 chime has struck, so there's no time to waste.

The moon is playing hide and seek among the scudding clouds, casting a ghostly light on the company blocks. Prickles go up and down my spine. Dodging from shadow to shadow, I'm in a highly nervous state. An age passes before I reach the clock tower and gingerly try the door. It opens so I slip inside, closing the door behind me and stand there in the gloom half wishing I'd found the door locked.

Tales of ghosts in the clock tower, apparitions, spectres and phantoms are in circulation to put the wind up the younger boys. Peering up the dimly lit stairwell, I brace myself for the long climb and am a good way up when the three-quarter chime strikes like thunder, filling the still, damp air like the hammers of doom. Rooted to the spot, I clamp my hands over my ears to stop the vibrations and wait until it comes to an end. I know I can't go back now. If Podger has told anyone what I have planned and it becomes known that I've been to the tower and left without doing what I said I'd do I would never live it down. And so, with pounding heart, I reach the top, panting for breath.

Calm now, I concentrate on recalling what the choirmaster has told us about clock mechanisms. At the right time, a cam drops into a fluted drum and sets the chiming mechanism in motion. With a wrench from the tool rack on the wall, I loosen the securing bolt of the drum I've selected and work it along the shaft and away from the peg poised for the next chime. That done, I put the wrench back on its rests and scurry down the stairs as fast as my legs can carry me.

Opening the tower door, I peer into the night to see if the coast is clear: not a soul is in sight. I make my exit, close the door and run for my life, flitting from shadow to shadow back the same way I've come. Back in bed, unseen and undetected, I pull the blankets over my head and curl up in a tight ball.

On muster parade the next morning, our Regimental Sergeant Major, late of the Grenadier Guards, forms all eight companies into a hollow square and faces the assembly with his back to the band who fill the open side of the square some distance away. The RSM – or Whacker Black as he is known – so named because he delivers with a six-feet long cane any corporal punishment the Commandant orders – is clearly hopping mad.

'Pay attention!' he thunders. Eight companies of khaki-clad boys under command of their company sergeants major prick up their ears.

'Someone among you who is listening to me right now ...' – the RSM pauses to let his words sink in – 'someone has been mucking around with the tower clock. I know who it is and I want that snivelling little wretch to step out here immediately.'

In his right hand, the RSM carries a pacing stick, an instrument with a hinge at the end. It opens like a compass for measuring distances on maps, except that the RSM uses his to measure the rate at which we march. On a route march with the band leading the way, the RSM marches with his pacing stick much to the irritation of the Bandmaster, who maintains that the band knows how to set the pace. The RSM waves his stick at his command for the culprit to step forward.

Being a clarinet-playing member of the band, I have a good view of the RSM's performance and listen with apprehension to his description of the wretched guilty party.

It's so happened, much to my dismay I should add, that instead of silencing the clock chimes I have caused the mechanism to chime the full midnight chime every fifteen minutes throughout the night. By the early hours of the morning, awakened by the persistent chimes, most everyone is awake in his bed. I hadn't banked on that happening, but it explains why the RSM is in such a fine fury.

Whacker flays about with his pacing stick like an infuriated Zulu on the warpath.

'If the culprit doesn't step forward this minute, not a single boy will leave these premises,' he hollers. 'Do you hear? Do you hear, I say?'

In the ranks of the band, boys look at one another in bewilderment and I try to look as surprised as anyone else. Witney, with the cornet section, turns and looks at me with wide-open eyes as much as to say, 'Blimey! I don't believe it, but you did it, eh?'

I grip my clarinet tightly, as much for self-confidence as fear for what I've done, and gaze rigidly ahead.

'Stop moving in the ranks,' hisses the Bandmaster.

The Bandmaster has a running feud with the RSM over that pacing stick, for the band set the marching pace, so he wants no criticism for not keeping the band under control. The RSM's opinion that we are a shower of halfwits is widely known, but I for one do not appreciate being described as snivelling. In the silence that follows Whacker's awful threat, I decide to give myself up and step from the file. I march towards the RSM, resigned to whatever fate has in store for me.

'Where the hell d'you think you're going, Fulthorpe?' the Bandmaster roars.

I stop. 'It was me, sir,' I say.

'Good grief! You?'

'Yes, sir.'

'May the Lord have mercy on you, Fulthorpe. Proceed to your doom, boy!'

With that for a benediction, the Bandmaster turns his back in a gesture of resignation and walks away. There's no point in his trying to soften whatever blow is in store for me.

The click! clack! click! of my studded boots on the asphalt sounds unnaturally loud as I march towards the RSM. I hold my clarinet by my side, parallel to the ground in the approved manner for marching when not playing, and affect a smart halt when I reach him.

The RSM has his back to me. He stands unmoved. The parade maintain an utter silence. In his own good time he turns and, for a fraction of a second, looks over my head. Perhaps he has expected a taller boy to be standing before him. When he looks down, I peer up at him and, from my vantage point, see half hidden by his waxed moustache, his nostrils as distant caves, black and cavernous.

He emits a strangled bellow: '*Whaaagh!*' and a shower of spit sprays my face.

In a small voice, I say, 'It was me, sir.'

'And who's *me sir*?'

'Fulthorpe, sir. Boy Fulthorpe, K 51, G Company, sir.'

'Mr Finn! Mr Finn! Get out here immediately,' he shouts to the distant figure of B Company's sergeant major.

'Yes, sir!' Paddy Finn answers.

'Give me two escorts, at the double, Mr Finn.'

Mr Finn turns back, detaches two boy NCOs from his company and sends them forward. I am taken into custody by being marched off the parade square to the headquarters building. At nine o'clock, the RSM marches me before the Commandant and in his presence I stand bareheaded, dishonoured and in disgrace while Whacker Black reads out the charge sheet.

'Boy Fulthorpe, K 51 of G Company, sar, is charged under Section 252 of the Army Act in that, prejudicial to the good order of military discipline he did, on the night of June 7th, unlawfully enter the clock tower and vandalise the regimental clock, sar!'

The Colonel, seated behind his glass-topped desk, gazes at me with a quizzical expression. His gleaming desk, a barren expanse of polished mahogany, is bare except for a marble base pen and ink stand at his right hand. I'm tall enough, but only just, to see the reflection of the Commandant's greying head and shoulders in the shiny surface of the desk. The sight of the mirror image of the Colonel seated at his desk is somehow mesmerising.

'Well, boy. What have you to say for yourself, eh?'

The Colonel, a fine gentleman with a ruddy complexion and a white, brush moustache, strikes me as having a kind and agreeable countenance. His red tabs remind me of General Knox. In putting his question, he cocks his head to one side and, naturally, his image in the polished surface of the table follows suit.

'Nothing, sir!' I say, looking not at him but at his reflection.

'Nothing?' He leans the other way and rests his jaw on his fist. His reflection in the desktop, in concert with his body, moves in attentive juxtaposition. It is like watching the reflection projected at the corner of a shop window when you seem to move both arms and legs off the ground. Now he's speaking again.

'Why did you do it?'

'It was the chimes, sir. They keep me awake.' I could offer no more convincing explanation on the spur of the moment.

A ghost of a smile appears on his face. He quickly subdues it. 'You didn't like the chimes, eh? Is that it? So you thought you'd vandalise the clock to make the chimes ring all night?'

He shifts his position, casting his eyes to the ceiling before looking at my Company Sergeant Major, CSM Johnson, also present and standing by my side.

Silence follows. The Commandant, late of the Royal Warwickshire Regiment, weighs the situation. I have no idea what's going through his mind, but I sense he's finding it difficult to look me in the face, for I have switched my gaze to looking directly at him. I sense he is keeping his emotions in check.

'Regimental Sergeant Major!' he says at last.

'Sar?'

'Get this child out of my sight.'

'Sar! Boy Fulthorpe! About turn! Quick march! Left-right-left-right-left-right,' the RSM bawls.

Having done an about turn, I smartly march out of the Commandant's office – left, right, left, right – and into the main hall where I halt at the RSM's command and replace my cap. Behind me, I hear a quiet 'humph' of laughter. Whacker Black is not as indulgent.

'I'll remember you, Fulthorpe,' he says. 'Let me catch you here again and you'll wish you'd never been born. D'you know what that means?'

'No, sir.'

'The high jump, boy, the high jump. Now, be off with you. Don't let me see you here again.'

By eleven o'clock the tower clock is back in working order, chiming its merry way, marking the passing hours of the day.

*

My brush with the authorities over, that little incident is the first but not the last of my tribulations. I don't need to be told that I've been singled out as a troublemaker and that I'll have to watch my step in future.

'I see you've been in trouble,' says Mum reading my Guardian's Report the next time I'm on leave.

'What trouble, Mum?'

'Don't give me that,' she says, cuffing me one. 'What's this here? Conduct – questionable. Could do better. Needs discipline.'

'They always say that,' I say, mounting a quick defence. 'But you know what you've always said, don't you, Mum?'

'What's that?'

'Don't get caught.'

'You cheeky devil,' she says with grudging approval. 'Then we'll hear what your father has to say when he reads this.'

7   Uncle Bill from Hopping Hill

OUR UNCLE BILL CRAFT married Dad's sister Ada – our Aunt Ada that is after whom Ada May has been named. Aunt Ada was engaged during the First World War but her fiancé was killed in the trenches of the Western Front. Everyone who knew her was shocked to learn that within six months of her betrothed's death she married Bill Craft. The shock was not so much because she had defied convention to wait for a year, as for the political views of the man she married.

When he married Aunt Ada, Bill was a pariah, an outcast from the community on account of his standing as a conscientious objector. He objected to anything to do with the war and refused to enlist when called up. Claiming conscientious objector status, he took a stand before the Review Board and went to prison for his unpatriotic views. Being outspoken in opposition to the war might be all right for academics, intellectuals and poets, but Bill Craft is none of these. He's a man of the working class, which is not to say he is uneducated and hence, as one might say, ignorant. On the contrary, he has been a lifelong member of a society with strong left wing political views.

It is possible that the death of her fiancé so turned Aunt Ada against the war that she clung to Bill as a survivor clings to the wreckage in a disaster as sea. This is speculation, of course, for I don't know anything about her circumstances other than hearsay and even that, coming from Mum, has to be highly suspect. But Bill and Ada Craft seem a happy, contented couple to me. They always make us welcome. Our Grandpa Fulthorpe welcomed us too, while he was alive, although he was short on conversation. It was to Aunt Ada that he had moved following the awful row over Ada May. Unlike Uncle Bill Craft, our grandfather was illiterate.

When asked, Uncle Bill says he's from Hopping Hill, has never worked and never will, which is quite untrue. He is a Northampton man born and bred and has never known anything but hard work. Hopping Hill, a hamlet nearby, provides him with a convenient name to work into a jingle for amusement. His humorous behaviour with children is one side of his nature. On the other and according to Mum, he exerts an undue and politically perverse influence on us Fulthorpe children.

She dismisses her brother-in-law as Craft by name and crafty by nature, for she has little time for him except when it comes to needing a favour. She allows us to visit, but questions us inquisitively when we get home. She doesn't visit the Crafts herself.

Uncle Bill is a jolly if rough-sounding companion who welcomes our company one at a time on his excursions to his smallholding a mile or so beyond Harlestone Village. One child is enough. He can't handle two. He makes his living off a smallholding of about thirty acres that includes pasture, an orchard, and intensely cultivated garden vegetables. The property includes a miscellaneous collection of ramshackle barns and stables filled to capacity with discarded implements, tools, harnesses, chains and cordage. As a market gardener, Bill works his land four days a week and, on the other two working days, Wednesdays and Saturdays, sells his produce by horse and cart in and around The Boroughs where, his past being unknown, he gets a warm welcome.

Short in stature and stolid in temperament in public, Bill has the strong calloused hands of a working man. He's got a sturdy, muscular frame too, developed over the years from intensive manual labour working his land, planting, hoeing, digging, bagging and heaving carrots, potatoes and other root vegetables. He seems impervious to the cold. Many a time as a boy, when I've been perishing cold, I've watched him cutting and loading skips of Brussels sprouts and cabbages laden with early morning ice and frost as though he were working in spring weather.

He dresses for work and comfort, not style. He secures his corduroy trousers with binding twine under the knee like a country yokel. It keeps his trouser bottoms clear of the dirt and his heavy working man's boots, which are often muddy. He wears a collarless flannel shirt with a polka-dot red handkerchief about his neck, knotted at the front. When humping sacks of root vegetables, he turns the peak of his flat-peaked to the back of his head like the coalmen who deliver coal by the sack. Summer and winter he wears a heavy jacket which completes his ensemble. He has short grey hair and a matching, nicotine-stained walrus moustache, for he smokes cigarettes he rolls himself.

Bill is impervious to the weather, rain or shine. Driving his horse and cart to and from his smallholding – the cart is always empty when he sets out and laden with produce returning to Jimmy's End – he folds his coat and lays it over the back of the driving seat. But he never serves customers without being properly dressed: he'll always wear his coat when serving his customers.

Working at the farm, he has maintained a strict, unvarying routine. He has no time to waste. When not ploughing or doing work requiring horsepower, he'll unhitch his horse Sally and set her free for the day to roam in a small field lush with fresh grass that never goes under the plough. That field produces an abundance of mushrooms, which I, or whichever sibling is with Bill for the day, is required to collect when they are in season. This back-breaking work yields an abundant harvest, which Bill sells during his next round of The Boroughs. If mushrooms are out of season, there is always fruit to gather, vegetables to bag, rubbish to clear away. Bill does the carrying, but anyone with him has to work.

The noonday break is unvarying. Bill eats an apple or two with Cheddar cheese, both of which he cuts with the sharp folding knife he carries with him. He gives me a Granny Smith apple and a hunk of his cheese. I have no need of a knife, but contentedly chomp away at the fruit and eke out the cheese, nibbling it a bite at a time. We sit among the cordage and rusting farm implements of his work shed, which has a water well in the centre. From this he draws ice-cold water for his tea, made in a working man's enamel kettle pot set to boil on a primus stove. We drink the tea from chipped enamel mugs with lots of sugar and no milk. When through with them we clean and put them in a glass cupboard propped against the barn wall and resting on loose cordage.

At the end of the working day, we load up the cart, back Sally into the shafts, and leave for Jimmy's End. I've sat on that seat with him many a time as a child and still love the thrill of the vehicle's rattle and jingle along the road, the steel-rimmed wheels crunching pebbles along the way. The smell of the horse's droppings when she is full from a day of rich eating will stay with me for the rest of my life. From having collected horse manure from the street in our barrow for the allotment, I don't find the odour of Sally's droppings offensive. It simply goes with that long journey back to Jimmy's End at the close of a hard day. A day spent working in Bill's fields is immensely satisfying. My uncle is knowledgeable about the town's history and vastly entertaining into the bargain with his songs.

With Sally clomp-clomping away along an empty stretch of country road with little traffic to impede our way, Uncle Bill will burst into song, singing with a will enough to burst his lungs:

Oh! Crack! crack! goes my whip, I'm happy, never sad
Who could lead a life so gay as Jack the carrier lad?
My horse is always willing and I am never sad,
Oh! Who could lead a life so gay as Jack the carrier lad?

'Come on, lad,' he'll shout. 'Open your lungs. Let's have the chorus from you,' and we'll sing that 'Crack! crack! Goes my whip' bit again and again after each verse. Rattling along the Harlestone Road, he fills my heart with joy and to me Bill is as lovely and jolly a companion as anyone could ever wish to have.

Once back at Jimmy's End, he has Sally back the cart under cover and then stables her for the night. The space for the cart is just enough to enclose it when the shafts are propped into the raised position. Bill feeds Sally, sometimes brushes her down and leaves her with a large galvanised tub of water and feed for the night before locking the stable doors. He rents a stable not more than two streets away from where he and Aunt Ada live on the Harlestone Road.

Their dwelling, the end one of a quartet of eighteenth-century ironstone labourers' cottages, has walls three feet thick and glass-bottle casement windows. The cottage, with its own well and rickety hand pump in the kitchen, has been in the Craft family for as far back as anyone can remember. For working people, they are fortunate. They own the cottage outright. The water pump was installed when the area was still country, which means they don't have to pay water rates either. They resist all attempts by the town council to connect them to the town water system.

The cottages are in strange contrast to the surrounding factories and modern buildings. They are a deviation, an aberration noticeable to anyone with an eye for architectural form and design. How could it be that in the sweep of nineteenth-century industrial development these four cottages have escaped the wrecker's ball? Uncle Bill says that it has only been in the last thirty years that slate has replaced their thatched roofs.

From the foot of Crane Hill where we live, Jimmy's End is reached via Spencer Bridge (named after the landed gentry, the Spencers) that goes over the River Nene and railway lines. Spencer Bridge Road, as it is called, forms a T-junction with Harlestone Road about half a mile distant from us. Still, for us Fulthorpe children, it is the end of the known world.

On Bill's Wednesday and Saturday rounds, the women of The Boroughs welcome him with open arms. His punctuality, his cheerful manner and his nineteenth-century garb are a breath of fresh air in the drab streets of our district. Housewives respond to our Uncle Bill's singsong call, as armies of old headed for the sound of guns.

'Greengrocer! Greengrocer,' he'll shout in his rich tenor voice. You can hear him in the next street. 'Come an' see my lovely potatoes for peeling, carrots for scraping, beans for running, peas for podding, sprouts for brusseling. Come along I say! Let us turn over a new leaf. Is red cabbage greengrocery? You can bet your life it ain't, m'ducks. Up an' down the market square an' round about the Drapery. When we get to Mercer's Row we'll stop an' spend a ha'penny.'

By the time he's finished his performance he'll have half a dozen customers lined up for business.

'Hello, m'ducks,' he'll say. 'What will it be today?'

The women emerge from their houses in all manner of dress, some of the skimpiest of clothes, a husband's topcoat over a nightdress, their hair in curling rags, odd shoes hurriedly put on to be at the head of the line.

'Yes, missus! It is a fine day to be sure.'

If it's teeming with rain and customers are in a hurry to be back in the dry, maybe he'll say, 'Yes, it's a foul day, missus, there's them as 'ave to work like you an' me.' He is easy and pleasant and friendly and works his rustic charm on them to extract the last penny from a customer's purse, but he never short-changes. If a customer requires two pounds of carrots then two pounds it is, no more, no less. He'll sort through the carrot box for a root of the right size or, failing that, break one in two to get the exact weight on his scales. Root vegetables go by weight. Cabbages and cauliflowers he sells by negotiation on size and density.

'Here's a lovely head, missus. I'll take fourpence for that. No? Too much? Threepence ha'penny then. Can't go lower, m'duck. Orright? Good! Here you go then. Open your bag.'

Bill's cart is a robust piece of engineering from the 1880s, a four-wheeler with iron hoops shrunk on to wooden wheels – a work of the cooper's art. A high-slung driving seat with support rails for the back gives one a good view over the horse's head. Hinged side boards fold inward when not in use but increase the carrying area when needed. Wood stave barrels loaded with vegetables occupy the centre area while orange boxes propped along the sides carry vegetables, fruit and, occasionally, buckets of flowers.

Bill does his rounds in all seasons of the year, dressed for peddling his merchandise as he is for working the land. His only concession to heavy, rainy weather is a folded potato sack formed as a cover for his head and shoulders like the leather cowls coalmen used to protect themselves when delivering coal. If the sack gets too wet, he replaces it with a dry one.

Mum is not among Uncle Bill's admirers. She regards him with barely concealed contempt; they are hardly on speaking terms unless one or the other wants something: Mum buying his produce, for instance, and never getting better treatment than anyone else but ever hoping she might. On his part, Bill Craft having trouble on his rounds and needing help will knock on our door and shout, 'Are you there, missus?' and she'll come out to see what he wants, which is how our Jack has come to work for him on a Saturday.

One cold January day before the war, not long before I start at the Duke of York's, he knocks at the front door and then calls through the letterbox, 'Are you there, missus?'

Mum certainly is, for she's been standing at the front window watching from behind the curtains.

'I'll go,' I say.

'You just stay where you are, nosey parker and you can get away from that window.' It's all right for her to look out but not me. Mum goes to answer the knock, humming to herself as though to make out she doesn't know who's there.

'Oh, it's you, Bill,' she says on opening the door.

'I'm having a spot of bother, missus,' he says.

'Is it trouble, Bill?' she asks in feigned surprise. She can be as smooth as Gordon's Gin when it suits her.

'The ice is too much for my horse. I need a hand, Mag.' He can be civil and pleasant when it suits him. Mum likewise, but mostly the two of them are as stiff and formal with one another as could be after that row with our grandfather, when the Gaffer had gone off to live with Aunt Ada.

Mum cranes her head over Bill's shoulder as though expecting to see the horse with a broken leg or something. She can be pretty dumb, too, when it suits her.

Sally and the cart are stuck on Crane Hill. The poor creature can't move the cart uphill no matter how she tries.

'I can't make it up the hill without cinders,' says Uncle Bill, blowing his hands in the cold.

She stands looking at him, trying to make up her mind what to do.

'Well, aren't you going to invite me in?'

'Yes, come in. Shut the door. It's cold,' she says, suddenly coming to life. 'Jack! Our Jack, come here, love.'

'Yes, Mam. What is it?' says Jack.

'Get your Uncle Bill a bucket of ashes, and a shovel, will you? There's a good'un.'

Jack goes into the back yard and returns carrying a bucket of coke ash and the coal shovel we use for collecting horse manure.

'I've got a couple of bricks for the wheels as well, Uncle Bill,' he says.

'That's good, lad.'

Jack follows Uncle Bill into the street and Harry slips out as well to lend a hand before Mum can stop him. Mary would have gone too, but Mum says, 'Not you, Miss Poverty-Must-Get-In. Get back. Serves him bloody well right the way he treats that animal.' She pushes the rest of us back in but stays on the front step to watch, half-closing the door behind her.

With a good few buckets of coke cinders and Jack and Harry to help, our Uncle Bill lays a trail for Sally to get a grip with her hooves. He stations Jack and Harry at the back wheels with the bricks, takes Sally by the bridle and begins tugging at it to get the mare, slipping and sliding, bit by bit, up Crane Hill. It is slow, hard work. Sally snorts clouds of vapour as she struggles and slips and strains mightily to move the load.

I'm watching with Mum at the front door, wedged between her thigh and the door jamb. She doesn't want me to see because she keeps saying, 'Git in, git in, you nosey parker,' but she's too interested herself to come in and close the door. She's humming loudly to herself all this time like she isn't really a spectator, but just happens to be on the front step watching the world go by.

Coming past Downs's shop, Uncle Bill changes places with Harry, saying, 'Here, boy! Take the bridle. She won't hurt you.'

At the rear, he lays Harry's brick on the tail board, puts his weight to the wheel spokes and heaves with all his might. Jack is doing the same thing on the opposite wheel. Neighbours arrive to help, two followed by three more and in no time half a dozen men and boys on the street have their shoulders to the wheel and those many hands make light work. The cart moves up Crane Hill like a breeze.

'Giddy-up, Sally,' says Harry to encourage the horse. 'Not much further, girl,' and he strokes and coaxes the mare like a regular carter.

Just when the struggling, straining mob of helpers have manhandled the load to the front of our house – there's still a long way to go – Mum shouts to Uncle Bill, 'I'll take two pounds of carrots and a cabbage when you're ready, Bill.'

Can you imagine that? I'm there and I've heard it. She can be really insensitive when the fancy takes her.

The look of anger on Uncle Bill's face is enough to sink a battleship and it wouldn't take much for him to belt our Mum a fourpenny one. She must have got the message because she hurriedly shoves me inside, comes in herself, and closes the door.

A short time later, Harry comes back with the cabbage and carrots. He's breathing heavily from the exertion. 'Uncle Bill says that'll be eightpence ha'penny, Mum.'

'What?' she says. 'That's full price. Is that how he pays me for lending a hand?'

Harry shows his exasperation, saying, 'What did you want to go and say that for when we were halfway up the hill, our Mam?'

'Tush! It was business for him, wasn't it?' She tries to laugh it off, but Harry doesn't think it's at all funny.

Jack doesn't come back for the rest of the day; he's in his early teens, working in one of Mr Barratt's shoe factories and now a man of the world. He stays with Bill for the rest of the day to help him on his rounds and comes home in the early evening with sixpence and an apple to show for his day's work.

Mum says it's sweated labour and something about our Uncle Bill being a sharp one, adding, 'Isn't that him all over?' Agitated, she clicks her false choppers and gives Jack the look of scorn she's probably inherited from her dour Scottish or bog-Irish ancestors – as though Jack were the one at fault.

'I don't know why you're getting hot under the collar, our Mam,' he says.

'Hm! Him and his workers' manifestos,' she snorts. 'Get socialists like him running the country and we'll soon know where we'll be.'

'Where's that, Mam?'

'In the poor house, that's where. Here! That can go towards the housekeeping,' she says, taking the six pennies from him.

'I'd like to know who's in the poor house now,' Jack says.

'You've got the apple, haven't you?'

'I'll sell it to you for tuppence.'

Mum laughs. 'Give it here, then. I'll make an apple dumpling.'

'Not on your life you won't,' he says. 'Isn't the labourer worthy of his hire?'

'Yes! I think that myself, often,' she shouts at him as he runs into the back yard to wolf his wages, core and all.

After that incident, Jack works regularly for Uncle Bill and is soon spending all his free hours with him. As time passes, he picks up Bill's habit of eating with a hunk of bread and cheese in one hand and a knife in the other, but gets short shrift from Mum for using bad manners at the table. He also starts talking about 'the workers' and 'the proletariat' at the meal table, which shows a side of Bill Craft that comes out in dribs and drabs.

As though being a conscientious objector weren't enough, Bill Craft is a committed communist who cheered the Bolsheviks for the 1917 Russian revolution. That sort of thing doesn't go down well in our king-and-country conservative family. We may be working class and our father a stoker, but Dad's been a soldier and is fiercely loyal to law and order as represented by the conservatives. Mum too.

'What do you know about the workers, my son?' Dad asks one day after Jack's been going on about the proletariat. Dad's very reasonable and doesn't raise his voice. 'You don't want to be listening too much to your Uncle Bill, my son. Oh, I know he's your Uncle Bill from Hopping Hill, who never worked and never will, or so he likes to say. But what you don't know is that he's never worked for any master but himself. It's all talk and paper learning from him. Emancipation of the proletariat indeed, dialectic materialism and capitalist instruments of production ... Have you any idea what he's talking about?'

'No, I haven't.'

'He uses big words, doesn't he? Can you spell proletariat?'

'No, I can't.'

'He uses those big words a lot, doesn't he?'

'A bit, I suppose.'

'Well, you can take it from me, the bigger the words the bigger the claptrap. Those bloody Communists are no better than the Blackshirts who gather on the market square every Sunday night.'

'He works hard, doesn't he?'

'Of course he does. So do I, so does your mother, so do all the men and women around here. We don't need lessons from him and his Bolshevik cronies to know which side our bread's buttered on. You mark my words. Once we allow those Communists to start running the country we'll soon all be lined up at a soup kitchen on Compton Street.'

Jack has no answer for that. Mum, having had all her thoughts spoken for her, nods her head in agreement. Our Dad is an articulate man who speaks with care. You can tell Jack's impressed with what Dad's said, by the way he lowers his head and challenges with a defiant stare anyone who looks at him.

Maybe it's a small matter, but I'm well aware from the time I spend in his company that Bill is opposed to all forms of violence. Sad to say though, his pacifist outlook doesn't extend to Sally, his Belgian mare, a lovely gentle creature. Our Uncle Bill is not above punching her on the snout when she's cantankerous about backing the cart into his stable. Taking his politics and jail record as a conscientious objector, which I come to understand gradually, it's hardly a wonder that old soldiers shun his company when he stops in a pub for a drink. Memories die hard.

*

Nothing stuns me about Bill's manner more than his changed attitude and the hostility he shows me in the summer of 1939 when I'm home for the holidays (we call it summer leave) and go over to Jimmy's End to see our Aunt Ada. I'm in uniform. I no longer even have any civilian clothes. Those I'd worn to school have been returned to Mum, who's altered them to suit Fred, the next boy in line.

'Don't you go coming here in uniform,' says Uncle Bill as soon as he sees me. 'Doesn't your mother have proper clothes for you any more? Come to eat us out of house and home, have you? Can't your Mam feed you? The army don't feed you any better, do it?'

'Leave the boy alone, Bill,' says Aunt Ada. 'It's not your fault is it, my duck? How's your Mam? Getting another little brother or sister, are you?' She has a way of changing the subject with great lack of subtlety.

'I don't know,' I say and think, even though Mum is walking the Barratt way again, it's none of anyone's business but hers, certainly none of theirs. Besides, I don't like the way they speak about our Mum. What I think about her is something else. It's none of their business. She's my mother and a good sort, so denying knowledge of her condition is the best way of avoiding discussion of the subject.

'Don't know?' Uncle Bill says. 'It's as plain as a pikestaff, I should think. Come on, then. I suppose you've come to eat us out of house and home.'

What a change has come over him since the time I used to go with him to his farm and come rollicking home along the Harlestone Road singing 'Jack the carrier lad'.

★

A week later, war is declared with Germany. Looked at in the light of what this means for the Fulthorpe family, it's none too soon either. Even with me going back to Duke of York's the house will be overcrowded. Until I return I have to sleep in the downstairs front room with Jack to make room for others upstairs. Jack tells me he's going to enlist and the very next day he comes home to announce the news. It's the day before the end of my summer leave.

'M ... Mam! I've enlisted,' he declares without fanfare.

As I've said before, under stress he's inclined to stutter just like the Gaffer. Whether this is inherited or learned I don't know. He certainly had a close relationship with Grandfather with whom he was a favourite.

'What? Not already?'

'Yes. I've got my papers and train ticket here. I leave for Portsmouth tomorrow.'

'Well, I'll be jiggered,' she says, turning white. 'Did you hear that, Jack?'

Dad's moving potatoes into the dark of the back place under the stairs.

'I heard,' he says, coming to stand in the doorway with dirty hands and looking sadly at Jack. 'I didn't expect he'd keep out of it for long. What's your Uncle Bill say about that?'

'I haven't told him yet.'

Mum stops kneading dough to dip her hands in the flour crock. 'He must suit himself,' she says to Dad, pushing back her glasses with a powdery finger. 'You must suit yourself, son, You always did. Them as makes their bed must lie on it. That's what I always say—'

'We won't make a song and a dance about it, Mag,' says Dad, interrupting her litany of all the things she always says. 'As for you, my son, I hope you don't think it's an adventure. War's a nasty business, very messy. It'll take a lot of killing before it's over, win or lose.'

'It'll be over by Christmas, Dad.'

'Like hell it will. That's what they said last time. It took a lot of slaughter before we were through and it'll be no different this time.' He puts his hand on Jack's head. 'So it's the Navy is it?'

'I've always fancied the Navy.'

'I can't say I blame you, the trenches are no place for a man. I only hope the Navy fancies you, my son.'

Although he's never one for dwelling on a subject, he can say a lot in a few words. I have a strong impression that Dad hates war even though he has spent a good many years in uniform. He shakes his head and goes back to putting the potatoes in storage.

Jack's almost 16 – his birthday's in October – and is doing well in the shoe factory, learning the leather trade from the soles up as they say. During his spare time he works for Uncle Bill Craft, still lending a helping hand, a job Harry soon takes on. Mum would miss the money Jack contributes to the family finances, but she doesn't really begrudge his leaving to do his duty once Dad has given his blessing.

Uncle Bill is more direct. I go with Jack to say goodbye because we're leaving together early the next morning.

'You silly young bugger,' says Bill on getting the news. 'You need your head examined. Fighting's a mug's game. Let them as have nothing better to do dig ditches. There's more profit in it for the working man than fighting.'

'Working man, my eye,' Jack retorts. He's now old enough to give as good as he gets. 'Some care you give for the working man, our Uncle Bill. You're always on about the working man, but the mingy wage you've paid me for the time I've spent helping you makes me want to laugh. You're nothing but a capitalist yourself.'

Uncle Bill looks at him in surprise. 'Did I ever miss paying you? You should've joined a union.'

Jack is stumped for an answer.

Aunt Ada intervenes. 'That's enough of that, you two. Here, Jack! Help me lay the table if you want to eat. You as well, our Arthur. Come on, look sharp, the both of you.'

To quote Mum, Aunt Ada keeps a good table. She can afford to live well having no children of her own, which is the reason, perhaps, why she enjoys having us visit her. I know she is always quizzing us in her quiet way about what is going on in our family. Only occasionally does she come to our house. She's fond of Dad, her only brother, but with Mum the relationship is distant, the atmosphere between them always strained and awkward.

We eat in silence, which is unusual at Aunt Ada's table. Bill Craft loves to talk about politics, the history of the town, horticulture, how Communist Russia was going to put the world to rights and, of course, the civil war in Spain in which, to Uncle Bill's chagrin, General Franco has been the victor. Uncle Bill offers Jack his calloused hands when we're leaving and slips a ten-shilling note into his pocket.

'Good luck,' he says. 'You'll be needing it, boy, because it's going to change the world, you mark my words.'

Walking home together, Jack says, with all the knowledge of the leather factory worker he is, 'It's going to be a working man's war, our Arthur.'

'Then what were you on at Uncle Bill about his being a capitalist for?'

'He's an employer. Employed me, didn't he?'

'What's a capitalist anyway?'

'A c ... c ... capitalist is a f ... f ... factory owner, like Mr Barratt. How can I expect you to understand?' This is another way Jack's beginning to be like Uncle Bill: asking a question to put you off.

'What? Him who built the Barratt Maternity Home?'

'Yeh! That's right.'

'What did Uncle Bill build?'

'Nothing.'

'Then he's just a little capitalist, isn't he? But how can he be a capitalist and a worker at the same time?'

'Th ...th ... that's because you don't know anything. You're just a squaddy see. If you were a matelot it'd be different, wouldn't it?'

'Will you write to me when you leave home?' I ask.

'W ... w ... what d'you w ... w ... want me to write to you for?'

'Because I'd like to know what you're doing, you know.'

'I'll th ... think about it,' he says.

I'm thinking it might be a good idea to keep a sort of journal about the family. After all, Harry might leave too if the war lasts long enough. By writing it down, I hope I'll get a good record of what the others are doing. It would help make up for my not being at home, which I miss a lot I must say though I never say as much to anyone.

The next day, Jack and I take the same train to London together. We part company on the Circle Line on the London Underground because he's heading to Waterloo for a Portsmouth train and I'm going to Dover from Victoria.

'T ... t ... ta-ra, then,' said Jack. 'I'll be seeing you.'

'Yeh! Ta-ra yourself,' I reply.

We are not to meet again for three years and, during the interval, the war will change everything – especially our Jack.

8   Getting the Corporal a Fag

THE WEEKLY routine at school continues unchanged following our return from summer leave although physical evidence of alteration is clear to everyone. Construction of the four soaring sky-high radio towers at the edge of the white cliffs is now complete and under armed guard. We know this because we taunt and scoff at the guards on our marathon across the Downs on a Saturday morning when a cross-country run is on the schedule. The guards give as good as they get and sometimes alarm us by giving chase. Our route is as far as the towers and back, although the run is stopped shortly before Christmas.

Not being used to running, the marathon practically kills me. Air-raid shelters have been built behind our H-blocks. The doorways of all buildings are now protected by sandbag blast walls put up during our absence, and blackout curtains have been fitted to the windows and the windowpanes have been taped over. The changes are all very strange.

Evidence of aerial activity comes on a fine day in October in a bright blue sky. We witness two Westland Lysanders in formation being harried by a German Messerschmitt, which is running rings around the Lysanders like a cat playing with a couple of mice. The Lysander, known as the flying carrot, is a sturdy, ponderous aircraft with wings shaped like a dragonfly. A group of us watch fascinated as the Messerschmitt loops a couple of times around the Lysanders, then shoots off over the English Channel like a speeding arrow, probably tired of playing games. There is no gunfire, so I think they are being very gentlemanly with one another.

We continue practising our evolutions and saluting drill on the parade ground, do our physical training, boxing, swimming, rugby, soccer and live our lives as the infant soldiers most of us are destined to be. Nothing much else happens to excite our lives until an anti-aircraft battery arrives. The gun crews dig up the playing fields, build protective sandbag revetments for the guns, and settle in for the duration. The crews are under canvas, also pegged on the playing fields, but ample space remains for us to play sports.

★

Before Christmas, we are issued with gas masks and instructed on how to use them. From then on we carry them everywhere with us in their cardboard containers slung over our shoulders. We feel more soldierly as we swing our swagger sticks when 'on pass' in Dover.

Christmas comes and goes and the new year's intake arrive before we return from Christmas leave. They have come, as I and my fellows did a year earlier, to take the place of those who have enlisted with the exception of some few who have returned to their parents or guardians. The presence of 'newchies' looking awkward in their khaki uniforms and behaving self-consciously fills me with a sense of accomplishment and satisfaction that I know the ropes.

Knowing what's going on is not limited to what goes on at school. In the library, we have newspapers to read and radios to listen to the news. In February 1940, a number of boys whose fathers are still serving are able to confirm the news we read in the national press of the British Expeditionary Force sent to France to help the French on the Western Front, which is a repeat of what happened in 1914. The BEF is commanded by General Lord Gort, VC, who was the inspecting officer on our Grand Day last July when we trooped the colours like any regiment of the line. General Gort, whom I saw close up, sticks in my mind because, like the Great Protector, Oliver Cromwell, he had an enormous wart on his chin. The ten divisions under his command have been able to do nothing to stop the German panzer divisions breaking through their front and putting both the French and BEF in retreat. In no time at all, remnants of the BEF have started congregating in the area of Dunkirk. The news is not good.

When defeat of our army is beyond doubt, and before the actual evacuation begins, the school authorities evacuate the school in a hurry to make room for the returning troops. The orphans among us are the first to leave. They are bundled off to the other military school run by the army in Dunblane, Scotland, which takes the children of soldiers of Scottish regiments. Then, over the next two weeks, a steady trickle of boys leave for their homes and guardians with their kitbags and gas masks slung over their shoulders. By the end of May 1940, 15 of us are still on the school premises, gathered together in one dormitory of G Company.

There has to be a reason why I don't go home with the others, but I have no idea what it is —a telegram misdirected or a letter lost in the post perhaps. I don't know. The Adjutant, who is responsible for the evacuation arrangements, has to make sure parents or guardians know we're coming. But having to stay doesn't trouble me in the least. With aircraft flying back and forth day and night, and all the shipping activity in the English Channel going on, there is enough excitement to keep those few of us who remain more than interested. Besides, my next door bedmate, Soupy Witney, and I are still together. The other boys remaining, a dozen or so, move into the opposite dormitory in our block. I don't know a single one of them. Witney is different.

Witney and I are in G Coy and have slept in beds side by side before he was moved to another dormitory to inherit the number of a boy who died of pleurisy last October. Everyone said it was a bad omen, Witney stepping into a dead man's shoes, I mean, but it didn't seem to worry Soupy a bit. He told me he'd had enough bad luck to last him a lifetime. His father, a sergeant in the Leicestershire Regiment, died in 1937 of the effects of gas poisoning from the First World War. The Leicesters are the 17th Foot, which means it's pretty senior among regiments of the line. I mention this because knowing the number of one's father's regiment comes as second nature to us. Dad's regiment was the 48th Foot, not among the most senior of line regiments, but by no means junior either. Anyway, his father having died, Soupy's mother worked as a charlady in Coventry and couldn't afford to keep him, so that's the reason his 'Petition for a soldier's son' was accepted and he got admitted to the school.

Witney is a true friend. We're two peas in a pod because he is always ready to defend himself, which is how he's earned his nickname Soupy. I'd made my mark with the clock tower incident and Witney his when he tipped his bowl of soup down Cartwright's front for trying to bully him into giving him his bread. Cartwright thought he could intimidate Witney because he was smaller, but getting a bowl of pea soup down his front soon put him in his place. The sight of him smothered in green goo, his mouth open in a cross between surprise and horror, put me in stitches, others too. It was no joke for him of course, but hilarious to the rest of us.

Witney became known as Soupy ever since he went up before the Commandant on a charge of 'conduct contrary to the good order of military discipline' and got two strokes of the best that Regimental Sergeant Major Whacker Black could deliver. This meant Soupy having his head gripped firmly between our Sergeant Major's legs up to the crotch with the tail of his shirt pulled out and his khaki trousers stretched tight. When all was ready, the RSM let fly with a five-foot long cane.

Soupy and I have stuck together like glue and since then my nemesis Cartwright has left us alone – and so, incidentally, has Corporal Miles. I've never talked about that experience to anyone – and try not to even think about it – but Miles too has left me alone since Witney poured the soup down Cartwright's front and I tried to stop the clock from chiming. I think they both got the message that neither of us were going to allow ourselves to be bullied.

We are, I suppose, two of a kind, for we're always game for shenanigans: after lights out, raiding turnips from the farm next to the school; upsetting the laundry baskets of other companies being wheeled to the laundry on the far side of the parade square. The first in line for the check-off means getting back to one's house first. This chore being done before the noonday meal on a Sunday means delaying other laundry parties by overturning their baskets.

At the end of May where there were so few of us left, there's no school and lots of time for walking-out passes. One evening near the end of May, we are in the day room, we are in a group of half a dozen drinking our cocoa and polishing our boots. We often pass our time this way, talking and cleaning our equipment, polishing our brasses. It is very quiet. Every now and again, someone will spit on his boots to mix the saliva with polish to get a better shine.

Then Sergeant Major Johnson comes stomping in and halts at the end of our table with his huge beer belly resting on the edge. He glowers at Soupy, who stands up and, with that innocent and neutral expression of a good soldier, faces the CSM. We know something's wrong, but can't imagine what it is. One of the first things a boy learns is to meet any show of authority with a blank and disinterested expression.

'Do you want to get killed, Witney?' asks the CSM, poking Witney in the chest. .

Soupy steps back to keep his balance. 'No, sir,' he says.

'What do you mean no, sir? You don't want to get killed or no, you haven't got an answer?'

'Both, sir,' says Soupy, who has a quick tongue.

Our sergeant major is one to talk about getting killed. He was the colonel's trumpeter in the Twenty-first Lancers at the Battle of Omdurman in 1898 and rode with him through thousands of milling Dervishes with no more than his trumpet. He used to tell us he swung his trumpet like a club to whack surprised Dervishes who got too close. I never believed that story. Soupy once asked him if he could still blow the trumpet afterwards. If our sergeant major was to be believed, he survived the forest of spears and swords with nothing more than a cut on his arm. Given his red face, pot belly and bandy legs, it's hard to believe he ever rode a horse let alone blew a trumpet.

He turns to me. 'And you, Fulthorpe! Do you want to get killed?'

'No sir.'

'Then keep away from the cliff, you young buggers, both of you or I'll knock the living daylights out of you. You know what I'm talking about, so don't look so innocent.' He has a fierce temper when he's angry.

'Yes, sir,' we say in unison.

'Don't let me hear of you being there again.'

We know well enough what he's talking about. Someone has seen us near the cliff and reported us. The four radio towers on the cliffs overlooking the Channel draw us to them as magnets attract iron filings. We often go to inspect them when we are on pass. They are fenced-off, protected with barbed wire and warning signs in large red letters state GOVERNMENT PROPERTY - KEEP OUT. That alone is reason enough to inspect them. Our khaki uniforms with their distinctive knee-length trousers, brass button coat and forage cap mean you can't do a thing within five miles of school without someone blabbing to the authorities. So this is what Sergeant Major Johnson is on about.

It's rumoured that the radio towers are part of Britain's preparation for war, a secret installation to give warning of enemy aircraft. We dismiss this as nonsense because, as our sergeant major who knows everything says, 'How can four 300 feet towers facing the coast of France be a secret?' He's right, of course.

The next morning about ten o'clock, we're in the day room being lectured by Paddy Finn, another CSM, renowned for his Irish humour and sage advice. He has just finished telling us to 'Always take care of your feet lads. You need them to advance at a steady pace and retreat at the double,' when the RSM comes in to order everyone to parade on the roadway.

Paddy Finn breaks off, saying in his rich Irish accent, 'All right, b'ys. Outside with you and get fell in.'

'But we've just got off parade, sir,' says Soupy.

'Then you'll just have to get back on again, won't you, Witney? All right, Corporal Perkins. Get them out.'

'You heard the sergeant major,' says Perkins. 'Everyone outside and fall in.'

We scramble out of the block and into bright sunshine. The sky is blue, not a wisp of cloud in sight, yet the rumble of thunder and a thud, thud from afar is in the still air. We form up in threes and march to the parade square where Whacker Black is waiting for us.

'Someone's copping it,' Soupy whispers from the side of his mouth. 'Is it you again, Fulthorpe?'

'Listen to me, lads!' the RSM shouts as though he were addressing the entire school instead of the twelve of us standing rigidly to attention before him. Three of our number left yesterday, so our numbers continue to diminish.

In his khaki uniform with its large hip pockets, his gleaming brown Sam Browne belt and world war ribbons on his chest, the RSM might have been dressed for the annual trooping of the colours, except that he is without his ceremonial sword.

'We are faced with a crisis, so I want everyone of you to pay attention. Our men across the Channel are in trouble. They're being evacuated and brought to Dover and other places along the coast. We're going to the harbour to help with the unloading.'

The RSM says we have a job to do, that we'll be working under the two sergeant majors who'll be coming with us. We will take the short cut to the harbour area by way of the Downs and a road that connects the town to Dover Castle. The port officer in charge of disembarkation will tell us what to do. The important thing is to behave ourselves and not get in anyone's way. Nothing as exciting as this has happened since we were at the Olympia Tattoo in June when we performed a mock battle to the music of 'The Parade of the Toy Soldiers' played by the school band. It was not nearly as thrilling as being marched down to help with the unloading.

'All right, lads. That's enough,' says Whacker with a nod to one of the CSMs. 'Sergeant Major Finn. Take them away.'

'Attention!' comes the command. 'Move to the right in column of threes. Right turn! By the left, quick march!'

We leave the premises by the main gate, cross the road and break step to cross the Downs under the morning sun and a cloudless sky. The gorse is in flower, a vibrant display of stippled yellow against the lush grass of the downs as far as the eye can see.

In the pale blue sky a flight of Hurricanes is streaking towards the distant coast well north of Calais. Much nearer to earth, a lone Spitfire trailing a thin stream of black smoke comes in from the sea and descends to some airfield inland. Nearer to the Castle we get a clear view of the Channel. It is a dead smooth sea. I've never seen it as calm as it is today, flat as a millpond. A few miles out, a stricken ship is settling low in the water with a black column of smoke rising sluggishly into the still blue sky. A number of small craft appear to be circling the sinking ship, but they are too far out to tell if they are lifeboats or pleasure craft. I should think they are there to help unload the passengers and crew. In the far distance, against the narrow line of the cliffs of Calais, more ships are attached to thin lines of black.

We have no idea what's happening on the other side of the Channel nor where the boom of the guns is coming from.

'Cor! D'you see that?' someone says.

'What?'

'That over there.' A large vessel packed with men and a smashed superstructure is nosing its way into the harbour. It looks a sorry sight.

The harbour area is utter confusion with vessels of every shape and size practically queuing for a berth. Others are secured to vessels already against the dock. Disembarking troops of various nationalities, but mostly French and British, move in orderly fashion from the outer ships to cross the decks of the inner vessels. The decks of no two ships are at the same height, which means troops have to clamber down to the next deck or up to it to get to the dockside.   The Dover seafront is just as congested as the harbour. Civilians from the town are mingling with the troops, bringing them tea and refreshments. The servicemen themselves are milling around, being ordered here and there by officers arrived to sort them and get them onto the waiting transport, which is a line of red, double-decker London Transport buses, green East Kent single and double-deckers, charabanc tourers with their canvas tops, and some army trucks, all nose to tail along the front road. As one bus is loaded and drives off, the line stirs and moves forward. It is an amazing sight. Soldiers, airmen, and some seamen who've lost their ships. You would have thought that no one knew where to go or what to do, which isn't true. The officers in charge are supervising the disembarkation with unruffled calm.

'Have you ever seen anything like it?' says Soupy.

'No, I haven't.'

There we are, standing at ease alongside a 1500 weight Bedford truck, waiting for Paddy Finn who's gone to get orders. A mixed party of Tommies passes us by, heading for the leading bus further along.

'Are you our reinforcements, lads?' asks one of the soldiers, grinning. 'God help us!' he adds to his companions.

'We'll have a go!' Soupy calls after him.

'I bet you would, too, mate,' says another soldier. The others, looking weary and exhausted, merely smile.

'Shut your mouth, Whitney,' Boy Corporal Perkins said. A moment later, he orders us 'Squad! Attention!'

Sergeant Major Finn has returned in the company of an elderly lieutenant who looks as if he's just climbed into a new uniform.

Paddy Finn issues his instructions. Six of us are to accompany him, he says, to collect rifles and ammunition. The other are to go with Lieutenant Summers to act as guides and runners for the Port Officer and his staff. The CSM salutes the lieutenant and, addressing everyone, says,

'Off you go, boys. Do your duty and report back here at four o'clock. There'll be a sandwich pack waiting for you.'

Soup Witney and I are in the Sergeant Major's party. We follow Paddy Finn to do as we are told.

The next two hours pass in a frenzy of activity. Exhausted men come off the ships in dribs and drabs depending on the vessels arriving, some little more than motorised pleasure boats. The ship we've watched enter the harbour is at the dockside now with blood everywhere, its superstructure a mass of twisted and distorted metal. Even before the last of its cargo has left, two of its crew are hosing down the empty, bloody deck. Steel hawsers and pulleys squeal as ships make ready to leave port. In comparison with the millpond calm of the Channel, the water in the harbour is in constant motion from the movement of ships.

A crewman of a small coaster about to make way shouts to men on the quayside, 'Let go fo'ard. Let go aft.'

I make my way along to the quay to the next vessel. It is unloading men. I stop one of the soldiers coming down the gangway.

'What d'you want, son?'

'Your rifle and ammunition, please. We've been told to collect them. We're making a pile of them, over there, see. RSM's orders.'

Their response to this is predictably unfriendly.

'Fuck the RSM. I haven't fought halfway across Europe to give up my bleeding rifle to you, sonny.'

'Get lost, mate.'

'Go back to your mother.'

'Who snatched you from the cradle?'

'My God, son. Are you our last line of defence?'

The talk is flippant, but their faces tell a different story. These are the faces of haggard, gaunt, exhausted men with weary limbs who drag themselves and one another from the ships. Watching the walking wounded and stretcher cases coming on to the dock gives me an overwhelming sense of sadness. The soldiers who mock or swear at me are right. Who has the authority to relieve them of their weapons? It is only later that I will discover that the country is in desperate straits for arms and ammunition, that their small arms are urgently needed by reserve troops settling in along the east coast to resist the expected German invasion. I feel a strangeness amidst all the confusion and chaos. Most incredible to see are the numerous dogs disembarking with the survivors from the rescue vessels.

In the distance, I can make out Paddy Finn having more success than I've had getting soldiers to hand over their weapons. He is handing rifles, ammunition pouches and the odd Bren gun to the two boys working with him. That's all right for CSM Finn. He has his rank and authority and the returning soldiers are still disciplined enough to obey orders from a sergeant major. They can easily ignore a boy in uniform though, and I can't say I blame them. I wouldn't give up my arms if anything like this happened to me.

Surprisingly, some hand their weapons to me without a murmur. They are glad to get rid of them. Others empty their ammunition pouches as well. A lance-corporal passes me a Bren gun he found lying on the deck and wishes me luck as I stagger under its weight to the dump. Not having all the luck the lance corporal wishes me, I wander off on a private tour of the dockside, sensing more than understanding the unreality of it all, I should think, in retrospect anyway. I walk further along the dock to where a stone parapet separates the dock area proper from the front road.

It's quieter here and not so busy and that's where I come across a lance-corporal lying on a stretcher with his head wrapped in bandages. I reckon someone must have dumped him there while they went away to find an ambulance. He beckons me over and I go to speak to him.

'Hello, Corp,' I say. 'Have they forgotten you?'

He raises his head and gives me a weak smile. 'Got a fag, mate?' he asks.

'A fag. D'you want a fag?'

'Give us a fag, mate.'

'Sorry, Corp,' I say. 'I don't smoke.'

'Get us a fag.'

A lump comes into my throat. He's no older than our brother Jack. His eyes are glazed with exhaustion. I stare at his deathly pale face. The epaulette on his shoulder with its tarnished Royal Engineers sign is hanging loose. Blood is showing through the bandage, a big and bulky field dressing someone has hastily applied. It has come undone and the end of bandage is hanging limply over his shoulder. His arms are resting outside the army blanket covering him, draped over his stomach.

'Get us a fag,' he repeats.

'I'll try, Corp,' I say. 'Hang on a minute, will you?'

I hurry away in search of someone who can give me a cigarette. I stand in line at a Sally Anne mobile canteen handing out tea and biscuits. A French private in a torn field coat and the odd-looking helmet French soldiers wear, turns and looks at me. He pokes his companion, saying something about '*petit soldat anglais*' and laughs.

When it's my turn, I decline the offered cup of tea and say to the Salvation Army girl, 'Excuse me, Miss. Have you got a fag?'

'A cigarette, my ducks? No, I haven't and you shouldn't be smoking at your age. It's not good for you.'

'It's not for me, miss,' I say. 'I want it for a corporal on a stretcher over there.' I point in the direction of the stone wall where the wounded sapper corporal lies.

'Sorry, love,' she says, 'but we're out of cigarettes.' As I am leaving the line-up to continue my quest, she calls out to me, 'Why don't you take him a cup of tea?'

'He doesn't want tea, Miss. He wants a fag,' I call back.

Further on, I come across a guards sergeant dressed in his webbing equipment and back pack. With helmet and rifle slung over his shoulder, peaked hat with the peak half hiding his eyes, he looks ready for parade. You'd never believe he'd just arrived from Dunkirk.

'Excuse me, sarn't,' I say.

'Sergeant to you, boy,' he says in a strong Welsh accent. He gazes down at me from a lofty height. 'What is it?'

'Please, sergeant,' I say, standing to attention, 'have you got a fag?'

'Fag? Fag? You mean cigarette do you? You're too bloody small to smoke, man. Put you on a two-five-two, I will.' His bark is awful.

'It's not for me, sergeant,' I say quickly. 'It's for that corporal over there, lying on the stretcher.'

'Oh, it is, is it?'

'Yes, sarge.'

'Sergeant!'

'Sorry, Sergeant.'

'I'll give you bloody sorry, boy.' He unbuttons his breast pocket and takes out a green paper packet of Woodbines. They looked as neat and tidy as the sergeant himself. He taps one out and hands it to me.

'Have you got a light, Sergeant?'

'Well, I'll be damned.'

Taking a single match from his breast pocket, he flicks the end with a deft movement of his thumb and bends over for me to light the weed.

'Give it here,' he says, realising I don't know how to light it. Using a second match and flicking it away, he hands the cigarette to me.

'Thanks, Sergeant,' I say. I turn and break into a run.

'March, boy, march! No need to run.' His bellow carries over the noise.

I slow to a smart step. By now, a lightheadedness has gripped me. I am happy, grateful to the point of ecstasy for having got the corporal a cigarette. You can't imagine what a wonderful feeling of accomplishment I feel. I am quite light headed as I hurry with the cigarette gripped between my thumb and forefinger to where the corporal lies. Eager with joy and desperate to run, I control myself because I think the sergeant may still be watching.

I reach the stretcher and bend down, saying, 'Here you are, Corp! Here's a fag for you.'

He doesn't move. For a moment I think, *Blimey! All that and he goes to sleep on me.* His head is turned, showing the brownish red patch on the dressing dried in the sun. I hold the cigarette in front of his face so that when I touch him on the shoulder he has only to open his eyes to see it. When I do touch him he doesn't stir.

Then I realise that he isn't asleep at all. He's dead. How I realise that he is no longer among the quick of this world I can't explain. I don't know how I realise, instinctively perhaps, for I have never seen the face of death before. The sense of grief that comes over me is instantaneous. It hits me like a blow in the stomach. It takes my breath away. I can't think straight. I desperately want for him to be alive. Confused thoughts race through my head. I tell myself I'm wrong, he's just unconscious. That's it. Could this happen to our Jack? Of course not. He would joke about it, only feign death. He's like that. I shake the sapper corporal again.

'Come on, Corp,' I say. 'Wakey, wakey! I've got your fag here. It's a quarter gone. If you don't take it soon there'll be none left. I can't hold it much longer. Please wake up and take it. It's okay. There're ambulances everywhere and if you just hang on I'll get someone to come and see you. I will, honest I will. Are you listening?'

But in my heart I know he isn't. I don't want to believe it. I sit on the stretcher with my backside against his still warm body and put a hand on his shoulder.

'Corporal?' I say, but there's no answer.

Inexpressible sorrow grips my throat. Oblivious to the noise around me, the bustle and movement, I take my hand from his shoulder and lower my head. Tears come into my eyes and stream down my cheeks. I quiver uncontrollably as I abandon myself to grief and sorrow for this poor dead corporal. I have no idea how long I remain with my head bowed, but it can't have been too long because the cigarette is still in my fingers when I become aware of a motionless figure before me.

Through the veil of tears I can make out two legs of khaki above scuffed black boots. I raise my head. The guards sergeant, the same one who's given me the cigarette, stands before me.

'What's the matter with you, boy?' he asks in his lilting Welsh voice.

'It's the corporal, Sergeant. He's dead.'

'Dead! Is he now?'

During the long silence that follows while the sergeant gazes down at me, I look back at him, unable to avert my eyes. We – the sergeant, the dead corporal and me – are like statues fixed in time and space. If I could distil the evacuation of Dunkirk into one moment, it would be this instant in time in which I sit gazing at the sergeant and he at me.

At last, he breaks the spell, saying not unkindly, 'What are you supposed to be doing, laddie?'

'Collecting rifles, Sergeant.'

'Well, you'd better get on with it, hadn't you?'

'Yes, Sergeant.'

'Go on, hop it.' His manner is now quiet and subdued.

'Yes, Sergeant. Very good, Sergeant.' I get up and walk away not looking back. But I haven't gone more than a few steps before he stops me dead in my tracks with a shout.

'Hey! You, boy.'

'Me, Sergeant?'

'Yes, you, boy. Put that bloody cigarette out or I'll tan your hide for you.'

I drop the cigarette butt and crush it under my heel.

'Be off with you, man, and don't let me catch you malingering again.'

'No, Sergeant.'

I march smartly away with tears still my eyes.

I leave Dover the next morning and travel to London with Soupy Witney in a train packed with Dunkirk survivors. It is the last I will see of my chum. I am later to discover that Soupy has been killed with his mother in the air raid that flattened Coventry in August 1942. In fact, the night over the Coventry air raid, I am home on leave, watching the bright bar of conflagration lighting the distant sky from the top of Crane Hill.

I have sobbed for the corporal on the stretcher, yet I'm not aware of being deeply affected when I hear the news of Soupy's death although, I must admit, it does sadden me a little.

9   T ... t ... Timber!

MY BROTHER JACK appears like a ghost from the past on the wooden veranda of the guard room one sunny Friday at noon in July 1943. He shows up from the dead with a bandaged head and is grinning from ear to ear when I hurry to the camp guard room to see him standing there. That's one hell of a shock. I haven't heard a word from him in three years, so he is the last one I expect to see awaiting me. He kept his half-hearted promise to write to me when we said goodbye and parted in London that day in 1939; he to Portsmouth to join the Royal Navy and me back to school. Meanwhile, what happened to him I don't know.

Jack wrote to me once on an airmail letter, folded and sealed to form an envelope with the address on one side and space for the return address on the other. I wrote a long letter back to HMS *Ganges*, which I know was a shore station, not a ship, so he was not yet at sea. After that, I had not so much as a peep out of him in three years. He might as well have disappeared off the face of the earth, but not entirely, for I did get word of him.

News of him came from home secondhand. From time to time, Mum had a postcard on which the sender had a choice of statements: 'I am well. / I am not well.' The one not applying had to be struck out. He wrote a proper letter once, but the censor did a thorough job of blanking out every scrap of information that might have been of use to the enemy: his ship, location, job, any reference to the tropics, to the North Atlantic, the South Seas, or writing from a home port. The Navy was more severe about censoring letters than the army, especially those from the men below deck. News of real interest was as scant as hair on a bald head.

For more than a year there was no news at all. We all thought he'd been lost at sea, naturally. It happened often enough, especially on the Atlantic convoys. The absence of a 'Missing in action' notice was cold comfort to Mum and Dad, which they expected any day. In any case, killed or lost-in-action notices often took months to get through the system. Was it any wonder that he'd been given up for dead? Thinking back, Jack had turned 16 the year he enlisted. That would make him 19 in 1943.

I lived my life as he did his, separate from the family. From Dover, the school moved to Cheltenham and from there to the north coast of Devon where we took over a hotel requisitioned by the government for the duration of the war. Our accommodation was confined to a single building on a headland overlooking a beach five miles long. Additional to the main accommodation block, various auxiliary buildings, including Nissen hut schoolrooms, made up the complex.

My time at the school ended in the spring of 1943. The colonel of my father's regiment signed my 'Petition for a Soldier's Son' with the idea of my becoming a musician in the regimental band. I had learned the clarinet and might one day have attended the Army School of Music at Kneller Hall, but the Bandmaster of the county regiment was out of luck because the Army had other priorities. That year, along with others in my year, I enlisted in the Army Technical School at Arborfield in Berkshire. The unit's abbreviation ATS was unfortunate because it was the same as that of the more well-known service for female soldiers, the Auxiliary Territorial Service or ATS for short.

I am in the ATS at Arborfield when Jack comes calling. I don't know it's him when, during our midday meal of corned-beef hash and Spotted Dick pudding, Markland, a runner from the company office, comes into the dining hall looking for me.

'Are you Fulthorpe?' he asks, regaining his breath.

'Of course I'm Fulthorpe, you twit,' I tell Markland, whom I knew well as we were in the same intake. 'Why the formality?'

'Report to A Company office immediately.'

'Oh God! What crime have I committed now?'

'You'll see. Come on.'

Worried sick about being put on a charge for a crime I didn't know I'd committed, I go with Markland to the orderly room and there the unheard of happened. Markland, smirking hugely for having pulled my leg, stands by while the company clerk hands me a 72-hour pass and a railway warrant and tells me to be on my way. It's like being given two weeks' extra pay with no questions asked. I ask all the same.

'It's your brother,' says Markland, still grinning.

'Yeh! Your brother,' the company clerk repeats. 'He's waiting at the guard room. I'd collect my things if I were you and scarper,' meaning for me to 'get going' and not to ask damned stupid questions.

'Thanks,' I say and scarper to my barrack block to pack. As they don't say which of my brothers is at the gate I naturally assume it is Fred, who is following the same path I've trod, first to the military school and then, when his time came, into the army as an apprentice tradesman except that wouldn't be for a while yet. Jack and Harry are both at sea, Malcolm is still at school, so it has to be Fred and it would be just like him to arrive without warning. Like all my siblings, he's a lousy writer and can't or, rather, won't string two words together on paper unless he needs something.

Five minutes later, mentally congratulating Fred on wangling me a weekend pass, I hurry round the corner of the gym and step smartly towards the guardroom when I catch sight of Jack. Seeing him standing motionless on the verandah with that beaming smile on his face is a shock. Cripes! I can't believe my eyes, but it's him all right. I'd know that face half a mile away and here I am not fifty feet from him.

I have another jolt, however, seeing him with his head swathed in a bandage. He reminds me of the sapper corporal on the stretcher at Dover. I don't mind saying that the sight of him gives me a queer turn. I'm happy, of course, but sick to my stomach at the same time, wondering what in God's name has happened to him. Is it a shrapnel wound, a bullet in the head, concussion from a shell blast? It could be one of a hundred reasons, except that he is alive and kicking. He has his Royal Navy hat perched at an angle on the back of his head, which would be funny except for the bandage. Getting nearer, I see a prominent bulge in the dressing at the back of his right ear. That explains the angle of his matelot's hat. He doesn't appear to be in pain as he takes his ease, leaning over the wooden rail of the verandah watching me approach. He has draped his blue, Navy topcoat over the rail and a half-full kitbag is on the deck at his side.

As I get nearer I think, God above, he looks deathly pale and thin. He's lost weight. His face is drawn, his eyes sunk in their sockets, his cheekbones stand out like the hind quarters of a starving cow. He has that deathly ashen complexion, the look of a man at the end of his tether, yet that triumphant grin of recognition with which he greets me is the pride of a successful warrior. It more than makes up for the rounded shoulders, the shrunken appearance, the form at which the casual onlooker might gaze with sympathy and commiseration.

Beaming with pleasure, I mount the verandah.

'Whatcha, scouse? Everything all right, then?' he asks by way of greeting.

'Yeh! Fine! And you orright, our Jack?'

We half embrace; nothing over-demonstrative. A squeezed arm or a punch on the chest in more normal circumstances might have served as well.

'Of course I'm orright, you nitwit.'

'What happened then?'

'W ... w ... what d'you mean what happened?'

'Your head.'

'Sod my head. That's not for you to know. Got your things?'

'I've got all I need here for the weekend,' I say, indicating my knapsack. 'But where 'ave you been?'

'Is this the inquisition? You ask too many questions, so why don't you just shut up and follow me?' He hooks his topcoat over one arm, throws his kitbag over his shoulder with the other, and goes down the verandah steps on to the road.

'Hang on,' I say. 'I've got to sign out.' I go into the guardhouse, show my pass and warrant to the corporal of the guard, sign the register and am free to go. I salute an officer entering the camp in a pick-up. He gives me a cursory glance, stops, opens his window and asks, 'Where are you going at this time of day?'

'Long weekend pass, sir,' I say.

He doesn't know me. I don't know him. Some officers are like that, always wanting to assert their authority.

'Humph! Carry on,' he says, glancing at my pass.

'Sir!' I salute him and hurry to the bus stop where Jack's waiting with his kitbag at his feet. I grin happily at him. He makes to knock my peaked cap off my head.

Jack likes to be in charge when Dad isn't around so he can tell the rest of us what to do. I know he's always thought I'm too big for my boots, especially after that first term at school when he took me into the back yard of the house and threatened to give me a pasting, goading me to put up my fists. Still, he didn't thump me in the end. He only meant to frighten me, and pretty well succeeded.

But there's another side to him. Liberal and generous with his money he is, even if he is bossy. Now, standing at the bus stop, waiting for a ride into Wokingham to catch the London train, he seems more relaxed than I've ever known him. He grins at me and I grin back.

'You okay, mate?' he asks.

'Yeh! I'm okay. How come you got me a long weekend pass?'

'Easy! I told your company officer I was on survivor's leave and could I have you for the weekend 'cos I didn't reckon I'd last much longer?'

'Blimey! Just like that?'

'Just like that!' He snaps his fingers.

'Cor! You are a good'un, our Jack. Thanks.'

'That's okay! Have they knocked you into shape yet, drained that cockiness out of you?'

'Me? Cocky?'

'Yes! Big head. That's what you are.'

I punch him in the shoulder. He punches me back, saying, 'Hey! Just watch it, will you? You're not too big to be clobbered.'

The bus arrives, crowded as usual with service personnel, men and women clutching their knapsacks, backpacks, kitbags going on leave or being transferred, everyone chattering like cackling geese. Everyone talks to everyone no matter who they are or where they're from. We work our way to the back, stepping over packs and webbing and kitbags and rifles. We both stand out from the crowd: Jack as a blob of blue in a sea of khaki, me because I wear a peaked cap and three-inch wide web belt –World War I issue. The web belt for battledress is a two-inch wide belt.

Jack stumbles over a rifle. 'I hope to God that's not loaded,' he says to the fusilier who reaches for the fallen weapon.

'Not likely, mate,' says the fusilier. 'They only issue blanks in our mob.'

A gunner gives up his seat for Jack and I hang on to an overhead strap to talk to him.

'Come on, then,' I say. 'Tell us what happened?'

'What d'you mean, what happened?'

'Your 'ead?'

'That's nothing. I was in hospital in Durban.'

'It looks bad.'

'It should do. They took my brains out; said they needed them for the army.'

I laugh. Everyone around us laughs. Jack winks at a nice-looking ATS Corporal sitting next to him – the women's ATS, not our lot, the Army Technical School.

'Why's that?' This from the gunner who's given up his seat.

'Urgent appeal. There's a shortage among your officers.'

More laughter. 'Right on, mate.'

A lot more flippant chat like this went on. When we got into Wokingham and were heading for the railway station,

Jack told me what had happened. The bus wasn't as crowded then, as a good many got off at the town centre.

'We were got into a bombardment with the Japanese off Singapore. Blimey! You couldn't even see the enemy except as dots on the horizon. I was on deck when we fired our guns and had no blast cap on my head. Summat happened. I don't know. The world went dead. Couldn't hear a thing. Next thing I know they took me to the Durban general ...'

'The General Hospital?'

'Yeh! and drilled an 'ole in my head, see.' He indicates a place behind his ear. 'And what d'you think? The ship sailed without me. Got into another fight, with a cruiser squadron in the Indian Ocean and our lot came off worst. I was sorry about my mates, but I'm glad about me because I'll be out shortly.'

'What? Discharge?'

'Yeh! So now you know and don't ever tell me I've got a hole in me head, 'cause I have, see.'

'I always reckoned you had.'

'Hey! Just watch it, scouse. You're not too big to get a pasting yet.'

Jack has a quick wit, but he leaves himself open for that one. My siblings are all same that way, quick on the uptake, I mean. I am the slow one and think up brilliant things to say long after I need to be quick-witted. When I do make a quick reply it comes out wrong, cocky like and biting, which was perhaps the reason Jack and I have had our differences in the past.

Perhaps I'm haughty and arrogant, I don't know. He says I used to be conceited and knowy and needed putting in my place. Being in a military school can be rough, for it coarsens the spirit and hardens the soul and you have to fight to stick up for yourself – like it or be bullied. There is that other thing, too. The business with Corporal Miles, I mean. I've kept that to myself, though it's changed me a bit, I suppose. If I'd told my brothers I dare say they would have beaten the living daylights out of Corporal Miles. It all happened a long time ago of course and Corporal Miles was now in the past, but it still hurt.

It is good to be with Jack again. He's changed a lot in three years, far more pensive than he'd been in the old days. His silences are more prolonged as though he is preoccupied with something, his head perhaps. Still, I have a feeling it was more than that. A sense of brooding, pensiveness, sadness is what strikes me when I come round the corner of the gym and first see him. There are moments during the bus ride when I detect the same thing, a sense of suffering, pain, despair; a wretched, woebegone look in his once lively countenance. Then he snaps out of it and seems to be himself again.

I ask him to tell me more about his time in the Far East, but he says, 'Oh, bugger the war. You ask too many questions, so shut your cakehole and be quiet.'

'Keep your shirt on. I was only asking.'

'You ask too much. Come on. Let's get off.'

The train to London is packed. We're crammed in the corridor alongside two fusiliers in battledress and full equipment. They look inquisitively at Jack's head wound and make a couple of sarcastic remarks, which I suppose they mean to be funny, about getting the worst of a scrap, though I don't believe they mean any harm.

'Th ... th ... thinking of taking on the Navy are you, mates?' says Jack after it has gone on long enough. 'If you want to try it, I'll throw you straight out the window.' He hasn't lost his stutter, or his temper – that's our Mum in him. Her Irish genes have affected us all to varying degrees. A pretty WAAF corporal at Jack's elbow smiles at him, admiring a matelot's pluck in being willing to take on a couple of khaki squaddies.

Jack reacts to her unspoken alliance and says, 'Thanks, love. What's your name?'

But then she turns a bit snooty, saying, 'None of your business, sailor.'

Jack laughs. 'Go on with you. An able seaman's at least equal to a flight sergeant in your mob.'

She cocks an eye as though impressed by his cheek and his bandaged head. 'Ah, so you want to take on the RAF now, do you?' Then, backing down, she says, 'You've been in the wars, I see.' Perhaps she thinks the stutter is from shock.

'Ain't that what war's about?' he says. 'People get hurt.'

The WAAF corporal must sense the irony in his reply, for her sympathetic response is unmistakable. Before you could say Jack Robinson, the two of them are deep in conversation while I'm a mere appendage to their tête a tête. As it's obvious they don't want me butting in, I gaze out of the window as the train clickety-clacks its way past the bombed-out and derelict buildings nearer the centre of London. The damage from the Blitz is huge: bombed-out areas with skeletal buildings and cratered streets from which clumps of grass are already sprouting. Then the train slows as we pull into Waterloo Station.

Jack's near the door and his belligerence shows again just as the train is drawing to a stop and one of the fusiliers is pushing with his kitbag to be first onto the platform.

'S-stow it, mate,' says Jack. 'WAAF corporals first. Now him' – meaning me –'now me. That's right.' The fusiliers hold back. 'Women and the walking wounded first.'

The fusilier takes it in good part. 'Okay, matey,' he says. 'Can't argue with that.'

Waterloo Station is a seething mob of uniforms. The military police are out in force checking for passes and travel papers, on the lookout for deserters and anyone going absent without leave. This is where Jack's head wound counts. 'Get your pack on you back and stick close to me,' he says. 'Pay no attention to the MPs. They ignore you when you're carrying a kitbag, see. It's like accosting a pregnant woman.'

I can't see the RN police stopping an invalid sailor. Sticking close to Jack, the two of us pass through the ticket barrier at which MPs from all three services are stationed and on the lookout for those who might be working a flanker, stopping personnel and inspecting their papers. We hurry along the main concourse, heading for the Underground. Sunlight streaming through the broken panes of the blackened canopy has a permanent blue sheen from the smoke. Waterloo with its concourse of platforms is a massive place under the press of uniformed humanity. It is as though civilians have ceased to exist except that this is obviously not so, for a fair sprinkling of civilians is among the sea of allied uniforms: Aussies, Yanks, Sikhs, Canadians, French, Poles, army, air force, navy, WRENS, WAAFS, ATS. Waterloo is the hub of the world at war.

Moving past the sandbagged doorways and avoiding the wagon trains of baggage easing a passage through the throng, we give up saluting officers with anything less than a red tab or, in naval parlance, a hatful of scrambled eggs. Jack says that only officers on home duty pull you up for not saluting. We get into the Underground along with the press of humanity. Jack buys us a couple of tickets to Charing Cross Station.

'Why Charing Cross?' I ask. 'We have to go to Euston to get home.'

'You want to see London, don't you?' he says. 'We'll stay in London overnight and go home in the morning.' He gives me a knowing look and winks.

'Staying in London? In a hotel? You're barmy.' I've never been in a hotel in my life.

Jack is hurrying along, going with the crowd. Pedestrians intent on their own journeys have little time for others, but easily give Jack space at the sight of his bandaged head. I stick to him like a barnacle.

'You're a worry guts,' he says. 'So why don't you shut up and keep close to me?'

I do. Sometimes he gets ahead, but he'll stop and wait for me to catch up. His beaming, weather-beaten face, despite its hollow and drawn appearance, is easy to pick out in the crowd. He's taking great care of me, making sure I don't get lost.

Posters throughout the London Underground are constant reminders about the war: CARELESS TALK COSTS LIVES. TURN IN YOUR POTS AND PANS. WALLS HAVE EARS. HELP THE WAR EFFORT. IS YOUR JOURNEY REALLY NECESSARY? Some posters are still pre-war. I notice those big Barratt Shoe posters on the Underground station walls opposite the platform, exhorting people to WALK THE BARRATT WAY along with the Guinness and Brasso metal polish advertisements.

We emerge from the Underground at Charing Cross Station and walk up the narrow cobbled lane to get to the hotel. The lane is the main entrance and exit used by taxis to pick up and deposit passengers. These black, honking conveyances careering up and down the lane make it a dangerous passageway for pedestrians on the narrow pavement.

The reception area of the hotel is crowded. Service personnel of every nationality are competing with some few civilians for attention. Web equipment, rifles and kitbags have been dumped wherever vacant space allows. Everywhere is confused and no one seems to mind, nor could the aged hotel staff have done anything about it if they did mind. The chances of my brother getting accommodation among this crowd are hopeless. I mean, how can an able seaman compete with the all the pips and red tabs and gold rings on arm sleeves milling around the reception desk? I reckon, of course, without Jack's pushiness.

He tells me to watch his kitbag while he goes to work. 'Excuse me! Excuse me!' he hollers, pushing his way through the crowd. 'Hey! Just watch who you're shoving,' he calls out, bold as brass. He elbows his way through the crowd; officers, senior ranks, naval types and air force heroes are all the same to him and far too polite to pull rank on a matelot with a bandaged head. It is enough to make anyone turning to see who's pushing and elbowing them move out of his way. What he says to the receptionist when he gets his attention I have no idea, but he's back in no time with a key to a double room on the sixth floor, a piece of paper, and a triumphant grin.

'Come on, scouse. We're in.'

'Crikey!' I say. 'You don't half have a cheek, our Jack.'

In the room, he drops his kitbag on the floor near the window and throws his coat onto the bed. 'Hey! What d'you think? Not bad, eh?'

I am dumbstruck as I look around the room. It's like nothing I've ever seen outside of the pictures, the cinema pictures I mean. I've never been in a hotel before let alone staying in one, so it's amazing to see the neatly made beds with their blue covers and matching curtains, the electric lamp on the table between beds, the red-carpeted floor. I go into the bathroom with its towels and a piece of soap on the washbasin. It's all so incredible, amazing. I come back into the room flabbergasted by the richness of it all and say, 'Cor! Our Jack. Innit marvellous? Fit for a king, wouldn't you reckon?'

'It's all right. Could be better.'

'Go on wiv you. I bet you've never been in a place like this.'

'Course I have. They have hotels like this all over the place in South Africa.'

After the bleakness of the barrack room, I am in heaven. It isn't just a room with single beds. It has a polished walnut chest of drawers, a writing table and, at the foot of each bed, a sturdy platform with bulbous legs that serves no purpose I can work out. I put my backpack on the bed nearest the door. The room must have set my brother Jack back at least seven shillings and sixpence. That's nearly a week's pay for me. I look at my brother with new respect. 'Our Mum'd never believe this, would she?' I say.

Jack is enjoying the impression that all his munificence and bounty is having on me. He stands there watching me, listening to me ooh-ing and aah-ing and lapping it up. As I've said, he is very generous at times even though he's bossy. Having sat on his bed and enjoyed, I suppose, the adulation and admiration heaped on him, he suddenly gets to his feet and goes to the window, saying, 'It's stifling. Let's get some fresh air in here.'

While he fiddles with the catch to open the window, I flop out on my bed to luxuriate in the comfort of it all. My feet are hanging over the end of the bed. I have my boots on. It won't do to muck up the bed with my boots. That would never do. I'm thinking, I could easily spend the rest of my life in this place, when a sudden exclamation of 'Oh, my God!' from Jack jolts me from my reverie.

'What's the matter with you?' I ask, lifting my head.

'Come here, quick.'

I leap from the bed and, in a single bound, am at the window looking out, but he grabs me and hauls me back.

'Not that far, you idiot. D'you want to be seen?'

'What d'you mean. I can't see anything.'

'Fool! Across the way, one floor down.'

He stands back, giving me directions. The hotel is H-shaped. The wing opposite us is bathed in a rich afternoon sunlight. Several windows are open to catch a breeze. In an open window directly opposite, an RAF type is unbuttoning his jacket.

'I can see a bloke taking off his jacket. He's disappeared now,' I say.

'You're as blind as a bat, our Arthur. God! I can't take you anywhere.' My brother steps nearer and cranes his neck, saying quietly, almost conspiratorially, 'Next floor down, over one, open window. See?'

'Oh yeh! I see what you mean. What's going on there then?'

'You bloody fool.'

A naked couple opposite, in full view, are locked in writhing embrace, their arms and legs entwined in an agonising motion I can only describe now as the excruciating and painful contortions of Hieronymus Bosch figures squirming in agony. I may appear naive and dim-witted, but I have no idea what they are playing at. I haven't the faintest idea what they are doing. The act of copulation is completely foreign to me despite my own traumatic experience at the hands of Corporal Miles. I simply do not make the connection and, were I not so ignorant I might have enjoyed my brother Jack's introduction to voyeurism. Instead, what I see strikes me as rather comical, ludicrous even.

Here is this man, a little heavy and stocky I'd say, with a trimmed black beard and a slightly balding head, pumping away for all he's worth, putting immense energy into his exercise. The woman, obscured by the body on top of her, doesn't stand a chance, I reckon. He is that much over her. Had she not held her head with its blonde hair turned towards the window with her eyes closed, I would have thought she was in pain except that she doesn't appear to be objecting to the punishment.

Suddenly, the rhythmic motion ceases and all is still. Then the bearded fellow rolls off to the side of the bed, which is when Jack yanks me back into the room and bellows across the intervening space at the top of his voice, 'T ... t ... timber!' in a long, drawn-out sing-song voice.

The timing is perfect. I don't see what happens next, but according to Jack, describing it all later when we've calmed down, the man hurtles from the bed like a startled hare and jerks the curtains closed, his face contorted in a furious anger. We are, neither of us, in a fit state to discuss the action we have witnessed rationally, for we are overcome with laughter.

Beside ourselves at the side, Jack reels against me and, catching his mood, I dissolve into a fit of hysterical laughter. Yes, that's it. We laugh and laugh until tears are running down our cheeks and nothing can stop it. Jack is gulping air between bouts. I laugh so much I have a pain in my stomach. We fall on to the bed and then sink on to the floor, with our backs against Jack's bed. I've never seen him so rollickingly happy. What medicine, what wonderful medicine for us both.

'Cor! Did you see his face?' Jack wheezes after we've calmed down and his breathing is becoming more regular. 'I'm going to die, I'm going to die if I don't stop laughing.' His face is lit up with a radiance I've rarely seen. It is infectious because, once we get going, it's hard to stop. When one of us stops the other starts again and so it goes on. Jack will calm down, look at me and wheeze 'Timber!' without a stutter, but magical all the same, for we renew our laughter. I think that half an hour of hilarity will last me for the rest of my days.

Eventually, we compose ourselves. Jack sits cross-legged on the floor facing me. Sitting there in his bell-bottomed trousers, his square-necked Royal Navy shirt and bandaged head, he's happy and relaxed, but with his bandage giving him the appearance of an eastern potentate, I must say he looks a bit farcical himself.

'I just hope that never happens to me,' he says.

'Me neither.' I mean it too. I could never imagine behaving so stupidly, especially for the amusement of other people.

My brother looks at me with a queer expression. 'I should hope not either,' he says. 'You're far too young for that kind of thing.'

'Is that right?'

'You bet your life it is, brother, and you'd better not tell our mother either. Come on,' he says, changing the subject. 'We're not staying here all day. Let's go out.'

We spend the rest of the day in the West End, Piccadilly Circus, Oxford Street, Charing Cross Road, mixing with the crowds around Nelson's Column. London has taken a pasting from the Blitz, but it isn't as bad in the West End as in the East End at Tilbury Docks. I don't see the damage myself, but there are lots of reports in the newspapers, which somehow never cease getting their editions out regularly.

I don't say people ever get used to the bombs, but going by the crowds of servicemen and women in the West End, the London bobbies on their beats and the crowds of civilians about on a warm summer's afternoon, everyone seems to be taking things in their stride. Even when the sirens went at dusk, no one hurried for the shelter of the London Underground. For our part, we simply move from pub to pub, working our way back to Charing Cross. Some pubs have beer, others have run out. We give those a miss, naturally. Jack enjoys a pint of beer like Dad. He doesn't get drunk, just merry. I'm sure he's conscious of having me in tow because he's forever saying, 'Are you all right, our Arthur?'

And just as often I'll say, 'I'm okay. Why shouldn't I be?'

'I don't want you getting into trouble or our Mum'll kill me. Things can get pretty rough in some of these places, see, for if anything happens you scarper outside and wait for me. You'll be okay.'

But nothing happens. People are pretty friendly with one another, the Yanks most of all. They must have money coming out of their ears the way they carry on buying rounds of drinks, but Jack isn't interested in men. He doesn't need their money. He has his own. His interest is in the numerous women in uniform. He has a knack of getting into conversation in a most casual way, chatting up every woman we meet. He'll say something like, 'Hello, love. Orright, are you? How's your war going?' with no trace of a stutter. Much of what he says goes over my head. It's double-talk and innuendo I can't understand. He must have many offers because he frequently uses me as an excuse, saying, 'Sorry, love. I've gotta return him to his mam. He's too young, see. I don't know how he got in here in the first place.'

'He does look a snippet, doesn't he?' one of his pick-ups says.

'A bleeding shame taking them from their mother's breast like that,' says another.

'It's the army, see. Got no standards, have they?'

I'm dead tired by the end of the evening. The noise, the chatter and the beer have made me woozy. I can't remember getting back to the hotel. Jack must have returned me and put me to bed, for I awake next morning with no remembrance of the last part of the evening. I do notice that he has a fresh dressing on his head, as clean and fresh a new turban as one could wish, so he must have gone to a hospital while I was asleep to have it attended to.

We rise early and breakfast in the dining room. Breakfast is included in the price of the room. We take the Northern Line to Euston, which is only about four stations north of Charing Cross. Euston is our London station for a direct train to Northampton. Trains leave for Northampton at least once an hour, so there's no hurry. We leave our gear, Jack's kitbag and my back pack in the reception area with a hundred others while we have breakfast. No one in his right mind would pinch a kitbag.

Jack is all business, anxious to be off. 'Eat up. We haven't got all day. If we get a move on we'll catch the 8.05. That'll get us home for ten.'

I'm finishing a slice of toast when I notice Jack's face turn visibly white, which is worrying. I think that maybe our night out has been too much for him. I mean, I know he's still ill.

'What's the matter?' I ask. 'You all right?'

'W ... w ... well, I'll be b ... b ... buggered.' Jack is sitting facing the main door of the dining room and I have my back to it, so I turn to see what he's looking at.

'Don't turn round. Stick where you are,' he commands, but he's too late. I've turned round.

The couple who've given us such vast entertainment the previous afternoon now enter the dining room. The man, easily recognisable by his black beard, is a captain in the Royal Navy, not a temporary one either with wavy stripes, but a regular officer, a three-ringer. And so, advancing in our direction comes this very senior officer in the Royal Navy. What's more, his advance in the wake of the head waiter is enough to freeze me with fright. His companion, an attractive Wren with straight blonde hair under her blue and white tricorn hat, is a sight to behold. What swain would not commend her? The captain looks old enough to be her father because she could not be more than 19 or 20, the same age as Jack. I see her peachy complexion after she's passed by, her cherry red lipstick in the style of Betty Grable, the US pinup star. The difference is, with contrasting dark eyes and brows to her blonde hair, the Wren is a stunning sight, fit to capture the hearts of ten thousand men.

Jack studies the brewing storm in his teacup and looks at me with steady eyes as the captain ploughs through the sea of tables. I'm conscious of Jack's grim expression as the captain approaches. I wonder what Jack will do. The Captain doesn't stop. He sails by with barely a nod of recognition for a wounded fellow serviceman and goes on his imperious way.

The Wren brushes my shoulder in passing and hesitates, turned to bestow a smile on me by way of apology, and moves on. That's when I take in her features and make-up. I blush crimson, overcome by her rich aroma of distilled perfumes. Not Jack.

He grabs his hat from the spare chair and says, 'Now get a move on and don't ask any silly bloody questions. Go into the lobby, pick up our things, and wait at the side door, the one we came in from the Underground. Got it?'

'Yeh! Then what?'

'I said don't ask questions. Just get going.'

I do as I'm told and Jack soon follows. Once in the lobby with the dining room door closed, he bursts into laughter. I swear he's almost as bad as he was yesterday afternoon. What's more, I know something's up. He has the very devil in his eyes.

'Have you got our things?'

'They're over there.'

'Pick them up and get going.'

'Why? What you going to do?'

'Just do as I tell you. Go on, hop it. Scarper!'

I know better than to question him further. I pick up his bag and my pack, and move towards the doors, leaving Jack hovering near the entrance to the dining room. At the exit I turn, like Lot's wife turning to take one last look at Sodom.

Jack opens one of the double doors to the dining room and, without stuttering, bellows at the top of his voice, '*Timber!*'

I exit through the door and take off down the cobbled street at a stretch gallop, running for dear life. I'm lumbered with Jack's kitbag, but next thing I know he's alongside me, grabbing his bag and taking off at speed. Laughing his head off, he turns to holler at me, 'Run, you bloody fool, run.'

I ran as never run before. With a pounding heart and the adrenalin pumping like mad, I took flight down the

street and into the station, my studded boots pounding the
cobbles. Then into the Underground I flew and bang! An
outstretched arm stopped me cold. It was Jack, hugging the
white tiles of the wall and panting for his life. Commuters
were milling around us.

'I'll meet you on the Northern Line, right? If not, get to
Euston. See you there.' With that, he disappeared among
the milling throng.

I was out of breath, couldn't run another step.
Moments later, beyond the crowd of pedestrians
descending the stairs, I caught a glimpse of the Royal Navy
Captain as he flashed past the entrance without his hat. My
God, I thought, he's missed us. With a palpitating heart, I
made haste for the northbound platform of the Northern
Line and got off at Euston without incident.

'You okay?' Jack said for the umpteenth time on our
way home to Northampton.

'Yeh! I'm okay,' I said.

I don't dare tell him how sorry I feel for the Wren. I
think he'd only laugh if I did. She is a creature of exquisite
beauty and I am sorely smitten. As our Dad said, we'd
learn the sweet mystery of life without help from him and
he was right, I'm just beginning to learn the sweet mystery
part of it anyway!

What's more, I love my brother Jack as never before.
You have to have a brother and to have had narrow escapes
with him to appreciate his true worth. My brother Jack may
have been in the ranks of the walking wounded, but he is,
as I've discovered, a prince of a fellow with an irrepressible
sense of humour.

10   Harry in a Foreign Dock

HARRY AWOKE to a world of total darkness. He tried to open his eyes, but they were locked, tightly shut. He knew he was conscious, which meant, he reasoned, he had been in a deep sleep and had not entered the next world, which might well have been his lot given the circumstances. So it was either a case of a deep sleep or something more serious. It was hard to tell and unreal. He knew there was light on the other side of his eyelids, but they were glued tightly shut. He didn't panic. There was no need for that. He was sufficiently awake and aware of his being, his existence, to know that he was, well, feeling easy and comfortable and – thank heavens for it - not in pain. That meant he could gather his senses together and think about things. He breathed deeply, but with difficulty because his nose was clogged and his mouth dry as parchment.

The common, everyday signals of recognition were missing. His sense of hearing, touch, taste and smell were wrong. The sounds about him were distant; so his ears were plugged too. He was flat on his back with arms out stretched at his side, palms down. At the slightest movement of his fingertips he felt smooth sheeting. He had a horrible taste of tar in his mouth. God! but his throat was bricky dry. His sense of smell was heightened with a pungent, foul smell of black, viscous oil about him, but the total lack of recognition of his surroundings troubled him. Again, with neither panic nor alarm because, apart from the difficulty of breathing, he was not actually uncomfortable. He searched for answers, hoping it would all come back to him .

I was not with my brother Harry then, of course, and could not experience what he felt or went through. I can only go on what he told me about his ordeal later. In relating this version of his experience, therefore, I've reconstructed what he told me in bits and pieces over a long, long time. As to its accuracy, I can affirm that Harry is straight as a die and tells the facts of his experience without display or pretension. Nor does he embellish or overstate as, say, our sister Ada May embroiders her tales. Mostly, he doesn't talk about his experiences unless they are funny – at least, he thinks they are funny in the way the gods played their games – such as returning from shore leave drunk and waking up in the brig to find that his ship had sailed without him. He should have been court-martialled, but was merely docked a couple of days pay and shipped out on the next sailing. The frigate he missed was torpedoed in the Bay of Biscay and lost with all hands, which surely was the gods playing games. In any case, I believe that in telling what happened to him I'm as near to the truth as will ever be known.

Harry read somewhere that smell is the most primitive of the senses, which is why he recognised that what he had in his mouth and nose was the rank stink of bunker C oil. Why it was called bunker C I don't know, but it was thick and gooey, like tar. He could 'feel the smell' of bunker C in his mouth and a revolting taste it was, too.

Something entered his left nostril and moved around and left. It came again and then went into the other nostril. It tickled. Too exhausted to lift even a finger, he twitched his nose and a muffled, faraway voice came to him.

'Ah!' said the voice, 'You're awake, are you?'

He had no perception of time or place, but he neither knew nor cared where he was. The simple fact of coming to his senses was proof enough that he was alive. He drifted in and out of fitful sleep as a drunkard seeks oblivion, but an inner will drove him relentlessly upward to reach the living world of light and comprehension. Gradually, the will to survive dominated and he knew he was awake for certain.

Fully aware now of the light beyond his eyelids, he made another effort to open them, but couldn't. He thought of rubbing his eyes, but the effort of lifting a hand to perform that simple task was too much for him. He first had to deal with an overwhelming feeling of nausea that came as an involuntary heaving in his chest, forcing his tongue between his cracked lips. He was powerless to stop the heaving, the retching, the overpowering desire to find relief.

Firm hands gripped him and turned him on his side, a queer sensation, this being lifted and moved without the slightest effort on his part. He heaved again, coughed and retched and, blessed relief, vomited.

With this involuntary physical effort, he became more aware of movement around and about. Someone wiped his mouth with a soft, wet cloth and a voice bid him try to vomit again. Next a cotton-covered stick poked about in his ear. Things began to register more clearly in his befuddled brain: a clinical odour was in the air, competing with the smell of oil. Metal clinked on metal, the same distant, soothing voice he had heard moments ago spoke again to him. He reasoned he was in some sort of sick bay, in the ship's sick bay perhaps; it was hard to tell, only they didn't have women on board ship and he could tell that the owner of the voice was definitely female. Frigates were too small to have large sick bays anyway. There came to him again this distant, hollow clank of metal like the sound of a spoon on the rim of an enamel bowl. Someone moved against his mattress; he felt it through his fingertips and the flesh of his forearms.

Strong arms and hands turned him onto his back again, his arms outstretched by his side. Harry tried again to open his eyes, this time succeeding in lifting a hand to them, but someone restrained him and addressed him in an unfamiliar accent.

'All right, sailor boy. No need to exert yourself. I'm taking good care of you.'

The accent was foreign, strange, cultivated. He opened his mouth to speak, but the voice shushed him and he felt a finger touch his lips.

'Not yet. All in good time, sailor. Now let's get those eyes open.'

The woman's voice that spoke was young and authoritative. He felt a warm hand grip one side of his head while another wiped first one eye with cottonwool then the other. The wool pad felt smooth and silky, soaked in baby oil. Competent fingers worked on his eyelids, applying a soft pad to remove the thick and viscous glutinous muck that held them closed.

He could smell a different aroma now, the nurse's perhaps. She was a nurse; he'd worked that out. It was a refreshing and lovely fragrance like nothing he'd ever known. Her face was so close to his he could feel the warmth of her breath. She spoke again.

'Sailor boy, you'll soon look as good as new and I'd sure love to see those eyes. Handsome fella, smooth cheek, a thick mop of hair.' Pause. 'It could do with a shampoo. Why! You're blushing, I do declare.' The face behind the voice laughed, a gentle, mocking laugh of pleasure.

Harry, who was pretty good at people's accents, couldn't place the voice. He again made an effort to open his eyes. They burned and stung and filled with water. He felt another wad of cotton wool on the lids.

'Take your time, take your time, sailor.'

Harry blinked and one eye popped open. It gave him a close-up view of the nurse. Her features were a blur. He opened the other eye, but his eyes wouldn't focus.

'I can't see proper, miss,' he said in a croaky voice.

'Close your eyes.'

The nurse worked patiently and without hurry, all the time speaking with quiet good humour to assure him.

'You're a lucky fellow. I had a patient last week who'd pricked his finger and it turned septic. We had to amputate his finger at the shoulder.' She laughed to tell him she was pulling his leg. 'So there you are. You can never tell. And here you come to us, sailor boy, plucked from a sea of trouble and not a scratch to show for it. Now be a good boy and open your mouth.'

He opened his mouth as instructed and, gripping his tongue in a piece of gauze, the nurse swabbed out the cavity, which Harry called his 'meat hole'. The pad wiped around his tongue and fingers carefully worked a tooth pick to remove lumps of oil from his teeth. One gauze pad after another went to work to be discarded once soiled with foreign matter.

'Now you're fit for me to take your temperature.' The nurse snapped her fingers, expertly flicking the thermometer to send the mercury down. 'Open your mouth. Under the tongue it goes, just like that. It won't take long. Sixty seconds are enough.' She smiled at him while waiting for the time to pass. 'I had a date once that lasted sixty seconds. It was all I needed. Sure hope it never happens to you.' She gave him a conspiratorial smile as she removed and read the thermometer.

Harry watched her at work, frequently blinking to clear his vision. He had her face in focus and scrutinised her intently while she wiped the instrument and put it in a glass tumbler of water on his bedside locker. She had a suntanned face, leaflike brown eyes, and an angular countenance with prominent cheekbones. Her apron and bibbed front showed a narrow waist. Beneath the cap with its stiff wide brim perched primly on the crown of her head, held in place by hairgrips, she had a mass of ginger red hair turned under in a tidy roll.

He was in a ward. Nurses were busy at work cleaning up men in much the same condition as Harry, a fact he picked up at a glance.

Aware, perhaps, that he was looking at her, she smiled. 'Welcome to the world, sailor. How are you feeling?'

'Orright, miss, thanks.'

'Are you all right, sailor?' she asked. 'Is something wrong.'

'You speak funny, miss.'

She laughed. 'So do you and what a delicious accent you have. Taking a fountain pen clipped to the inside of her starched bib, she flipped the page of a clipboard and said, 'What's your name, sailor?'

She had the oddest way of addressing him. He had known immediately he heard that word 'sailor' something was not right. No one called a naval rating 'sailor', not in the Royal Navy. Everyone knew ratings were seamen and addressed them as such. Harry was Seaman Fulthorpe to all and sundry. His superiors addressed him as Fulthorpe and sometimes not that, but, if they had his eye, it was 'Hey, you!' which was enough. Harry was disoriented by his surroundings, confused. It was the nurse's accent he couldn't place. She wasn't a Scot, Welsh, Irish, Geordie or southerner.

''Arry, miss,' he said.

She looked at him as though she hadn't heard him properly. ''Arry? she asked. She leaned closer. ''Arry? Do you mean Harry with an aitch?'

'Yes, miss. That's wot I said. ''Arry. What do they call you, miss?'

'Rebecca,' she replied, with a quizzical smile. 'Harry what, sailor?'

There, he thought, She said it again, sailor. 'Fulthorpe, miss.'

'Very well, 'arry Fulthorpe,' she said mockingly. 'Let me see ...'

It was then that it all came back to him with crystal clarity. They had been at sea, out of Boston, Massachusetts no more than a few hours. It was the spring of '42. A US coastguard ship was way off their port beam. Harry was an Asdic operator, a submarine spotter the Canadians called a ping merchant because they listened for the telltale echo of an acoustic ping from submarines lurking below. He was on deck, heading for the bridge with a thermos of tea when it happened. They were going full speed towards a torpedoed oil tanker settling low in the water. The next instant the frigate copped a torpedo on its portside. The U-boat had found another easy target.

Harry had been going off watch at the time, passing through the galley to his berth when the chief petty officer told him to take a thermos flask of tea to the captain.

'Why me?' He had argued. 'I've been cooped up in the Asdic hole half the watch, chief.' His was the worst job of the Asdic crew, for someone had to raise and lower the echo-sounding probe in the pod at the bottom of the ship to make it operational. Then he'd spent his watch one hour on, listening for the ping-ping echo of a submarine and the next hour on deck searching the surface with binoculars. It was exhausting work: the time spent with earphones clamped on the head played strange tricks. He even heard pings in his sleep. The operators knew this, so fresh ears were welcome. The end of the watch left everyone exhausted.

'Don't chew the fat with me, Fulthorpe,' the chief snapped. 'Get up to the bridge with that flask and put your bloody lifejacket on. D'you think you're on a seaside pleasure boat?'

Harry's ship was cramped for space like all ships smaller than destroyers. It wasn't normally on duty in the West Atlantic. The Canadian Navy took care of western approaches, but Harry's frigate had called into the Boston roads as its sea approaches were known, in the States for some reason and was on its way to join an eastbound convoy.

Harry had enlisted as soon as they'd take him, but he had reservations about Asdic operations. Duty in the Asdic hole – known as the ship's arsehole – was perishing cold, so he had on his duffle coat and sea boots and, going off watch, he carried his lifejacket loose. When the chief PO told him to take the thermos of tea to the bridge he dropped his lifejacket on the mess table and the chief told him to put it on.

'Come on, Chief. I'll only be a minute. I've been wearing it all watch.'

The chief got snarky. 'Don't argue, Fulthorpe. Do as I say, and don't give me your backchat. Go to the bridge without your jacket and you'll be in the brig,' he said, meaning the ship's cell.

'Right you are, chief. Just as you say.'

A torpedo hitting the frigate was not unlike harpooning a mackerel. A strike in the right place was fatal. Besides, the frigate was an enemy warship and a lethal adversary to a U-boat. The explosion, directly beneath Harry's feet, threw him from the ship like a cork popping from a bottle of champagne. He felt himself sailing through the air, cartwheeling in total silence because the explosion had deafened him. He hit the water feet first and went down, down, down, the wind knocked out of him.

A rush of adrenalin kept him struggling back to the surface gasping for air. Without his duffle coat and lifejacket he might have plunged to the bottom like a javelin. Coat and lifejacket and his sea boots had provided him with a certain buoyancy. There, on the surface of the sea, rising to the crests of the waves before plunging into the troughs, he caught glimpses of the ship, far away. She had sucked in water like a sponge and was heeling over, settling quickly down into a watery grave.

He kicked off his sea boots and struck out for the ship as though it were still worth reaching for life, support and the company of his mates, but it was a waste of energy and he knew it. If he got too close to the ship he'd be sucked under. Still, it was a tangible and solid structure in an empty ocean while it remained afloat. He looked for signs of others in the water, debris, life rafts, anything, but there was nothing left. The sea was as blank as the bellman's map of the ocean.

The sea was also cold, but that, he supposed, was the initial shock of being dunked. The duffle acted as a blanket under the lifejacket because his hands were colder than his body. He reasoned that his body warmed the trapped water next to his skin and that explained why his hands were colder. He decided against wriggling out of his coat, figuring he'd waste too much energy getting that off and donning his lifejacket again. His sea boots were an encumbrance and so, with some difficulty and much struggling, he kicked them off and felt better for it. He still had on his thick woollen sea socks. Next, to conserve what little body warmth he had, he pulled his legs as near to his chest as he could, in the foetal position. Someone had once told him to do that if he ever landed in the drink.

Now, lifted on the sea swell, he got the idea the sea was calmer where he'd seen the ship sinking near the tanker. The tanker had by now disappeared, but the sea was certainly calmer where it had once been. He moved on his back slowly towards that area. The lifebelt kept his head high. He coughed and gasped to avoid swallowing seawater. No one else was in sight, but there had to be other survivors. If only he could find them. He used his strength sparingly. At seventeen, he was young and fit. His year in the Navy had put beef on him. He tried swimming the breast stroke for a while. When he tired, he turned on his back again. He found it easier to keep afloat and his head above water even though the lifejacket restricted his movements. He couldn't know that in striving to reach the calm patch spreading over the sea he was seeking safety where the greatest danger lay. The calm area was a growing blob of oil from the tanker's ruptured tanks. He realised his error too late.

Oh my God, he told himself, I've got to get away. He had visions of immolation in a sea of fire if anything set it alight, though commonsense told him there was no chance of it catching fire now. The ship was gone. He struck out, using his energy to get clear of the oil patch. His hair, face, eyes, ears, mouth and hands were soon matted with the black, oily mess. It was worse than liquid tar with its rank and acrid smell.

After what seemed an age, a long way away, a conning tower broke the surface and he shouted and waved to attract attention. He didn't mind being taken prisoner. Anything was better than drowning. The conning tower was on the far side of where his ship had gone down. Just as quickly, the conning tower disappeared beneath the waves. Bugger me, he thought, what luck.

He concentrated on keeping himself afloat. There was no point in trying to swim. He had nowhere to go, but God! the water was getting colder. With the oil on his face, he had difficulty seeing clearly. He'd tried rubbing his eyes, but the rubbing made them worse. The oil stung. It clung to his face like a death-mask. It filled his mouth and nostrils. When clear of the oil, he took in a mouthful of seawater and spat out what oil he could, but the taste remained. God, it was awful, like eating raw tar. He reckoned he had no more than a couple of hours at this rate.

Floating on his back, he let his arms fall free under him and used his legs to propel himself forward. The pain in his feet from the cold was excruciating. At the rate he was going, he knew he wouldn't last long, but he was determined not to give in until he had to.

He did his utmost to conserve energy, snorting and spitting seawater every time he broke surface from the wave action. His mind began to wander. He shook his head to clear his brain. He tried opening his eyes for another look at the morning sky. Sometimes, he thought he could see the grey overcast through the slits of his oil mask. Mostly though, the world was a grey blur. The salt and oil in his stomach made him retch. It was such a drag to keep going. He knew he was weakening, but still he clung to life with fierce tenacity. Blimey, he thought, if only our Mam could see me now.

'You dirty little devil,' she'd say. 'Get to the sink and make yourself decent. You're not fit to come to the table.'

'Silly devil yourself,' he replied. 'D'you think I want to be like this?' He laughed to himself.

'Don't you get lippy with me, our Harry. You're not too big yet for a clop across the chops.'

'Is that right, Mam? I'd like that right now. Honest, Mam, I would.'

'You can cut that out. Your father'll be home soon. Then we'll hear what he has to say. You're a bloody disgrace.'

'I know, Mam, but I can't help it.'

What Harry didn't know was that US Coast Guard vessel that had been on the frigate's port bow plucked him and other survivors out of the water two hours later and headed full speed for the nearest US port. The Coast Guard had shared company with the Royal Navy ship while they were still in the US. Harry had no recollection of his rescue nor what the action of the Coast Guard vessel had been when the U-boat surfaced and immediately dived below. For their part, his rescuers thought he was dead when they fished him out of the water like hauling in a marlin, and they treated him like a cadaver until he stirred with life. They fished out others, too, an overwhelming number of merchant seamen and RN personnel from Harry's ship.

In the sick bay, the crew of the Coast Guard were inundated with the sheer number of survivors. They did what they could to keep everyone alive by providing warmth, hot coffee for those capable of drinking, and they also did what they could to remove the worst of the black oil that clung like bitumen to cloth . Harry was one of the more severe cases of those soaked in Bunker C. It had clogged his respiratory system and filled his stomach.

Addressing him again, Nurse Rebecca brought him out of his reverie. 'How old are you, Harry?'

'Seventeen, miss.'

'Seventeen? Seventeen? I can hardly believe it.'

'How old are you, miss?'

She burst into laughter. 'I can see you're all right. Mint fresh and no mistake. Never you mind how old I am.'

"Aw, come on, miss.'

She drew herself up and looked aloof at him. I'm nineteen, sailor.'

'Cor blimey, miss. Then I don't believe that either,' he said through his coughing and spluttering.

She laughed her appealing laugh again. The public ward was filled with survivors, each being attended to by the overworked nursing staff. It was a civilian hospital unused to the casualties of war. The naval station had reached the limit of its capacity and called on the civilian medical services for assistance. The hospital had had survivors from the sea before, of course. It was inevitable considering the war in Europe had been going on since 1939. Unknown to Harry then, Nurse Rebecca had recently graduated, so Harry was a new experience to her.

'And where do you come from, Harry?' she asked

Harry looked at the smiling face and thought her question a silly one. Didn't everyone know where he came from? England, of course. Lying in this hospital bed was stupid especially when, he knew, there was nothing wrong with him. The only time he'd been in hospital before was when he had scarlet fever. He'd been thirteen at the time. The ambulancemen came to the house, swaddled him in red wool blankets, and carted him off to the isolation ward of the Northampton General. It was the only time he had known Mum lose her composure. He saw the fear in her eyes and knew from the way she went on about 'Harold, Harold, my poor sick boy' and 'Whatever shall I do?' how frightened she was.

Later, when he was fully recovered, she confessed that she had visited the priest to plead for divine intervention whatever that was. 'I lit a candle for you,' she said, but Dad would have none of that nonsense and said, 'Come on, Mag. Give it a rest.'

'Where are you from, Harry?'

Now he understood. She meant his home town, which was different. 'Northampton, miss,' except that he pronounced the name of his home town with the hint of an f, as in Norfampton.

The nurse gave him a strange look, and shook her head slowly from side to side with water filling her eyes. She spoke to him gravely and with sincere compassion, for it hadn't taken her long to catch on to his odd and peculiar lingo.

'Oh, no, Harry,' she said, 'It's not possible that you come from Northampton. You can't have come from Northampton.'

'I am from Northampton. Course I am. Our house is on Crane Hill, just up from Paddy's Meadow, next to the Twenty-Fives, opposite the Welcome Inn—' and here Nurse Rebecca interrupted him, for all these public house references meant nothing to her.

'No, no, Harry. You cannot come from Northampton with that accent of yours,' and she gave him another weird look, as if he were demented.

'I tell you it's true, miss. Honest to God it is.'

Nurse Rebecca was silent for a moment, wondering perhaps if she should break the news. 'Well, you see, the reason is, Harry, you're in Northampton now.'

Harry struggled to sit up in bed, startling her by his sudden burst of energy.

'In that case, can I see my Mam? She'll want to see me, miss.' His excitement was unmistakable and his coughing severe..

The nurse took his reaction as a further sign that Harry's mind had wandered. She tried to calm him, laid a hand on his shoulder to make him lie down, saying, 'Please, Harry, lie down and rest. You'll get me into trouble.'

The two struggled: Harry to have Mum come, Nurse Rebecca to calm him. Then Harry was overcome by another fit of coughing.

Grabbing the kidney bowl, Rebecca held it for him to vomit into and, when he'd calmed down, wiped his mouth. About that time, the head nurse, attracted by the commotion, appeared at the foot of the bed and asked, 'What's all this, Nurse Fine? Having a problem, are we?'

'It's simply that—'

'—Nurse says this is Northampton, miss.' Harry butted in, raising himself on one elbow to make his point.

The head nurse's hand shot up. She was clearly one with supreme authority. 'One at a time. You first,' she said, inviting Harry to speak.

'Well, it's like this, see? I come from Northampton an' nurse here says I don't, but if this is Northampton, I think you'd better let me Mam know 'cause she'll want to see me. She don't know I'm here, see.'

'Well, bless my soul,' said the senior nurse, her expression relaxing. 'Northampton, you say? Northampton, England? You mean, north of London?'

'Yes, ma'am. That's what I've been saying, haven't I?'

'Then you are a special case, sailor boy, for this is Northampton, Massachusetts, in the good old U.S. of A.'

'Cor, stone the flipping crows,' said Harry.

'What's your name, sailor?'

'Fulthorpe, ma'am, but it's Seaman Fulthorpe, not Sailor like,' for he now understood why Nurse Rebecca had called him 'sailor'.

'Well, of course, Seaman Fulthorpe,' she said. 'That's a good English name and we're going to take excellent care of you while you're with us, Seaman Fulthorpe. How old are you?'

Nurse Rebecca was going to answer, but the head nurse waved her to silence.

'Seventeen, ma'am – and a bit.'

'Seventeen and a bit, eh? Then you are a man of the world, Seaman Fulthorpe, and Nurse Fine here is going to take special care of you, I can assure you of that. Nurse?'

'Yes, ma'am.'

'Special care, mind.'

With that injunction, the head nurse sailed majestically on her rounds, leaving Nurse Rebecca Fine to do her duty.

Harry's recovery was slow. The oil in his lungs bothered him and there was nothing but time and lots of milk to clear them, the doctors said.

News of his rescue by the US Coast Guard and the coincidence of his origin in the twin town of Northampton, England, made Harry the object of inquisitive attention. Doctors and nurses attended his every need. He blushed easily when questioned, but couldn't help feeling pampered with all the attention, but Nurse Fine had made him willingly captive to her will.

For her part, and as instructed, she made him her special charge, imitated his accent – not successfully – and mocked him, getting a thrill that it so easily brought colour to his face. What is more, she proudly and repeatedly told the story to her colleagues in the cafeteria of their misunderstanding.

A week had passed and Harry was allowed to leave his bed to walk through the hospital grounds. Nurse Fine, whom he had addressed from the beginning by her first name, invited him to her home for the weekend. He was shy about going and made excuses: he was without a hat, he had only the clothes he stood up in, which were his hospital pyjamas and convalescent coat. What's more, he had no money. There were many reasons why he had to decline.

Rebecca persisted and said, 'Not to worry. It's all right.
Come and see how we live. No one's going to take your
head off.' And she laughed at him, which made him love
her to distraction. 'Besides,' she said, 'we've forgiven you
about 1776 and all that,' which amused him immensely.

Harry, never lost for a response, said, 'You can always
come back if you like. I'm sure the King won't mind,'
which made her laugh at his cheek and gave her more to
share with her colleagues in the cafeteria.

'You'll come then. We'll be friends?'

'Orright, miss, if you think it's okay.'

She picked him up at the hospital in the family's
Packard, a cherry-red tourer so big that it sailed the
highway like the *Queen Mary* and Harry was amazed. In
one bright June afternoon, dressed in US Coast Guard
supplied convalescent clothes, he stepped into an alien
world of immaculate lawns, wide avenues, with every house
on its own lot. He couldn't believe there were no sandbag
blast walls, no soldiers, sailors, airmen, no redbrick terraced
houses, no airraid shelters.

At dinner in the Fine house, Harry felt ill at ease. He
wasn't used to the elegance Rebecca so took for granted.
He answered the questions of her parents and two elder
brothers with a simple yes or a no, but was not to be drawn
out to elaborate. There were many things about the way the
family lived that he found strange and unfamiliar: the grace
spoken by Rebecca's father before the meal began, the food
they ate, their manner of cutting their meat and leaving the
knife at the side of the plate while they ate with their
impaled food on their forks. He had sharp eyes, too. On a
conducted tour through the kitchen, he noticed there were
two soapdishes: one with white soap and a blue dot centre,
the other white with a round red centrepiece.

During the meal, when he was feeling more confident,
he leaned close to Rebecca and questioned her in a whisper.
'What's your dad wearing a shawl and hat for? The hat's
ever so small, isn't it?'

She whispered her reply. 'It's just a long-standing custom of ours, Harry. Our dad's ultra orfadox.' She had picked up Harry speech pattern like an expert linguist.

'Orfadox what?'

'We're Jewish, Harry, originally from Poland.'

'Oh, I see,' said he, but he didn't.

Back at the hospital the following Monday morning, a Royal Navy–US liaison officer, interviewed Harry for his account of the loss of His Majesty's frigate of the Royal Navy. With his Oxford accent and superior manner, the officer made Harry feel he was back on duty.

Harry told no more than the bare facts.

When the interview ended, the lieutenant handed Harry the papers he would need to join another ship. 'Well, Fulthorpe. I expect you'll want to be joining another ship, won't you?'

'I hope I'm going to get survivor's leave, sir.'

'I suppose it's possible if you really need it, Fulthorpe.' From the way he spoke, he made it clear that he didn't expect Harry to quibble over his rights. 'After all,' he said, 'there is a war on and we must all pull together.'

Harry was not to be put off. 'I didn't have any last time, sir. Two days in Scapa Flow an' they shipped me out on convoy duty again. I don't reckon that was fair, d'you, sir?' He stuck to his guns, making sure that his papers to return to England and duty included written authority for survivor's leave.

So to England he returned, with his eyes opened to the new world and his outlook changed forever. He told the story of his torpedoing once and never mentioned the subject again, though it had been the second time in less than a year. About Rebecca, Harry loved her more than Romeo could ever have loved his Juliet, but couldn't put it into such powerful words as the bloke who wrote about them, he said. He set his heart on returning to the United States if he survived the war, but that's another story. In return, what America gained was a dyed-in-the-wool Americanphile that would hold firm for the rest of his days.

Harry writes to Rebecca from time to time. He never shares what she writes in reply with anyone, but keeps it to himself. I've seen some of the photographs she's sent. She is the most beautiful of creatures in her nurse's uniform and, it seems to me, the exquisite Mona Lisa-like smile in every photograph is there for Harry alone – as though they share a secret. Some photographs are like that.

I can't help feeling a little jealous of Harry and wishing myself in his place, but no, that's not true at all. He went through hell and Rebecca, I've come to believe, is his angel who's captured his love and devotion.

11   Tribal Gathering

THERE IS no joy, excitement or pleasure to compare with that of going home. It begins with recognising familiar buildings and places that flash by as the train nears the journey's end and draws to a stop on the platform. I get that feeling every time I return to Northampton Town via Castle Station, but never more strongly than one special day during the war when the London train stops in clouds of steam and Harry and I get off together, cross the footbridge and emerge from the station. We are home.

As it turns out, this is a memorable weekend for two reasons. First, we have never ever been together as a family at the same time, for I left home before the last two of my siblings were born. And then of course, the others enlisted at various times. Secondly, it's the first time ever that Mum's persuaded a couple of us to take her to mass – but I'm getting ahead of myself again.

Harry has travelled to London from Scotland on the overnight express, crossing London from Liverpool Street Station to Euston, and there finds me waiting for him. He has a 72-hour pass and has called the technical school to wangle me a weekend pass. A light drizzle is falling, so Harry lifts his overcoat collar coming out of Castle Station, His hat is perched jauntily on the back of his head with the black band on the rim bearing only the gilt letters 'H.M.S.'. For security reasons, sailors' hats no longer show the name of the ship to which the wearer belongs.

Though the cobbled yard of Castle Station yard is familiar, the place has a distinctly different air about it. Gone are the cast iron railings that formerly lined the pedestrian walkway into the station, removed to feed the war effort no doubt, although the ironstone wall that encloses the coalyard is still there. The wall is all that remains of the castle that once stood in this place. The main structure was demolished a long time ago and the iron stone recovered used for construction elsewhere. The square once filled with pre-war taxis waiting for fares is now crammed with army trucks bearing divisional emblems on their tailboards. These, standing empty, are waiting for the arrival of new contingents of troops.

The Yanks are in evidence too. President Roosevelt's 'Day of infamy' call to arms over the Japanese 7 December 1941 attack on Pearl Harbor was two years ago. Now US Army trucks are competing with five-ton British Army trucks for parking space in the yard. Their drivers, gathered in small groups under the station's canopies, are awaiting the arrival of fresh drafts of troops. Over the road bridge that crosses the railway tracks and leads to Jimmy's End, a convoy of more US Army trucks slowly grinds its way towards the centre of town. Why it has to pass through the centre of Northampton is probably a way of showing the flag. Who knows? The Yanks are everywhere.

I feel uncomfortable in my khaki uniform with its throat-choking collar and brass buttons. Beneath my greatcoat, I now wear a two-inch web belt. Half of us apprentices have been issued with regular battledress, but I'm not one of them. I'll have to wait my turn for them, which can't come about soon enough for me. My army apprentice's uniform and shoulder tabs with ARMY TECHNICAL SCHOOL are conspicuous. We shoulder our kitbags and begin the walk home.

Since being in hospital in the States, Harry has made his first journey to Murmansk in Russia on Arctic convoy duty. His face shows the strain he's been under, for his eyes are dark and his cheeks hollow. He still has that easy grin of his and he tells me a little bit about his time at sea, but not much. Much of the time we're together on the train he's quiet, deep in his own thoughts. He doesn't look at all well; wan and melancholy, I think, but who would after what he's been through? I've seen enough footage of Pathé Newsreels to know that escort duty for small warships is no picnic. U-boat packs, it's said, lie in wait in Norwegian fiords waiting for supply convoys heading north.

Every Royal Navy ship on Arctic escort duty carries a Russian commissar. The Soviets insist on this to guarantee safe passage into Murmansk once the convoy reaches its destination, but Harry says everyone knows the commissars are there to report everything that goes on, on board ship.

'What a change,' Harry says, looking around Castle Station yard. 'Not like this before the war, was it?'

'No, it weren't,' I say.

The Yanks are friendly, ever ready to chat you up. One greets Harry with 'Hi there, sailor.'

'Watcha, mate,' Harry replies.

'Gum? Smokes?' The Yanks are extraordinarily generous with their largesse and you can't help liking them.

Harry grins. 'No thanks, mate.'

'What about the toy soldier there?'

'He's our secret weapon; deadly with a right hook.'

The American laughs and elbows one of his companions in the ribs. 'Doggone it, Jim, what'll these Brits think of next?'

We walk up Lion's Gate Hill, the unending convoy of US Army trucks still grinding its way into town. It is an artillery unit with black American gunners crammed against the tailboards yelling and waving to pedestrians along the way who stop to watch the convoy pass by. The American gunners are a happy lot, tossing packets of gum to the grinning children and packets of Lucky Strike to adults. Trouble is, we can't understand a word they say.

'Silly buggers. They must be just off a trooper and going round the bend,' says Harry. He has lost his flat Northampton accent, which is no surprise. Mine went long ago under the influence of a military life.

As we're turning the corner at Lion's Gate to go along Chalk Lane – the highway's steep there, so vehicles have to gear down to climb the hill – a lorry backfires. The noise distracts me slightly, but Harry leaps like a startled rabbit and stands there a long time, shaking and recovering. His face has turned as white as a winding sheet and his left hand trembles violently as though he were suffering from a bout of the DTs. His nerves must be in a frightening state.

I reach out to help, saying, 'You all right, Harry?'

He doesn't speak, but gestures energetically for me to keep my distance. It's alarming. The sight of him shaking so has upset me. When he's recovered from his attack of nerves, he says, 'It's okay. I'm all right, I'm all right. Let's get going.' Then, a little bit further on, he says, 'Blimey! That didn't half give me a start.'

I don't understand. I always thought Harry had nerves of steel, but of course I don't know what he's been through or what's going on in his head.

We walk through the back streets of The Boroughs, taking the shortest root to Crane Hill by way of Chalk Lane, then Lower Cross and Crispin Streets to Compton. The cobbled lane alongside the burial ground has a low ironstone wall with picket fence gates to lone pathways and vegetable gardens leading to labourers' row houses. The burial ground itself, also enclosed in an original ironstone wall, is laid wall-to-wall with gravestones and the vast expanse has now become a play yard. Over the years, children have scuffed out any inscriptions that might have been evidence of the untold legions of monks laid to rest beneath the flagstones.

In contrast with Harry's shoes, my studded ammo boots echoe eerily in the cobbled lane. The iron railings that once defined the burial ground, I notice, has been removed like those at Castle Station; war effort again and only the stub ends remain.

At the corner of Crispin Street and Spring Lane where the infant school stands, Harry steers us downhill to the next street, saying, 'We'll go along Compton Street. Then they won't see us out of the back window.' He likes to surprise our mother that way. From our back window, one has a clear view of the length of Lower Harding Street, which is how we can tell when Dad's on his way from the gasworks.

Along Compton Street, we pass neighbours standing on their front steps watching the world go by, women mostly, but a few old men are out too. The women stand sentinel in their flat caps and aprons, arms folded across their chests. Their husbands, sons and daughters of call-up age are in the services, unless of course they are in reserved occupations: the police, munitions work or precision bearings. We say hello to faces we know, exchange greetings and pleasantries, get a nod of recognition or a thin smile and sometimes a question about how the war's going. Everyone is anxious to hear first-hand accounts of the war from anyone in uniform. The people of The Boroughs are an inquisitive lot.

We turn the corner at Downs's off-licence grocery store and in another ten steps are at the front door of the house. Harry flattens himself against the street wall.

'You knock,' he says. 'Mum's not expecting us. She doesn't know we're coming.'

I notice that, like me, Harry now calls her Mum instead of Mam. He no longer drops his aitches and also pronounces his 'th's. He used to say 'Norfampton' – now it's 'Northampton'.

I knock on the front door and hear the familiar footsteps coming along the passage. Then the door opens and Mum fills the doorway. Seeing me, she screams with delight.

'Ooh! Our Arthur!' she says with happiness. 'Bless your heart and cotton socks, what a lovely surprise.' She clasps me to her bosom and shouts over her shoulder into the house, 'Here, all of you. Just look what the wind's blown in.'

Harry is so happy to hear Mum's voice he can't stand being hidden any longer, so he steps into view and Mum gasps in surprise.

'Oh, my God! It's our Harold.' Her eyes fill with tears of joy. 'Oh, Harold, Harold, my lovey, how are you?' She clings to him for dear life, looking up and down the street with a triumphant and happy face, hoping everyone is on their doorsteps to witness this joyful reunion.

'I'm all right, Mum.'

Everyone comes rushing to the front door: Dad, Jack (still with his head bandaged), Mary in her ATS uniform, Ada, Fred from military school, all the younger ones. There is much rejoicing and the passageway is in an uproar; beaming faces, broad grins and arms outstretched to greet us. Harry tries to squeeze past Mum to get inside, but she blocks the doorway and Harry says, 'Come on, Mum. Let's get inside. You don't want the neighbours seeing everything.'

Mum steps into the street to let Harry go in. I follow and turn for Mum to come into the house too. Instead, she stands on the pavement for a while, preening herself, fiddling with her hair, looking up and down the street to see who's watching, making a right spectacle of herself, I reckon. She's practically doing a jig for joy. It's embarrassing. I find nothing more awkward and uncomfortable than the sight of Mum putting on a display for the neighbours.

'Would you please come inside, Mum?' I ask. 'I hate the neighbours watching.'

'Don't you be so bossy,' she says. 'Let them watch. It costs nothing, does it?' and she hums aloud to herself in that tuneless way of hers.

I go inside and she follows, but not before taking one more peek into the street before closing the door. In the kitchen, there's chaos with everyone talking at once. Harry is being passed around from sister to brother to father and back again to answer questions, for everyone has something to ask.

What a homecoming and what luck this Saturday afternoon. It is amazing. We are all home. I mean to say, here we are in the middle of a war and everyone is at home. It seems nothing short of a miracle, unbelievable. Who would have thought it possible that we could all arrive home en masse at the same time?

Our Dad stands in the midst of all his children, his face beaming with pleasure, his choppers on display from his wide grin. What elation and satisfaction we all feel. We're beside ourselves with happiness.

'Oh, Jack, Jack!' says Mum. 'I'm ever so happy. To think, all of them home. Is it possible?'

'It's remarkable, Mag. I'll say that.' Dad is too overcome with emotion to say more.

Mum is suddenly in her element, calling for order and attention. She says, 'Listen everyone. Listen to me. Ada! Will you shut up? Now, we must all get dressed up and go to Jerome's down Drapery Street to have our picture taken.' Jerome's was the only commercial photographer we know. No one is in favour of Mum's suggestion, so we follow her announcement with moans and groans.

'Oh, come on, don't be spoilsports. Let's have our picture taken altogether. Mary can see if she can get a pork pie from Browns, the pork butcher. Then we'll go to the Saracen's Head for a drink and come home and eat. What d'you say?'

Browns, yes, Browns the pork butcher. Even during the war we have specialty butchers who somehow remain in business: the meat and poultry butcher; the lamb butcher who sells nothing but lamb and its by-products; then the pork butcher who sells pork and ham, bacon, giblets, pork pies and the rest. Mary has worked for Browns before enlisting, so she's the best choice for getting a pork pie under the counter and anything else that might be going.

Then Fred pipes up. 'What do we want our picture for? Why can't we just eat?'

'That's enough from you, my lad,' says Mum. 'Life's just a great trough to you, isn't it?'

She's being unjust, but it is her nature to have a crack at someone. In fact, our Fred is as fit and trim and slim as any one of us with not an ounce of fat on him.

'Leave the boy alone, Mag.'

Mary picks up Kathleen and holds her close, for our second littlest sister is overwhelmed by the excitement of it all and on the verge of tears. She hardly knows any of us older ones.

'Come here, m'ducks,' says Mary, calming Kathleen's fears. 'It's all too much for you, isn't it? Well, my lovey, there's no call for tears.'

Dad begins banking up the fire, then sweeping up the ash fallen on to the hearth. 'It's a bit steep, going to the

Saracen, isn't it? Where's the money coming from? Why don't we get a jug of beer from next door?'

Mum gives him a warning look and says, 'Tush!' as is her habit when dismissing opposition. 'I think I can go dibs for the Saracen,' meaning she will pay.

'It's okay, Dad. We can look after it,' Harry says.

'Yes, don't worry, Dad,' says Jack.

'You can do with not worrying so much yourself, my son,' Dad says to Jack, getting up.

He's right. Jack doesn't look in any better state than Harry. His face too is thin and drawn, his eyes sunk in their sockets, his bandage changed daily at the hospital is stained from the weeping wound behind his ear, but he still manages a grin.

Fred says something again about it being better to eat and save the drinking for later, which irritates Mum. She flashes him a look of exasperation and snaps, 'Okay, mister wise guy. That's enough of that from you. I know you think your mother's an SOB at times.'

A deathly silence falls on the room. What on earth has got into our Mum to use that kind of language? She has a rich enough store of her own without resorting to newly imported Americanisms. Harry's jaw drops. Jack looks quizzical and raises his eyebrows. Mary, familiar enough with foul language, blushes. Foul language is not in the lexicon of the Fulthorpe family and SOB is at the lowest level of offensiveness. What is she thinking? It will be hard to believe in contemporary society, but coarse and offensive phrases beyond the odd 'sod' or 'bloody' and that sort of thing are not the regular language of the realm. SOB and SNAFU ('situation normal, another fuck up') are strictly Yankee imports.

Very slowly, and with a stutter, Jack asks, 'Do you know what you've just said, Mam?'

'Of course I know. What d'you take me for, a simpleton or something?'

'No, we don't, so what d'you think SOB stands for, Mum?' Harry asks.

Mum hesitates, and then dismisses the question with a haughty 'Tush!' and her face breaks into a broad grin. 'Good gracious, boy! You in the Navy and you don't know the meaning of SOB? Silly old bat, of course, what do you think?'

There is an outburst of laughter. We hoot and laugh and punch one another merrily at the joke. Mum's naivety is hilarious. Even Dad laughs – not that he understands the joke any more than Mum does, but it gives him immense pleasure to see us all so happy.

That Mum doesn't like being the butt of a joke is evident from her face. Revealing her ignorance of something as simple as SOB is a small thing, perhaps, yet it demonstrates her vulnerability to criticism. I begin to realise that she is not the all-knowing Mum who has raised us. I begin to see her in a new light, not a critical one but in the light of understanding. She recovers her composure soon enough and is back in command of the situation.

'After we've been to the photographer, Malcolm can bring Margaret and Kathleen home and look after them till we get back ...'

'Why, Mum? Why can't we come?'

'You're too little. They won't let you in.'

'I went with Dad last Sunday.'

'You'll get in the way.'

Jack chips in with 'Sister Anna will carry the banner.' This stops Mum cold. She doesn't know what he's talking about, but Mary does.

'But I carried it yesterday,' she protests.

'You'll carry it today,' Harry replies.

'I'm in the family way.'

'You're in everybody's way,' we sing in chorus.

'What are you all on about?' Mum asks, mystified.

'Forget it, Mum. Let's all get ready and go.

Mum submits to the decision with a small grimace of protest and, without another word, goes to dress. She returns in a yellow woollen dress with a wide red belt and does her make-up in the kitchen mirror.

When she's ready, we troop to the Drapery, a main street in the town centre in a close-knit bunch. We're boisterous and happy. Mum won't hear of Jack or Harry paying for the family portrait session, though they're both well off from their long months at sea with nothing on which to spend their money. It's the same in the Grafton Arms, which Dad happens to prefer to the Saracen's Head, and in there we crowd together to drink our beer.

I wonder if Mum has enough money to go on paying. Our Dad only gets a small wage, so where on earth does her money come from? I go with her to the bar to get the second round of drinks and see her take from her leather handbag a thick wad of notes. There must be a hundred pounds in the roll.

My curiosity gets the better of me. 'Where did you get all that money, Mum?'

'You mind your own business and don't ask impertinent questions. You know what they say in Yorkshire, don't you?'

'No, I don't because you want to tell me, so what do they say in Yorkshire, Mum?'

'Cheeky devil. You're too clever with words for your own good. See all, sup all, say nowt and remember this, my son. It's an ill wind that blows no one good.'

'I don't know what you mean,' I said.

'Work it out for yourself, you fathead.'

You have to take Mum's choicest remarks with a good pinch of salt. In any case, there's no chance of pursuing the matter further because Harry comes to help carry the drinks to the table, and Mum clamps up tighter than a drum. We push our way through the crowded saloon with trays awash with spilt beer and hand out the drinks everyone has ordered. Then Mum takes her place without so much as a glance in my direction.

The sight of so much money in her purse is troubling though. How could she have acquired so much? Dad's income from the gas works is no more than four pounds a week now, five at the most. Perhaps Jack and Harry have added to her coffers from their unspent earnings. I know they're well off from long months at sea, but they could hardly have given her that much. Mum is in possession of a fortune. But I'm unlikely to discover the mystery of her new-found affluence because she remains tight-lipped from that time on and studiously avoids my eye.

By the time we set off for home, a mere five hundred yards down the street, we're as jolly as a bunch of drunken sailors on Saturday night leave in Margate, and none more so that our Dad. He is well into his fifties, but he does cartwheels on the street with the agility of a twenty year old. Mary carries Kathleen on her shoulders, Harry holds Margaret's hand. The four of them run helter-skelter around the rest of us all the way back to the house. The activity is frenzied, but progress is slow on account of Mum's legs. She bears herself bravely, glowing with pride and satisfaction being surrounded by all her children. Her happiness is complete that she can show them off to the world.

We pass the front room windows uphill of the door and there, displayed on sloping boards like goods in a shop window, is an array of secondhand clothes: hats, overcoats, three-piece suits hanging from a brass curtain rail at the back. Summer dresses are laid out to show them to advantage; jumpers in pastel shades of lime green and red and yellow; high quality skirts; and flower print blouses. I must have been blind not to have seen the window display when we left the house earlier to have our photograph taken.

What Mum said to me at the Grafton Arms now makes sense. She has turned the front room into a secondhand clothes shop, and that's the reason she's making money hand over fist. Going by the loot she has in her handbag, Dad's wages would be of small consequence to the family finances. How brilliant of her, how clever and astute.

Never one to take answers at face value, it doesn't take me long to work out Mum's wartime racket. Well, I shouldn't call it a racket; exploiting an opportunity would be more like it. Mum began her little enterprise by selling the secondhand clothes Lady Boldwell, the Colonel's wife, brought to her. It was the perfect way of making money during the war with clothing coupons in such short supply. I learn later that she has a constant stream of customers knocking at the front door for something or other they've seen in the front window. Mum's raking it in.

For the rest of that magical day we're crammed together in our small house. There are no boyfriends or girlfriends, no Aunt Ada or Uncle Bill from Hopping Hill, just us, all by ourselves. Proof of the importance of the occasion is our Dad forgoing his Saturday afternoon nap – an almost unheard departure from his weekly routine.

Mum, with her customary vigour, organises the preparation of a grand supper to celebrate the event in our lives. Feeding a large family is a huge undertaking even at normal times. Now, in the middle of the war, it might seem that the problem is insuperable, but the extra rations coupons save the day. The fact that anyone on a 72 hour pass got ration coupons for a week means that Mum is flush with the additional rations those coupons we have brought home would bring. It means that Margaret can be sent to Kingman's on Regent Street for butter, tea, sugar, cheese, bacon – all of which food is severely rationed. What a magnificent windfall that is for Mum.

Mary alone is without ration coupons because, as usual, she is absent from her unit without leave. To be absent without leave or AWOL or 'taking French leave' is taking a risk. That she could be picked up by the military police at any time worries Dad no end. I don't know how many times he warns her she'll get herself into trouble, but she pooh-poohs his concern with a wave of her hand, saying, 'It's all right, Dad. You worry too much. My mates are covering for me. The officers all take off for the weekend anyway, so why shouldn't I?' Mary is sixteen now, a year behind Harry.

Harry agrees with Mary. 'Our Mary can look after herself, can't you, Mary?' He's been in the brig himself for the same thing, so it's nothing to write home about.

'You bet your life I can,' she says. 'They can always fire me, can't they, m'ducks? I mean, aren't we all doing our bit?'

'What d'you do anyway, our Mary? Work in the cookhouse?' This is from me.

'Not bleeding likely. What d'you take me for?'

'Language, language,' Mum warns.

'Huh! Just listen to the pot calling the kettle black.' Mary is standing at the back wall of the kitchen, languidly tucking loose bits of hair into her hair roll. 'I was on predictors for a while,' she says, 'but I've graduated, see. I'm gun-layer on a Bofors 40 mm gun in an anti-aircraft battery and, like I tell the Yanks when they ask, it's the only bloody thing I lay.'

Jack and Harry laugh. That's another North American import: 'being laid', 'getting laid', 'laying someone', I mean. I don't know what it really means although by now I've got some idea of its sexual connotation. Still, it sounds funny. The Yanks have a lively way of expressing themselves. They bring new and refreshing vigour to the language. Dad gives a little smile; he is reserved in reacting to sexual allusions. Mum isn't as subtle. She doesn't think the joke funny and gives Mary a withering look of disapproval for her coarseness.

'Oh, our Mam, don't look so severe. We're grown up now, you know.'

'Well, I'm surprised at you with such talk. Why don't you save it for the barrack room?'

'Better be blunt than get demobbed under Para. 11, don't you think?'

'And what's that when it's at home, as if I can't guess?'

'Walking the Barratt way, ATS style.'

Dad can't help but laugh at this one. As for Harry, Ada and me, we holler and hoot and slap our thighs till tears come to our eyes. Fred isn't in on the joke. He's busy telling Malcolm about an airman he found washed up on a beach in North Devon; Kathleen is on Jack's knee telling him a likely tale; and Theresa is squawking for her bottle.

There's so much noise going on you have to shut your ears to the babble to concentrate on what you want to hear.

Chatting up a storm, we bustle about laying the table with good things from our walk-in pantry: pickled onions, red cabbage and piccalilli, plum jam, potted meat and cold potato pie with a thick, brown crust. You wouldn't think we were at war and starving for food. Also in the pantry, Dad had a five-gallon barrel of Northampton Brewery Company beer, which he's been saving for a special occasion and this is one. There's freshly baked bread, Haslet and pig's trotters on the table from Browns, a large pot of beef stew and dumplings on the fire. Margaret returns triumphant from her errand to Kingham's Provisioners, Mary unwraps the large pork pie from her excursion to Browns and, somehow – but don't expect me to explain how – everyone squeezes around the table to begin the feast.

'We need plates. We've forgotten the plates. Go and get the plates, Fred, there's good'un,' Mum says.

Fred goes into the back place. I still have this vision of him returning, his hands full, poised dramatically at the kitchen door for his entrance when catastrophe suddenly strikes. He takes one step forward and our precious plates begin slipping from his ham-fisted hands. Bang! crash! crash! bang! bang! they drop to the floor, smashing into a hundred pieces. Harry leaps from his chair at the sudden noise and dives into the corridor; Mum jumps up from her chair in alarm and stands staring at the devastation with her mouth agape; Theresa yells her head off in fright. The plates are irreplaceable. They are all we have.

Dad breaks the silence and the tension that follows, remarking, 'Well, bugger me. We're having a smashing time, aren't we?'

Fred nods his head vigorously in agreement, grinning from ear to ear until tears fill his eyes. No one feels this more than him and, abandoning himself to the comedy of the situation, Fred is soon convulsed in laughter. Others follow suit. Mum looks at Dad, at the grinning and laughing faces about her, and shrugs. Like the sinking of the *Titanic*, the disaster is so great it leaves everyone speechless.

'Pick up the pieces,' she says quietly. 'Jack! Lend our Fred a hand. Mary, Arthur, Malcolm; go into Compton Street and see if you can borrow plates or we'll be eating off the floor.'

We return from our errand with more than enough crockery to see us through the banquet. How we tuck into the feast Mum has prepared that memorable day is beyond description. Nothing can suppress our spirits, no morbid thoughts of what the future might bring nor what fortunes, good or ill, might befall us. We live for the present and let tomorrow take care of itself. We're together as a family, one and united – temporarily anyway – and who could ask for more? As Mum says, it's an ill wind that blows no one any good, which is true enough.

The next morning, we're all up early ready for another good day together. Then Mum announces, 'I think I'll go to nine o'clock mass this morning. Who'll come with me?'

It is enough that she's made that announcement. If she'd wanted to go in the past she'd slip quietly out of the house and leave the rest of us to get on with our Protestant lives.

'Come on,' she says. 'Who'll come with me.'

One by one, we shake our heads.

'No! Not me.'

'No thanks!'

'Me neither.'

'I thought we had an understanding, Maggie,' says Dad, 'to keep the bloody Church out of our lives.'

'You don't understand, Jack. It's different now. These are our children, every one of them. We've never been together like this before and I'd like to thank my God for their safe return.'

'Then do it on your own, Mag,' he says.

'Won't one of you come with me?' she asks. There's a heartfelt appeal in her voice. 'Someone? Surely. I don't ask much. You don't have to pray. I'll do that.'

'I'll come with you, Mum,' says Harry quietly. 'And he'll come too, won't you?' he says to me. 'Get your hat on, scouse. Let's get Mum to mass.'

I've been on church parades every week since I left home, sung in the choir. I like the hymns but not the sermons, so I'm indifferent to churchy things and don't give a toss about religion one way or the other. Still, I think, that's the Church of England. What would mass be like?

I soon find out. We have a half hour walk to Roman Catholic church on Marriott Street just off the Kingsthorpe Road. Mum walks on air, so pleased is she to be having us two for company.

'You don't need to be afraid,' she assures us. 'There'll be lots of people there. It's well attended and no one will notice you.'

But it's different from what I'm used to. Mum lights a candle at the entrance for some reason and places money in one of the collection boxes provided. One is a poor box, another is for missionary work, yet another for something called the 'vestment fund'.

Then Mum leads the way down the aisle and ushers Harry to an empty row before bending on one knee and having me sit on her other side before kneeling to pray.

'What did you pray for?' I ask her when she's done with praying.

'That's none of your business. Just you be quiet and follow the service,' she whispers. I think she's feeling very proud as she looks around to see who she can see, with Harry in his Navy uniform on one side and me on the other in khaki.

There's no point in describing the mass because everyone who's ever been to one knows the form without a reminder from me. Most of the mass is in Latin, but the priest gives some notices in English, which I think is pretty decent of him because not everyone understands Latin like him and Mum. Then it's all over and we three walk home together. Our Mum is as proud as a peacock and I know we've made her day.

Then we're back home for dinner, having waited for Dad and brother Jack and the others to return from a round of the local pubs and – well, that's it really. Mary has to set off early to hitchhike back to her anti-aircraft battery in Suffolk and Jack has to report back to Portsmouth. Still, all in all, it's been a memorable weekend.

12   In and Out of the Slammer

THE WAR has to go on without Jack's help – which I don't say lightly. He is discharged as unfit for further service. Jack takes up the trade of cobbling, which is the business of boot and shoe repairs; Harry goes back to sea on further escort duty for the Russian convoys going to Murmansk for which I don't envy him; Mary hitchhikes back to her Bofors gun battery in Suffolk; Ada lies about her age to enlist in the Women's Auxiliary Air Force (the WAAFs); and Fred is soon old enough to enlist to serve an army apprenticeship as I had done. Malcolm, Margaret and Kathleen are still at school; our infant sister Theresa, being a cretin child, poor creature, has died. And that accounts for everyone in the family in the weeks following our tribal gathering.

There's another death in the family too: our Gaffer, who's been bedridden for months in Aunt Ada's and Uncle Bill's house. I'm at home with Mary the weekend Aunt Ada calls at the house to persuade Dad to visit his father. He agrees and takes me with him on his journey of reconciliation. Aunt Ada must have been watching for us because she opens her front door immediately we knock.

'Hello, Jack,' she says. 'I'm ever so glad you came.'

'Hello, my old Tuppence. How is he?' he asks. Tuppence is his nickname for her. He calls our sister Ada May Tuppence, too, so there's a connection there.

'He's not good, Jack. He's not good. Come in, come in,' she says in hushed tones. The house is small and a word spoken in one corner can be heard in every other. 'I told Dad you might visit him. He was ever so pleased. He'll be expecting you.'

Aunt Ada is not a demonstrative woman. Although she looks prim and severe she is soft-spoken and has a kind manner. Like Mum, she wears her hair in telephone buns over her ears, only it's auburn coloured whereas Mum's hair is jet black. Aunt Ada is always smartly dressed too. There's no need to wonder why though. She and Uncle Bill have no children. They own their house and pay no water rates so their expenses are minimal, which is to say they're up to their bellies in clover like cows in a summer meadow.

Dad's sister ushers us into the comfortable living room of her terrace cottage, a welcoming coal fire flickering in the grate. The cottage walls are a good three feet thick with casement, bottle-glass windows set in them. When the Craft cottage was built a couple of hundred years ago, one of four joined labourers' cottages, the builders didn't spare the ironstone. Although the furniture, floor and ornaments are polished and spotless, the cottage itself has a distinctive patina of its own. Aunt Ada bids us be seated, but Dad remains standing.

Having listened to her report on Gaffer's illness, Dad says, 'All right, my girl. I'd better go up and see him.' Our Gaffer is dying of lung cancer caused, they say, by too much coke dust in his lungs, but I'm pretty sure that all that black shag plug tobacco he cut and mixed and stuffed in his clay pipe has a lot to do with it.

'You don't need me, Jack,' says Aunt Ada. 'He's in the small bedroom.' She opens the door at the bottom of the stairs and I get up to follow, but she says, 'Stay where you are, my ducks. Your dad'll want to see your Gaffer alone. Why don't you help me make the tea?'

She doesn't need help making tea, so I lay the table. When I'm done, I go to the casement window overlooking the Harlestone Road, which runs past her house and sit on the polished ledge and watch the traffic roll by. Long convoys of military trucks fill the road with just a few civilian cars mixed in. Road traffic is light at the best of times. With petrol rationing, civilian cars are few and far between.

This cosy room with its polished oak beam spanning the ceiling has restricted head room so that anyone taller than five feet nine has to duck to pass under the beam. A Tiffany-style lampshade for the only electrical light in the cottage hangs from the centre of the ceiling. Aunt Ada had electricity installed four years ago with the light switch fitted to the door frame leading upstairs. We have gas lighting in our house on Crane Hill, so it's still a novelty to switch on Aunt Ada's electric light and we marvel at the instant light available at the flick of a switch.

A large table with four matching sturdy upright chairs occupy the centre of the room, one at each end and two opposite the fire place. Two comfortable leather easy chairs stand between the fire and table, one for the Gaffer, the other for Uncle Bill. Cupboards and shelves with doors are built into the wall on either side of the fireplace. A carpet covered with expensive rugs is on the floor, making everything trim and snug. The contrast between Aunt Ada's place and our home is striking, for we have a rag rug in front of the fireplace over the worn linoleum that covers the living-room floor.

Dad's gone more than an hour. When he comes back down, he ducks his head to get through the doorway and looks very serious.

'Are you all right, Jack?' Aunt Ada asks.

'Yes, I'm fine, lovey. Don't concern yourself. We're all right now. Had a nice chat and made up, we did.'

'I'm so glad about that, Jack. I shouldn't like to think he had left this world on the outs with any of us. He can go in peace now and I'm ever so thankful for that.' She goes into the kitchen to bring the teapot to the table without pausing in her conversation. 'I'll just nip up an' see as he's all right and would like a cup of tea. Then we'll have one, should we?'

'There's no need now, Ada.'

'Oh!'

'He's gone. He said he was hanging on for me.'

'I'd better go,' she says in a quiet voice. With heavy feet she climbs the narrow stairs to see her father for herself and comes down again a short time later. Dad's waiting. She puts her arm on his shoulder and, with watery eyes on the verge of tears but not crying, she rests her forehead on the side of Dad's head for a long time. After a silence all that time she lifts her head and kisses him on the cheek.

With his arms wrapped about her, Dad speaks in a tone I've never heard him use before. 'He was a good man, Ada, and a good father to us,' he says sadly.

'Yes, he was,' says Aunt Ada.

'He had a good life and lived his allotted span.'

'He did. That's true.'

'And can rest in peace.'

'He can now, Jack. He can now.'

Aunt Ada won't have us stay. She says she can look after things if Dad will arrange for the undertaker to remove the body, which he does on the public telephone on the corner.

We're all sad our Gaffer has died, naturally, but it's not our way to gnash our teeth and smite our breasts over a death in the family. It's not done and as for viewing the corpse in the coffin, which I believe is common in other societies, nothing is considered to be more vulgar or offensive in the culture of The Boroughs. We bury our Gaffer at Dallington Cemetery on Tuesday afternoon following a burial service by the military chaplain of the Garrison Church of the Holy Sepulchre, called Holy Seps for short. Gaffer served his time in the regiment and is entitled to a military send-off. Afterwards, we all go to Aunt Ada's for scones and tea.

★

It's convenient for Mary the day Gaffer dies because for a change she happens to be on a weekend pass. She's promptly telephoned her unit officer to get an extension on compassionate grounds of there being a death in the family.

Mum's threats 'to bloody well crucify you in a minute' to Mary were so frequent before she left home that by now they've come to have no meaning. Mind you, Mum still shouts with equal enthusiasm and fervour at the rest of us, though she seems to have it in particularly for the girls.

Mary long ago learned to give as good as she got. She's honed her style over the years and has become so adept at answering back with the same unsheathed rapier of a tongue that she's developed impregnable defences. They can still go at it hammer and tongs, so if Mum comes out with one of her 'I'll bloody crucify you' threats, Mary will reply, 'Isn't that what Pontius Pilate said?'

'Don't come the acid with me, girl. Crucify, I said, and crucify I will.'

Mary's developed the habit of lowering her voice when argument with Mum heats up. 'You won't, you know. That's against the law now. The National Society for the Prevention of Cruelty to Children have put a stop to that kind of thing now and they'd kick up a stink if they found you out.'

Mum has to listen hard to catch what Mary's saying, which only increases her fury. 'God forgive me if I don't kill you before I'm through.'

'Oh, come on, Mam, be fair. Not with a wooden spoon you won't.'

When it suits her, however, Mum's quite capable of fostering good relations, especially when she's been pregnant and has needed Mary's help. Then it's 'There's a good 'un, our Mary. Do the washing up for us, will you?' or 'Help us with the washing, there's a love. I'm not feeling so good,' but between babies, when our Mum's fit and active, the battle of wills is fast and furious.

Mary is from the same mould as Mum. She's kind, considerate and protective, but not as mercurial as Mum, who jumps like spit on the hob when it takes her fancy. I have to say that Mary is a good-looker as a teenager. She has a trim figure and looks smart in her ATS uniform. Being a gunner, she's among the first ATS personnel to be issued with khaki slacks. Beneath her cherubic face is a will of steel. She began asserting her independence from about the time she reached her twelfth birthday. This bid for freedom stemmed I believe from her taking over housewifely duties during Mum's lying-in with successive children. The experience gave her the moral strength stemming from the exercise of authority and having to prepare our meals.

She can bake or steam a steak and kidney pudding or cook a stew or make spotted dick pudding as well as anyone. She can organise the housework and direct the rest of us without the confusion and turmoil of Mum's regime, for we're all well trained. When Mum's fit to take her place again, Mary reverts to her normal place in the family, though with increasing strength of spirit.

In her early teens, she shot up tall and willowy, which might explain why she was able to enlist so young. With short, dark hair and those hooded, almond-shaped eyes, she's striking and confident.

Following Mary's short stay at the Royal Soldiers Daughters Home, Mum said with disguised meaning, 'Yes, my girl, you're a disciple of St Paul, aren't you? Every finger a fish hook and no mistake.' If I knew then what I know now all would have been clear to me, but at the time only Mary knew or got the intent of Mum's words, for she went very quiet. It was one time she was stumped for an answer.

When war was declared, Mary left home to join the Women's Land Army. By the time half the country was in uniform, hers was a pair of khaki riding breeches, a green shirt and a wide-brimmed safari-style bush hat. She was sent to work on a manorial farm a few miles from town 'A worker to the manor born,' as she says. She stuck it for a year before deciding that hoeing turnips and cleaning out pig sties at the wages she was paid was not for her.

'I couldn't stand the land army, my ducks,' she told me. 'You're nothing but a labourer doing man's work at half the pay. Bed and board and Betty Martin's your Aunt Fanny as they say. There's no future in that.'

Months later, in one of Mum's weekly letters, which began as always

My dear son, Thanks ever so much for yours 15th inst. to hand

she continued without pause or punctuation:

our Marys been and gone and joined the ATS and that's a nice cup of tea if ever there was one working in the kitchens doing what she does best cutting spam and making corned beef hash so I told her she can bring some corned beef home any time ha!

Mother writes the way she speaks, which leaves you breathless.

Working in the cookhouse, apparently, wasn't Mary's cup of tea either. She badgered her Commanding Officer for a transfer to an anti-aircraft unit for gun-crew training and became a gun-layer in anti-aircraft gun battery equipped with 40 millimetre Bofors guns. The Bofors gun fires a 40 millimetre round of ammunition, fed into the breach in clips of four or five rounds and can be fired off automatically in quick succession. One round in each clip is a tracer, which means it shows up in the dark. Her battery is situated somewhere on the Suffolk coast.

Mary was seventeen when she became a gunner. She wears her long brown hair rolled in a neat ring that circles her head but with a loop that comes down to her neck. With her peaked, soft top khaki hat worn squarely on her head, her collar and tie and battledress top and trousers, she looks as smart a lass in uniform as anyone.

What with the Gaffer dying and Mary getting a bereavement extension to her weekend pass, Mum gets on to her again about being absent without leave. That means only one thing. She doesn't know Mary has a pass, for ration coupons come with long weekend passes. As Mary hasn't handed them over to Mum, it can only mean that she's sold them instead. What a laugh. It isn't so much not getting ration coupons that upsets Mum and having another mouth to feed as Mary flouting the rules by going AWOL. Mum's a stickler for obedience to the rules.

'By God! You'll be in for the high jump with your commanding officer when you get back, my girl,' she says to her after the Gaffer's funeral, 'and that won't half serve you right.'

We're back home, sitting in the front room, just me, Mum and Mary.

Mary laughs. 'No I won't. I'll tell the CO I've got me period, cramps an' all. I can't half put it on, you know.'

Mum's shocked. She draws a deep breath, puts a steadying hand to her chest, and rolls her eyes like Sarah Bernhardt in a dramatic role. 'Ooh! I'm surprised at you,' she hisses. 'That's not the sort of thing for discussion in front of him,' she says with a protective look at me.

'Why not? It's natural, isn't it? He'll know sooner or later, won't you, my duck?' Mary says, addressing her question at me. I don't know what she's talking about, so I shrug and remain silent.

Before she leaves to hitchhike a ride back to camp, I ask her why she's used up her weekend leave on coming home when all she seems to do is quarrel with our Mum. She's only enlisted to get away, but she gives me a knowing wink because she's caught Mum listening and says aloud, 'She's me Mam, isn't she? You are, aren't you, Mam?' Then she mimicks her, saying, 'Aye! You know what I always say, don't you? Blood's thicker than water. It is, ain't it, our Mam. That's what you always say, don't you, Mam?'

Mary can be vicious when it suits her. She's been taught so well that Mum is now quite out of her depth in dealing with her. Mary's imitation of her is also so strong that it reduces Mum to simmering, impotent anger.

Mum purses her lips in a tight knot and shakes her head from side to side. 'You can be a right nasty piece of work, can't you? I always said you'd be Mary, Mary, quite contrary.'

Mary laughs. She's had her fun, wound our Mum up like a coiled spring and is now ready to let her unwind. 'Don't take on so, Mam. I still love you for all your faults, so be a good 'un and give us a pound. I'm short this week.'

Recovering her composure and looking hard at Mary through her thick lenses, Mum say, 'You only come to me when you want something. You don't deserve anything, I can tell you. Where's my purse? Get my purse for me.'

'Oh! You are a good 'un, Mother.' Mary only says 'mother' when she wants to impress us with how refined she can speak when the occasion requires it.

Before she leaves to catch a bus to take her out of town to the Bedford Road, Mary has the brilliant idea that I should visit her battery. 'It's not far from Reading to Hellesley,' she tells me.

'Where will I sleep?'

'Don't worry about that. We'll find a bed for you and you can always sleep with me if it comes to that.'

'Go on with you. You're not allowed to do that.'

She giggles. 'That'd have heads wagging, wouldn't it?' Mary could be quite brazen.

Two months go by before I can get a leave pass to make the journey.   Because I can't get a rail travel warrant I have to spend my own money. I've got enough for a return ticket to London with some over for the Underground. I go to the end of the Central Line to Unger and, from there, thumb lifts to Martlesham and on to the village of Hellesley. I walk the last two miles in the pouring rain so that I'm completely waterlogged by the time I arrive at Mary's battery.

The camp is a bleak and desolate clump of corrugated Nissan huts surrounded by a double barrier of barbed wired. East of the huts, close to the shoreline, the sandbagged gun emplacements and ammunition bunkers sit like warts on the landscape. A more barren and godforsaken spot would be hard to imagine. No wonder Mary's always doing a bunk for home. It must be a miserable hole to be stationed in.

A battleaxe of an ATS sergeant with close-cropped hair and ballooning chest confronts me at the gate and practically marches me into the guardroom. She demands to know my business and, before I can tell her, says, 'Don't you know coast batteries are out of bounds?' She is horribly officious. 'Where's your AB64?' She means my Army service book.

I take it out of my breast pocket and watch in silence as she thumbs through it. She looks me up and down as if I were a lump of cat's dirt on her carpet, and clicks her tongue. 'As if we don't have enough trouble with one bleeding Fulthorpe without having to put up with another.'

'I'm here to see my sister, sarn't,' I reply. 'She's expecting me.'

'Don't sarn't me. She can go on expecting you because she's under arrest. You can't see her and that's that. You're wasting you're time.'

'I don't see why not, so why not?' I haven't come all this way to see my sister without putting up a fight.

'What d'you mean, why not?'

'Just that, Sergeant. Why not?' She's a right old cretin this one, the meanest-looking lump of suet pudding I've come across since I got into khaki.

'I said she's under arrest, close arrest, so skedaddle. Be on your way.' The sergeant could have been shouting orders on the barrack square.

'Is that you, our Arthur, m'ducks?' comes my sister Mary's voice from the far end of the guard hut.

I look past the sergeant into the semi-darkness. Beyond the guard room table, a filing cabinet and two sets of wooden bunks, I can just make out the grills of four cells, two on each side of the walk space. I can't see Mary, but her voice is unmistakable.

'Hello, our Mary,' I shout.

'Quiet!' the sergeant commands. 'No talking to the prisoner.'

At this moment, an ATS officer enters the guardroom. I snap to attention and salute. The sergeant gets to her feet and salutes, but she's not so quick off the mark. The officer, a tall, slim lieutenant with her hair tucked inside her peaked cap, looks at me in surprise. I see in her a familiar face I can't place. I don't suppose she's that used to seeing a soldier apprentice dressed in a pre-war jacket with brass buttons and wearing a peaked cap like a guardsman.

'Hello! Who do we have here, Sergeant Baxter?' the lieutenant asks.

The sergeant still has possession of my service book, opens it and reads aloud, '2548686, A/T Fulthorpe, ma'am.'

'I've come to see my sister, ma'am,' I blurt out.

'Hold your tongue and speak when you're spoken to,' Sergeant Baxter snaps.

'Let him speak, Sergeant. Let him speak.'

Now I recognise the lieutenant's accent, definitely a Northampton county accent. She reminds me of Colonel Boldwell's wife to whom she bears a striking likeness, only a younger and more attractive version. She doesn't look that much older than our Mary, though I've no doubt she is, being a full lieutenant.

She gestures to the sergeant, who hands my AB64 to her. She scans it for a moment or two then says, 'Fulthorpe? Where are you stationed A/T Fulthorpe?'

'Arborfield, near Reading, ma'am. I've got a weekend pass to visit my sister.'

'Gunner Fulthorpe's under close arrest, ma'm.' Sergeant Baxter seems determined to throw me out on to the road.

'I'm aware of that, Sergeant.'

'I'd like to see my sister, ma'am. I've come a long way and I didn't know she was in the slammer, honest I didn't.'

It has been raining steadily all day. A constant tinny patter of rain has been chattering on the corrugated iron of the Nissen hut since I arrived, but at this moment a clap of thunder breaks and rain falls in a deluge, rattling the iron sheeting like a hundred kettledrums.

The lieutenant leans over to answer me. 'Yes, I'm sure you do. Well, let's see if we can't just arrange something. Sergeant Baxter!' she commands above the din, 'Release Gunner Fulthorpe. She can be confined to barracks for the time being.'

The sergeant is not overjoyed to carry out the duty lieutenant's order, but she does as commanded. A short time later, Mary comes out of the cell, buttoning up her jacket. The officer gives her what I think is a look of recognition a little more than the usual indifference with which officers treat the other ranks. Mary returns her superior officer's not unfriendly recognition with an expression of gratitude and says, 'Thank you, ma'm.'

Without further word, the lieutenant turns and leaves the guardroom, plunging into the teeming downpour.

My sister grins triumphantly and, ignoring Sergeant Baxter, hugs me to her, saying, 'Hello, m'ducks. It's lovely to see you. Came at the right time, too, didn't you? Now you stay right there.'

Without so much as a word of explanation or by your leave, she returns to her cell and comes back carrying two ground sheet capes, one of which she's borrowed from her next door cellmate. Every soldier has a cape in his or her equipment. In wet weather, it serves as a rain cover over a full load of battle equipment. It can also be used as waterproof protection on waterlogged ground; a handy item really.

'Here! Put this on yourself or you'll get soaked to the skin,' Mary says.

'I already am.'

'I'll be back to report before bye-byes, Sergeant,' Mary says cheekily.

'I'll wipe that grin of your face soon enough, Fulthorpe,' Sergeant Baxter replies.

'Yes, Sergeant. Very good, Sergeant. Come on, our Arthur. Let's get out of here. The place gives me the creeps. We'll go to the NAAFI. It's always open.' She slings her gas mask over her shoulder, puts on her tin helmet and cape, and leads the way through the downpour into a quagmire of mud.

Over steaming mugs of NAAFI tea, Mary sits facing me, grinning, holding my hand across the table. 'You know who that was, don't you?'

'That bloody awful sergeant?' I ask. 'How should I?'

'No! The officer?'

'I haven't a clue, except her face seemed familiar.'

'Lieutenant Boldwell.'

'Go on with you. Can't be. Is she really?'

'Yes, that's right; Daphne Boldwell. Bit of luck, eh?' Daphne Boldwell is the daughter of Colonel Boldwell of our father's regiment and his wife, Lady Boldwell. Mary beams with pleasure.

'Well, I'll be blowed. I thought she gave me a queer look when she spoke my name.'

'It's a small world and it pays to know the right people. She's our battery commander an' ever so good to me.' Mary screws up her nose. 'Of course, I daren't let on we know one another or they'll have it in for me, especially Baxter. She's a right pig.'

'Why were you in the clink?' I ask.

'Oh, the usual thing. Baxter caught me leaving camp without a pass and is charging me with insubordination. It's OK, she can't do anything.' With her supreme self-confidence, Mary is nonchalant about her service life. She knows her job and I later discover that she's a crackerjack of a gun layer into the bargain.

We spend a lovely weekend together, though she's confined to barracks, which means we can't go into the village or walk along the country lanes. Instead, Mary gives me a conducted tour of the camp and guns in dry but blustery weather. We're also able to walk along the sea-shore and suck in the salt sea air. We skim pebbles along the water and laugh and joke. Her knowledge of guns amazes me. I reckon that what she doesn't know about the Bofors gun and how it works isn't worth knowing – and to think she's only two years older than me, amazing.

She explains how the gun is operated and what they have to do to keep it fed with shells. So all in all, she gives me an impressive introduction to anti-aircraft guns. Her battery is nicely spaced, covered in camouflage tarpaulins with each gun enclosed in a protective wall of sandbags. The ammunition bunkers are some distance away, sunk in the ground with a heavy earth covering and sandbagged entrances.

'Can you see the shells when you're firing?' I ask.

'Course you can. It's like a peashooter if you've got your eye to the shuftiscope.' What she means is, that as the gun layer, Mary can see the trace of shells leaving the muzzle through her telescopic gunsight.

Being among ATS women gunners of Bofors gun battery this weekend is an exciting experience for me. Mary's comrades treats me like someone from another world. They are all young, spirited and sharp-tongued, and they make witty remarks I only partly understand.

'Where did you get him from?' one asks.

'How do you do it, Fulthorpe?' asks another.

'Let us give him some training, Mary!'

'Does anyone want to find out why he's called monster?'

The women in the NAAFI canteen screech and hoot with laughter. Most of their talk goes over my head, especially our Mary's, who deflects saucy questions with her rapier tongue and talks about hiring me out for a bob a knob – whatever that means – to anyone interested. I'm not so dumb as not to get some of the allusions, but still green enough about the ears to miss the meaning of a lot that's said. The women, more than a dozen gathered together, are free and easy and good-natured; lots of fun to be with, I think. Most of the exchanges between them are directed at my sister and the fact she has me for company. She's quite a girl is our Mary, I discover, and popular among her companions.

The next afternoon, following an uneventful night – for in consideration my virtuous state, I sleep in a single room of an NCO on leave – Mary gets me a lift in a 15 cwt Bedford going to Ipswich and says goodbye to me at the main gate. The ghastly Sergeant Baxter stands on the verandah of the guard room to make sure, I suppose, that Mary doesn't hop on to the truck. The sun is out full and warm in a clear blue sky, so I set off in high spirits to get back to camp before my leave pass expires.

★

Two months later, the Germans begin a fresh onslaught on London by launching their V1 pilotless flying bombs, known as doodlebugs. The Fuhrer has threatened to flatten London with his new secret weapon and this is it. These bombs are fitted with early jet engines called ramjets. The contraptions are catapulted off a ramp to go phut-phutting on their way to the target, flying across the North Sea a few hundred feet above sea level until they run out of fuel. Then they fall and explode a ton of high explosive. They head straight for London mostly, but sometimes fall short when they run out of fuel or overshoot the city to hit the outskirts if they have an excess of fuel. When their jet engines cut out they drop like bricks and Mary's battery is in the direct line of fire.

According to Mary the day begins soon after daybreak when the siren alarm blares and everyone turned out at the double to man the guns. Mary is again behind bars for some transgression, but on the first wail of the siren the guard releases her from her cell and she runs hell for leather across the grass to her gun emplacement, searching the sky for signs of enemy aircraft.

'Get your damned helmet on,' yells the battery sergeant.

'Keep your shirt on, Sergeant,' Mary shrieks back. 'It's going on now.'

'Report to me on the all clear, Fulthorpe. I've got a charge in store for you,' the sergeant yells as she hurries away to chivvy the loaders at one of the ammunition bunkers.

Mary swears that some women NCOs are worse than men. She rams the helmet on her head and pulls the chin strap tight as she heads for the gun. The rest of the crew are already there, unclipping the ammunition boxes and loading. She mounts the bucket seat, stuffs her khaki hat into her trousers pocket, the peak sticking out, and elevates the gun muzzle to the ready position as she searches the sky for aircraft.

The site bustles with activity as latecomers race to their guns, loaders emerge from the bunkers, and officers and NCOs shout orders. In these few moments before all hell breaks loose, Mary takes in a number of things: Lieutenant

Boldwell entering an ammunition bunker, the commanding officer getting out of her utility van, the low overhead at about 500 feet, a shaft of sunlight striking the water through a break in the clouds. Mary searches the eastern sky to anticipate the range and bearing she expects from the predictor crew. It comes soon enough. The battery sergeant, listening on her headset, shouts her orders.

'Bearing! Eighty-two degrees. Elevation! Eighteen hundred. Range! Two miles V1.'

Mary is correcting the range and bearing, her eye glued to the shufti-scope, when a deafening roar comes from her right quarter. A lone German Heinkel is upon them without warning.

'Starboard!' she yells, traversing the gun carriage hard to face the incoming bomber. She has no time to reflect. The bomber, heading in low with its bomb bay doors open, is coming down her barrel. She fires – '*Vrump! vrump! vrump! vrump!*' – at what seems like point blank range.

A cluster of bombs leave the aircraft's belly and come sailing towards her, no time to duck. Again she fires – '*Vrump! vrump!*' – and gets in a couple more rounds before the Heinkel, with a thunderous roar, is overhead and behind her. The bombs explode in quick succession, first on the seashore then into the camp – '*Crump! crump! crump!*' The explosions are deafening as the bombs strike home.

Number one bunker a hundred yards away blows up. Clods of earth and debris come flying through the air, thud-thudding back to ground. The blast of the bomb and exploding bunker hits Mary. She hangs on to the gun mounting for her life. An ammunition carrier caught in the blast from the bunker, lies on the grass, naked, but still wearing her helmet. The sight is unreal.

One of her own loaders is down and bleeding from the head. Mary screams, 'Pam, don't move!' Smoke is everywhere in the still air and the stench of cordite is overpowering. Each second lasts a lifetime. At this moment, a sledgehammer of a blow strikes her hip and she gasps from the pain. She feels herself all over frantically, convinced she's lost a leg. It's still there, and although the hurt in her thigh is excruciatingly painful, the hat she's stuffed into her trouser pocket cushions the blow of whatever has hit her.

Through the smoke comes the sergeant's voice again, loud and firm as a linchpin. 'Incoming doodlebug. Bearing 82, elevation 79. Range, half a mile. Number three, lock on, lock on. Fulthorpe, Fulthorpe, d'you hear? That's you, you idiot!'

Mary presses her eye to the gunsight and seats the rubber pad of the sight firmly about her eye as she pushes it to cover her forehead and cheek. She brings the cross-hairs into focus and gets a clear view of the trail of puffs from the jet engine of the incoming V1. She figures it would be crossing her position at an angle, passing slightly to the south of the battery. Calmly she swings the barrel of the Bofors, giving a lead on the approaching bomb. In their excitement, many a gun layer would have let rip, but not Mary. She takes her time, waiting for the Doodlebug to get nearer. She adjusts the elevation and leads both to give the outgoing shells enough front room as one might say. Fire directly at the Doodlebug and it would be miles ahead of the shells by the time they arrived.

'Ready, ready, steady!' she speaks calmly to the loaders, not taking her eye from the sight. It is a warning to be ready with the next clip of shells. 'Here we go!'

She fires. Her eyes never leave the target as she follows the outgoing shells. With the adrenalin flowing in her veins she forgets the pain in her side as she traverses the gun to keep the V1 in her sights. Another tap on her back tells her the next clip of ammo's in place. She fires again: two twos, '*Bup! bup!*' '*Bup! bup!*' and follows with the final shell, '*Bup!*' Has she given enough lead? God above! It has happened, a miracle. There, a thousand yards out, over the sea, a mighty explosion engulfs what had only seconds ago been a deadly Doodlebug heading for London.

Mary takes her eye from the sight for a broader view. Incredible! Unbelievable! The V1 has disintegrated into a thousand pieces as large chunks fall into the sea. A whoop goes up from the gun crew. From under her helmet, she looks around, grinning. She's scored a direct hit – no doubt about it – and those left of the crew agree.

'Good for you, Molly,' her number two shouts.

They might have rested on their laurels, but there's chaos all around and no chance of letting up. The Heinkel has come and gone unscathed, a lone hit-and-run raider. The alarm and stand-down orders are on and off all day, for there's no shortage of V1s 'phut-phutting' past the site en route to London. Some are near enough to fire at, but most are out of range. Orders come from higher up of when to take on the flying bombs. When RAF fighters, Hurricanes mostly, are in the vicinity developing a technique to deal with the V1s all action ceases. The pilots fly alongside the flying bombs, nudging them off-course by using the tip of the aircraft's wing to lift the wing of the V1 and send it plunging into the sea. It's dangerous work and not always successful. Miscalculation has cost many a brave pilot his life during the course of the onslaught. The gunners witness many an encounter. Only when the sky is clear of RAF fighters are they free to put their gunnery skills to the test.

Between watching the RAF at work and bouts of action, the women gunners have time to eat, help clear away the debris of the bomber raid, and snatch a rest. Mary hobbles about painfully. She figures she's been struck by an empty shell case sent flying by the explosion. They store their casings alongside the bunkers to be returned for scrap. Although Mary considers her wound minor compared with some of the casualties from the raid and she has no broken bones, she is sore enough to report to the medical officer as soon as she can.

The dead included two ammunition carriers from her platoon, the sergeant who bellowed at her to put her helmet when the first alarm sounded and, more personal to her, Daphne Boldwell. Daphne was in the bunker when the bomb struck and no trace of her body has been found. Knowing the Fulthorpe family through her mother,

Lieutenant Boldwell has been Mary's protector, so it's sad she has gone in more ways than one.

Before the day is over, the battery has claimed two more V1s of which Mary's crew can claim credit for one. It is a missile coming in over the North Sea at 1800 feet. A well-directed shell shatters the V1's port wing so that, through the gunsight, she has a clear view as the bomb veers in towards the coast and plunges into the sea with an explosion clearly heard ashore. Her mates cheer the kill and swear their gun layer deserves a medal for her day's work at the very least. But Sergeant Baxter thinks otherwise and comes to return her to the guard room cell – also before the day is over.

Marched before the CO the following morning, Mary gets ten days confined to barracks for her insubordination and is docked three days' pay. She doesn't mind having her pay docked, she later tells me, because she knows she can get money from Mum now she's rich from her 'war profiteering', as Mary calls it. The ten days' CB she resents most because she is due leave.

And Mary takes it anyway by going AWOL as soon as her punishment is over.

13   The Gospel According to St Fred

FRED IS the lucky one of the family, always falling on his feet, taking care of the main chance like the time in Woolworth's when he nicked lead soldiers from a rotating display table. He stuck his hand on the table, swept the entire show of soldiers from the top and into his coat pocket, then calmly left the store. No one twigged his villainy – he was about seven at the time. Nor did a policeman come to the house. Fred had committed the perfect heist. When he tired of his new possessions, he dropped them one by one into the town drains. Being lead soldiers, I shouldn't be surprised if they are there to this day, getting nicely settled for discovery by some archaeologist in a millennium or two.

Fred's luck arises from a firm conviction in him that the very opposite is true, that he is the unluckiest one of all us Fulthorpe children. Why he feels this way I don't know, yet he claims it as his lot in life to be unlucky. Being near the middle of the pack, he has to assert his right to attention like the cuckoo in the nest with an ever-open beak for whatever is in the offing. That he is a chubby fellow when growing up is not surprising, for he frequently complains of a rumbling stomach, which he claims to be a clear sign of approaching starvation. What is more, he is ever ready to demonstrate the depth of his deprivation. For instance, one morning while we were awake in bed and talking, he said, 'I'm so hungry I could eat the brass knobs on this bed.'

'Go on with you,' said Harry in the next bed, enjoying the last few minutes of waking sleep. 'I'd like to see you try.'

'Then just you watch,' said Fred and, from the bottom of the bed, he unscrewed from the frame a small brass knob the size of a glass marble and popped it into his mouth. Down his gullet it went in a single gulp, just like that.

'What? Swallowed a brass knob? The little bugger!' said our Mum in astonishment when news of the event was brought to her bed. 'He's got a lot of brass, hasn't he?' and, struck by the cleverness of this observation, she rocked from side to side with laughter until her eyes filled with water. She laughed so hard she ended in a fit of coughing, calling out, 'Oh dear, oh dear! Oh deary me.'

I could have sworn she'd choke herself to death with all that coughing and laughing and carrying on. If that happened she would be following our Grandmother Tobin of Welsh chapel fame who choked on beef stuck celebrating the relief of Mafeking in the Anglo-Boer War as I've related. Mum could laugh and so could we gathered about her bed and we did. Only Fred failed to see the funny side of it. He stood at the foot of Mum's place of rest looking as solemn as a judge about to pass a sentence of death on a convicted murderer.

For all this hilarity, Fred's plight was a serious matter and something had to be done about it. Who could tell what damage he might do to his innards? A brass knob coursing through his system, wasting his gastric juices and lodging in his intestines could seriously hazard his health. Mum rolled out of bed in her nightdress and led us in procession downstairs like a jubilant posse with the prisoner captive.

'Get the castor oil,' she commanded. 'Hurry up! Look sharp!'

In an emergency, her mood can change with the speed of summer lightning. Mary brought the castor oil from the pantry. Mum selected the right-sized serving spoon from the kitchen table drawer. At the same time, Jack, Harry and I stood by to help. With so many willing hands holding our unwilling brother, Mum filled the spoon and put it to his lips. He struggled and howled and yelled and, honest to God, shouted that a bowl of porridge would serve as well, but to no avail. No one paid a bit of attention to his protests. Action was called for, not words, and the first spoonful went down his throat.

'Hold him still, can't you? Grab his nose. Extreme ills need extreme cures,' said Mum, applying spoonful after spoonful to his protesting lips. As much spilled over his cheeks and jaw as went down his gullet. The level of oil in the bottle fell alarmingly. Fred was as slippery as an eel by the time the operation was over.

'There! All done. Now we'll wait and see,' said Mum.

Fred was let go and, like a fish taken off the hook and slipped back into the water, he disappeared – but not for long. They also serve who only stand and wait as the saying goes or, in Fred's case, sit when he felt the castor oil taking effect. Mounted on a chamber pot placed in one corner of the kitchen, he sat looking glum and indignant.

'Don't worry. There'll be a successful outcome, I've no doubt of that,' Mum said. More laughter. 'Don't stand gaping you lot. Mary! Get the table laid. The rest of you, get washed.'

We obeyed our platoon leader and sat in our chairs for breakfast. There we waited for the castor oil to work. From time to time someone asked, 'Anything happening yet?'

'No,' Fred said, sullen and resentful.

'Leave him be,' Mum said. 'It'll work. Mind your business and let him mind his. The truth will out as the castor oil said to the brass knob.' More laughter. Mum did like a joke, especially those of her making.

'I think I'm going to be sick,' said Fred.

'Nonsense! It'll do you the world of good. Keep it down.'

Our Dad was on the night shift. He got home about 7.30 and, seeing Fred sitting in the corner like little Jack Horner, said, 'Hello! What's all this?'

Mum recounted the events of the past hour.

'Come here, my son.' Dad sat Fred on his knee in his shirt and bare bottom. 'Let them laugh, boy. He who laughs last laughs best, eh!' He was like that, our Dad, always siding with the underdog. 'Should us have breakfast on our own?'

Fred leapt from Dad's knee, scrambled down and flew to the pot. Just in time, the dam burst and a metallic clang of the brass knob colliding with the enamel chamber pot was striking evidence that Mum's cure had worked.

We laughed, we clapped, we shouted 'Hooray!'

'Bless my soul,' Mum said. 'He's a lucky blighter that one. I couldn't believe my ears when they said, Jack, but anyone who survives a brass knob in his insides has to have a cast iron stomach.'

'That's enough, Mag. Stop teasing the lad. The rest of you clear out. Go on with you. Off you go. Leave him alone.'

We had finished our breakfast of porridge and a dollop of damson jam each from the stone jar, so we left the table. Later, alone in the kitchen with Dad, Fred ate a hearty meal of fresh bread with the rissoles and thick gravy Dad had made just for the two of them. We were envious because we could smell and recognise what Dad was cooking. Rissoles served with brown Windsor gravy for breakfast are a rare delight: a mixture of minced cold beef, potatoes, onions and bread dunked in flour and fried in a pan of hot fat, they make a succulent, mouth-watering and delicious meal.

★

Ever since the bed knob affair, Fred has liked to boast that he is as good as his word. Who else would eat brass bed knobs to satisfy their hunger? It was an indication of the lengths to which he would go. What's more, he hoped it was a lesson for our Mum and that she'd pay more attention to his starving state in future.

Early in the war, Fred joined the same military school to which I'd been admitted. Unlike me, however, for I accepted the fact without objection, Fred's admission wasn't at all to his liking. With Jack and Harry in the Royal Navy, Mary in the Women's Land Army at the time, and Ada about to be in uniform, Fred had been the eldest sibling still at home. There was prestige in being the eldest, which he was loathe to give up, but it was more than that. He resented having to leave home for being, as he thought it, cast out.

We had little contact at school. Fred had his friends and I had mine. We fought sometimes, but settled our differences without ill will and, truth to tell, we were companionable with one another. We shared what we had when something came from home and sought one another's company when the other got into trouble. Other than that, we went our separate ways. Fred resented being called 'Fulthorpe Junior', which was the standard term of reference for brothers in the school. With the Bullers, who numbered three, the second one was known as Buller Middle. Unlike other groups of brothers in the school (there were several brothers at that time as a result of early high casualties during the war), who stuck together, Fred was independent from the start.

The significance of this is that Fred and I have never been very close since we left home. Life in the military school made our subsequent careers in a military life inevitable. As a consequence, wherever I have gone, Fred has followed. We have, of course, travelled home together on leave and back again. During those times at home, we've shared a closer friendship. At school, we both played in the clarinet section of the band and followed the trade of electrician once we began our military apprenticeship training. Fred has had a strong urge to excel, which might have had something to do with our drifting apart as we got older. We've been fiercely competitive, yet he was the one who excelled, for he did well in everything: at sport, music and at school. As compared with mine, his school reports glowed with marks and notes of achievement, yet he fostered this notion of having bad luck.

Fred is always short of money and tapping me for a loan, frequently prefacing his appeal with a taunt, which goes something like this:

'Do you know the trouble with you?'

'No. What?'

'You've got a big head.'

'You're a fine one to talk.'

'All right! Then lend us a shilling, will you? I'm famished and 'ave got to get some food inside me. I'll pay you back Friday.'

'What's my big head got to do with lending you a shilling?'

'You don't think I'm going to say something nice just to borrow a shilling, do you?'

'Where's your own money?'

'I gave it away.'

Now this was the thing about Fred. I have no doubt that he did give it away, for when he's flush with funds he casts his bounty around like a farmer of old, broadcasting seed. When he's skint, he begs and borrows and makes extravagant promises to repay his debts. Swearing on a stack of bibles he's the unluckiest fellow alive. Despite this weird twist in his personality he always manages to come out on top, which gives truth to the saying about it being better to have been born lucky than rich.

Dimly and without being able to articulate Fred's qualities or traits of character I've been aware of these quirks in his personality and have accepted them without criticism. Why not? He's helped me out often enough, so when he says he's given his money away I call him a dope and give him what I have with a warning – something like, 'Here, take it. Just make sure I get it back.'

'Cor! Thanks,' he'll say. 'I shan't forget it,' and off he'll flit, happy as a mudlark who's come into a fortune.

In short, while we aren't bosom pals we are not sworn adversaries either, just brothers who take one another pretty well for granted. We are again together at the Arborfield Technical School for a while. There it's everyone's lot to undergo battle training.

Every soldier who's ever donned a uniform has battle training as part of his routine no matter what his function – sapper, pioneer, infantryman, signaller, gunner or cook of the Army Concrete Corp. The equipment required for battle drill includes backpack, side pack, gas mask, ammunition pouches, water bottle and dummy hand grenades (dummies during training) strapped onto his webbing. Every platoon carries extra or, rather, common equipment as well: wirecutters, trenching tools, the platoon

Bren gun and spare magazines. Fully equipped, an infantryman's load is about sixty pounds.

One sweltering July afternoon late in the war, the platoon sergeant orders Fred to carry the Bren (machine) gun on the battle-training exercise. The exercise is a five-mile romp through the rolling countryside of Berkshire through farmers' fields and copses, glades, along cow tracks, shady lanes and a stretch of abandoned and grassed-over railway cutting. It is, as soldiers of old sang, 'Queen Anne commands and we'll obey, Over the hills and far away.'

Fred objects to carrying the Bren at the outset.

'Why me?' he asks Sergeant Dorking.

Foolish question.

'Because I said so, Fulthorpe.'

'But I've got a bad back.'

'Have you reported sick with it?'

'No, Sergeant. I thought I'd carry on as best I can.'

'Then your best today is to carry the Bren on your back and don't argue. Report sick in the morning. Meanwhile, if you collapse, we'll get you back to camp. The lads'll be pleased to help a comrade.'

The platoon sets off with Dorking in the lead, following a set route that leaves the main road to Wokingham about a quarter of a mile from the guard house. From there it skirts the hedgerow of a farmer's field and through a copse. On the other side of the wood is a whitewashed farm with a walled-in farmyard. Platoon leaders have orders not to damage crops, leave farmers' gates open, disturb the livestock or disturb the peace of the countryside. (Farmers, of course, are as much a part of the war effort as miners, factory workers and everyone in uniform.)

Everyone knows the route and the form. Two-thirds of the way along the platoon rest to allow stragglers to catch up. Platoons return to camp in formation, not strung out like schoolboys on a paper chase. It's a hard slog, but Sergeant Dorking, at the peak of physical fitness, moves back and forth along the way, urging the laggards to catch up. In his movements, he travels twice as far as anyone else.

In the heat of the afternoon, Fred soon lags behind. Dorking drops back a couple of times and urges him on. Fred tries his best as he said he would, but it's no use. The gap between him and the platoon gradually lengthens until he's left on his own. He figures he'll catch up when the platoon stops to rest. Besides, he knows the platoon won't re-enter camp without him. He shifts the Bren gun to a more comfortable position across his shoulder, balancing the weight on his backpack with the muzzle well forward so he can grip the foresight in a raised hand. With the load adjusted, he plods on until he enters an embowered country lane.

He thinks that getting out of the sun he'll feel cooler, but that's a mistake. Rivulets of sweat run down his face and neck. His shirt is wet with sweat and very uncomfortable under his battledress top. He wishes for a cold shower and thinks how pleasant that would be. The sweat drips from his chin on to the gas mask strapped to his chest. By pushing his head forward, he can rub his chin on the top flap of gas cover, but doing that causes his helmet to slip over his eyes.

The thud of his ammunition boots on the packed cart track sounds unnaturally loud as in an echo chamber. No other sound penetrates the leafy canopy of the lane, no sound of aircraft engines overhead, no engine noises. He has the sense of tramping through an old railway tunnel with its still air. The flies are a nuisance. They have that uncanny knack of finding moisture of which there is an abundant supply on his face. He swats the flies with his free hand and wipes his face on his sleeve and plods on.

At the far end of the lane he can make out a circle of sunlight as he moves steadily towards it in a state of reverie when a quiet sound of sobbing brings him to his senses. He thinks he is imagining things, but no – there it is again, louder and close at hand. Fully alert, he searches for the source of the sobbing. It suddenly gets louder in an opening in the foliage – a farmer's five-barred gate hidden from view until he's on top of it. And there, leaning languidly against the bottom rung of the gate, a deeply distressed country girl comes into view. The sight of her stops Fred dead in his tracks.

'Hello,' says Fred. 'What's the matter with you?'

She doesn't answer but stares at him with moist, bovine eyes as though surprised by his sudden appearance. She is wearing a short-sleeved, smocklike dress of light grey with a collarless open neck and voluminous skirt, the hem of which partly covers her legs. With one bended knee raised slightly higher than the other, the hem of her smock reveals a bare expanse of leg. Her chest heaves as though she has her sobbing almost under control as, with one outstretched arm resting on the bottom bar of the gate, she gazes at him with a wan expression. She holds a plain white handkerchief in her free hand and gently dabs her tearful eyes.

He waits for her to speak, to answer his question, but she only looks at him in her distress, so he asks again, 'Is there something a matter with you, miss? Are you ill or something? Are you hurt?' He's genuinely concerned.

She gives another mournful sigh and shrugs her shoulders with a careless toss of her head. Thick tresses of uncombed hair fall over her shoulders and half-cover her face. She inspects him from head to toe, sizing him up. She's hardly that much older than him.

'I asked what was the matter?' he repeats, wanting to be helpful. 'Can I do anything for you?'

'It's you,' she says at last. 'That's what.'

'What d'you mean? Me? What have I done?'

'No, but it's what you're going to do.' She drops her voice. 'You're going to molest me. That's what.'

Fred explodes with a loud, 'What? Don't be so daft. You don't even know me.'

'Yes, you are,' she says, speaking with firm conviction. 'You're going to molest me.'

'You're crackers,' he says, easing the Bren gun from his back pack and dropping the butt on the ground with a thud. It's a relief to get the load from his back. He takes a piece of towelling from his ammunition pouch and wipes the sweat from his face. It feels good. She has to be out of her mind to think he'd hurt anyone, let alone molest her.

'How the heck can I attack you in this get up?' he says almost angrily. 'Just look at me. Go on! Do I look as if I could hurt a fly in this outfit?'

Her 'Yez you do!' only eggs him on.

'God! Miss. Just look at this lot. This bren weighs a ton and that's on top of all this equipment. There's no need to smile. It's not funny I can tell you with all this paraphernalia strapped on: my backpack, pouches, gas mask and this damned Bren, I'm sagging at the knees, ready to collapse and that's a fact, I can tell you. What's more I don't go around molesting people like you call it. So what makes you think I can with all this load I'm carrying?'

Throughout his earnest and angry protest of innocence, not to say implied assurance of honourable behaviour, the girl says nothing. Then, with a lethargic movement of her hand, she moves her hair to reveal full and striking features that gaze at him with unblinking candour. Hers is the stare young children often give strangers – firm, innocent, guileless. With a voice of quiet conviction she repeats, 'Oh yez you are. I know your kind. You're going to ... well, you know; I don't have to tell you.'

'Don't start that again. How the heck can I molest you in this get-up?'

'Well, you can hang it on the gate, can't you?'

And he does.

★

I'll not speculate on how they occupy their time for the next while, but I have no doubt that Fred and his beguiling damsel in distress explore the sweet mystery of life of which our Dad has so often spoken.

When Fred, whose conscience has been bothering him, says at last that he has to get going, the maid of the Berkshire countryside uses the desultory charm of a lotus eater to persuade him to stay. He insists that he has to go.

'No, I can't, miss. Our Sergeant'll kill me if I don't catch up with the others.'

'You're still hot,' she says sweetly. 'Let me wipe your face,' and she sits astride him and wipes his face with the hem of her dress, all but smothering him in its folds. 'There, izn't that better?'

Fred nearly succumbs to her blandishments to repeat their wonderful experiment, but resists the temptress with gentle words. 'Come! Let me get up. I really must be on my way, miss.'

'Yez, I know. You have to catch up with the others. They're not far ahead. I watched them paz by a while ago,' she says innocently. 'But let me help you on with your things. You'd like that, wouldn't you?'

'Did they see you?'

'No. I recognised some of them from where I zat. Nice lads be they. I thought it best not disturb them in their efforts,' she says, helping him on with his equipment which she seems able to do with effortless ease.

When he's ready, she walks with him, holding the muzzle of his weapon while he holds onto the butt. He feels refreshed all right, but is worrying about being missed. She turns to smile easily at him and chats happily with the confidence of one completely at peace with the world.

'Do you come often this way?'

'No, I don't. Do you?'

'Now and then when the fancy takes me. I meet a lot of you soldier boys from the camp that way.'

'Cor! I bet you do.'

'They're not all as nice az you.'

'D'you say that to everyone?'

'No, honest. Cross my heart an' hope to die, I don't.'

'What's your name? I don't know your name.'

She has no chance to answer, for at that moment there comes a bellow from the end of the lane, loud and unmistakable.

'Where the hell have you been, Fulthorpe?'

Outlined in the light like an emissary from some heavenly court, Sergeant Dorking, unmistakable in silhouette against the light, presents himself in awful aspect. He could be Mephistopheles appearing from the flames of hell, come to claim Fred's mortal soul.

'He fell down,' says the girl disarmingly when Dorking is almost upon them. 'I helped him up. Is that all right, zir?'

Sergeant Dorking looks the country girl up and down. 'I've seen you before, young woman.'

She returns his gimlet stare with a Mona Lisa smile, a picture of comely virtue and innocence.

'Come on, Fulthorpe. Get your skates on and join the others. You'll be too late for your own funeral, you will. As for you, miss. I'd get home to your mother, if I were you. Go on now, hop it.'

'All right, zir. I'll do as you zay, zir. I waz only helping your soldier boy.' She stops and watches the two of them walk into the sunlight.

'You're a bloody sly one, Fulthorpe, and you can wipe that grin off your face,' says Sergeant Dorking as soon as they are alone. 'You're not fooling me. Anyone'd think you were born to sainthood with that look of bloody innocence on your face. D'you think I was born yesterday?'

'If I am I'll be the first, Sarge.'

'First what?'

'St Fred, Sarge. I don't think there's a St Fred in *The Lives of the Saints*. Personally, I think they could do with a St Fred, don't you?'

'Don't be so bloody cheeky! Get a move on and at the double.'

14   Dead Reckoning

ONE SATURDAY afternoon in the spring of 1945, four of us are seated at the kitchen table about to play crib. The cribbage board is set on the table with matches stuck in the holes and the cards are ready for dealing. A short time earlier, Dad has woken up from his afternoon nap, which he always has following his jaunt to the Grafton Arms or whichever pub in the area has a good supply of beer. The pubs are busier than at any time before the war because of the influx of servicemen and women from overseas stationed in camps dotted around the surrounding countryside.

Since the Normandy Invasion in June 1944, there has been a dramatic decrease in numbers of foreign troops, naturally, but new arrivals have come to fill the places vacated by those in Normandy or their graves. The newcomers, including black American soldiers, have taken to pub life like bees to the honeypot. The new Americans duly make their appearance in our house along with other visitors in uniform; our parents make everyone welcome. Still, I have to say the welcome mat is put down throughout The Boroughs.

But here we are alone for a change: Mum, Dad, Malcolm and myself. The younger ones, Margaret and Kathleen, are in the front room playing dress-up with Mum's secondhand clothes. Mum draws the high card to deal and has just shuffled the pack when there's an almighty crash at the front door, which flies open and hits the wall with a bang. Mum leaps to her feet in alarm and claps a hand to her chest as though about to have 'one of her turns'.

'What in God's name ...?' she exclaims, looking at Dad in alarm.

'Cut the cackle, Mag, and deal the cards. We'll know soon enough who it is,' he says and, as though on cue, there comes the voice of Ada May from the front door.

'It's only me, Mam. I'm home.'

'Oh! It is, is it?' says Mum, settling herself down again, not bothering to look. If it had been one of the boys she'd have been out of her chair in a flash and down the corridor to greet them.

Then Ada's square-bashing shoes come clomping along the passageway and I'm up to greet her as she appears in the light framed in the kitchen doorway, wearing her WAAF uniform and soft-topped, peaked hat at an angle on her head with her knapsack slung over her shoulder.

'Hello, our Ada,' I say, embracing her, but I'm brought up short at the sight of the right side of her face. It's a ghastly mess. No wonder she's wearing her hat at a rakish angle. She gives me a crooked smile with swollen, scabby lips and a fading black right eye that extends part way down the right side of her face. Then I realise she isn't smiling at all, but the nasty gash running from above the blackened eye to the lobe of her ear gives her a distorted grimace. The stitches and her shaven right eyebrow make her look hideous. I hold her to see the left side, which our Dad would see from his chair and Mum, too, if she only bothered to look. Ada's right arm is in a sling, her hand swathed to the fingertips in a bandage.

'Jesus! our Ada,' I say. She's been in one hell of an accident.

'We'll have less of the blasphemy from you, my son,' says Mum without looking up.

'Hello, my lovey,' says our Dad. 'Are you all right?'

Ada turns her head slightly to look at the back of Mum's head, which is when Dad gets a good look at Ada May and it's his turn to be startled. He gets out of his chair immediately and squeezes by Mum to take a closer look, saying, 'My God, girl. What on earth's happened to you?'

Mum twists round to see what the fuss is all about, so it's then her turn to cry out, 'Holy Moses, Ada! What's happened?' She has turned ashen-faced; her indifference has vanished.

There's no room for the four of us in that confined space. Dad has Ada May clasped in his arms, Mum is

trying to squeeze in, but can't. Full of concern now, for she
is not as indifferent as she appears, she tries to take hold of
Ada May, only Dad has her in hand.

'Oh! my lovey, you have been in the wars.' He is
overcome with emotion. 'Come in and sit down.' He
removes her hat and slips her knapsack from her shoulder,
handing it to me. 'Here! Take these, my son. He would
have her be seated, but she stands her ground, looking at
him with such a painful expression I think she's going to
burst into tears any moment.

A look of understanding passes between them. She
touches the side of her face with her bandaged hand in the
sling and says, 'It's a long story, Dad, but I'm all right.'

'All right be blowed, my girl. You should be in bed.'

'It's enough that I'm home,' she says, 'an' I'm here;
that's the important thing.'

'I should think so, too, my lovey. So will you be seated
and tell us what happened?'

'I will, but not now.'

All this time, Mum's doing her utmost to see Ada's
state at close range, but Dad has charge of the situation. He
pulls out the chair at the table next to Mum and gets Ada
to sit in it. Mum, feeling left out and not really seeing the
state of Ada's injuries, turns back to her chair, clicks her
tongue on the roof of her mouth and rolls her eyes to the
ceiling as much as to say, 'She's at it again, our Ada.
Poverty must get in.' She wouldn't be so dismissive if she'd
had a good look at the wounds.

The truth is my sister looks truly awful. Her once pretty
face, so full of mischief and devilment, will be disfigured for
the rest of her life, I'm certain of that and could so easily
weep for her, seeing the state she's in.

Ada changes her mind about where to sit. She holds on
to my shoulder to squeeze by and takes a seat at the table so
that now her face is bathed in the light of the kitchen
window and in full view of Mum, who's stunned into
silence, speechless for once at the sight of Ada May. She
puts a hand to her mouth and draws in a deep breath,
finally managing an 'Oh! My God! You poor thing.' Her

complexion has again taken on a deathly pallor, yet she's practical and ready to do what's necessary for the best. 'Let's get some boracic acid and bathe your face,' she says.

'No, it's all right. It's been washed in Acraflavine so I'm all right. I've bin well looked after,' Ada replies.

'All right indeed,' says Mum, a little miffed.

I'm not saying she's mean-spirited or anything like that, but why she has to be so theatrical all the time is beyond me. First she reacts to the crash of the front door to convey shock. Then when she learns it's only Ada come home she can hardly say more than, 'Oh! It is, is it?' Next comes an expression to indicate she's been stabbed in the heart and then, assured Ada's wounds have been attended to and her help is not needed brings another expression as much as to say, 'She's alive and well, isn't she? Talking and with the walking wounded,' but she isn't finished yet. She leans across the table for a closer inspection, like Florence Nightingale doing her morbidity rounds at Scutari.

'Should I make a pot of tea?' I ask.

'Yes, why don't you do that, son?'

I go into the back where we keep the pots, to bring back the family teapot. The kettle is simmering on the hob. Dad sets it more central on the coal bridge to bring to the boil while I lean across to get the tea caddy from the cupboard next to his chair. While I'm about this business, Dad gives Ada his attention and, in response to Mum's question 'What d'you think? Jack,' he says, 'She's a tough 'un. She'll survive.'

He holds Ada's hand while he inspects the wounds more closely. 'Have you hurt your leg, too, Tuppence?'

'It's nothing. Just a scratch.'

'You look like a ghost, our Ada,' says Mum.

'Not half as much as you do,' Ada shoots back, smiling weakly at her own wit. It takes a lot to put her down; Mum manages a smile, too.

We can none of us take our eyes off our wounded warrior, which attention she takes in her stride, calmly looking first at one and then the other. Finally fixing her eyes on Malcolm who, all this time, has not spoken a word, she says, 'It's all right. It's not the end of the world, you know.'

Margaret and Kathleen, attracted by the noise, have joined us from the front room and seated themselves at the kitchen table.

'Humph,' says Mum, shrugging, a gesture she uses when lost for words. 'I'm sure it's not. When did this happen, love?'

'A while ago.'

'You didn't tell us. You should have done. We'd have come to see you.'

'I couldn't. I was in dock, wasn't I?' She means the camp hospital.

'You could have sent us a message. I'd 'ave come to see you.'

In justice, Mum is concerned now that she realises the gravity of Ada's injuries. Her eyes have turned watery, which goes to show that underneath that belligerent shell of hers there's a streak of anxiety. In an agony of suspense to know what has happened, she ferrets around with words of concern '... poor thing ... terrible ... agonising ... how distressing ... poor thing ... tell us', trying every means of persuasion she knows to get Ada to talk.

Ada won't be drawn. 'Later, later. I don't want to talk about it now. Besides, you wouldn't believe me.'

'I don't know. I give up,' says Mum, frustrated by Ada's unwillingness to be drawn out, but she doesn't. She coaxes, flatteres and cajoles for all she's worth without success and when that coaxing fails she tries another tack.

'You've been fighting. Is that it? Is that what you mean by not believing you?'

'No, I haven't been fighting, not in the way you mean.'

'What other meaning can fighting have? You were in a car accident?'

'No, not that either.'

'All right, I give up. You fell down the stairs?'

'Give over, Mag. Let the girl take her own time. She'll tell us when she's good and ready.'

At our Dad's insistence, the matter's left at that, but not without Mum having the last word.

'I knew no good would come of her joining the WAAFs, I said so from the start.'

'I said, give it a rest, Maggie,' Dad insists.

'This is what comes of letting her have her way.'

'Oh! Do put a sock in it, woman.'

Mum's referring to the day a year earlier when Ada enlisted. I was at home that day so I can bear witness to it. I don't want to give the impression I've spent my life on leave. I don't get home more than twice a year now that I've finished my apprenticeship and have become a sapper, transferred to the Corps of Royal Engineers. Anyway, I remember that morning a year ago particularly well, because of the way Mum blew her top when Ada proudly announced her news ...

★

'You'll do no such thing, my girl.' Mum's eyes blazed with fury. 'You're not allowed. You're under age, so don't talk so much rubbish.'

'So was Jack and Harry and Mary, and what about him?' Ada shot back, pointing to me. 'Didn't you get rid of him before the war. Wasn't he under age?'

'That was different. He went to school.'

'Same thing. I don't see no difference. They stuck him in uniform.'

'I'm not having it. Wait till your father comes. We'll hear what he has to say.'

'I know what you're thinking, Mam, but I swear to God he can strike me dead if I tell a lie.'

'Strike you dead? One word from you and you'd make Jesus Christ swear.'

Ada will never change. She can tell a tale as soon as look at you, and the more people she has for an audience the better the yarn. I can count on all the others including Fred to a degree to give a truthful account of themselves. Ada May is different. She is her own invention from top to bottom, first to last, which is not to deny other commendable traits in her personality. Generous beyond measure, she'll give away her last farthing, her rations, clothes, cigarette ration, her shoes to the down and out, the shirt off her back as they say. She'll also tap you for your last penny, just like our Fred, but that's by the way.

'No, Mam,' she'd said. 'Fair's fair. Hear me out. I was standing outside the recruiting office on Barrack Street minding me own business like I always do, when this officer comes out an' says, "It's cold out there, m'duck. Why don't you come inside for a cup of tea?"'

'M'duck? M'duck? What are you talking about? Officers don't speak like that, you liar.'

'No, but that's only my way of saying it, Mam. Actually ...' she said, putting on Mum's blue-ribbon accent, 'He said "miss" and I says why not? There'd be no harm in that, so in I goes an' what d'you think? They bring me this lovely hot cup of tea ...'

'... And crumpets no doubt?'

'No. Biscuits as a matter of fact. You know, Afternoon Tea biscuits! They had a big square tin of Peak Freans, but I only took one.' Ada's ability to add such touches to her stories, like an artist who adds a dab of paint here, a dab there, gives them the ring of authenticity. She has the master storyteller's touch. 'He asks if I'd like to wear a uniform and what about a smart ATS outfit of khaki and I says no, I rather like blue myself, so it would have to be the WAAFs or the WRENs, and he says the WRENs are full up so what about the WAAFs?

'Well, you know how stuck up the WRENS are. I'm not surprised. The WRENs are full of toffee-nosed types. That sounds OK by me, I says, and he says OK, the WAAFs it is then, but was I sure I was old enough and I says, to be truthful, I'm six weeks and a day short of my eighteenth birthday, and he says that's not a problem then, so why didn't I sign the paper and I did, so that's the long and the short of it.'

'You brazen little liar.'

'Honest to God, Mam, if that isn't the smitten truth.'

There was more to the exchange, of course; I've given but the gist of it. When Dad came home and heard the tale, he said, 'If that's what she wants, Mag, then let her do it.'

'Oh, well,' Mum said, resigning all opposition, 'them as makes their bed must lie in it.' She had no difficulty capitulating to our Dad in small matters like serving your country.

★

And so, after less than a year in the service, Ada May (aka Toni as she now liked to be known) is home, displaying her wounds. The evening of her return as a wounded warrior we have visitors and she is again the centre of attention. Our guests are two black American GIs and a Canadian corporal whom Dad has befriended in the Grafton Arms. The GIs arrive about seven in the evening, armed with supplies from the PX store. The Canadian corporal brings a couple of tins of bully beef and a can of tinned ham, from the NAAFI he says. Nothing is ever like that in our NAAFI.

From our Dad's service in India and the North West Frontier alongside Sikh, Hindu and Moslem soldiers fighting the Pathans, he's always had a liberal attitude to people of other races. Our Mum, too, having been seven years in India and what today is Pakistan, took to the life of the lesser British Raj like she'd been born with a silver spoon in her mouth. What is more, having the strong streak of the Irish mimic in her, she learned to speak Urdu like a native.

Servicemen and women come to our house in droves from the beginning of the war only to disappear and never to be heard of again. It's no secret that black and white GIs don't mix well, but in our house it's the exception. Mum sees to that. She won't stand any nonsense when it comes to prejudice – though she has her own – and keeps the peace without trouble. The black GIs love her for it.

'In here, you're all the same,' she'll say if things look like getting out of hand. 'The Colonel's lady and Judy O'Grady are just the same under the skin – and the same goes for men.' If some visitors don't like it, they have to leave.

So it is this evening of the day Ada has come home all knocked up: we're all squeezed together round the kitchen table with our visitors, drinking beer brought in from next door. The fire's blazing; the back window, wide open behind the blackout, is letting in the leathery air from The Boroughs; and the inside air is thick with tobacco smoke.

I watch the Canadian corporal take a packet of cigarettes from his pocket and offer one to Ada. From the attention he's paying her he has obviously taken to her, so her injuries make no difference. She declines his offer, saying she prefers Lucky Strike. The GIs, Chuck and Brad, shy giants from Louisiana, have brought a carton of Lucky Strike. Unopened packets from the carton are strewn over the table among the empty plates and bottle of pickles and bread and cheese.

'That's a nasty cut you've got there,' says the corporal by way of making conversation.

Ada shrugs it off. 'The medical officer says I'll never notice it once it's cleared up.'

'Accident?'

'Well, wounded,' she tells him.

'Anyone with their arm in a sling is wounded,' Mum says, chipping in. Assured now there's nothing wrong that time won't heal, she's back in form, even with visitors present.

'I got hurt in an air raid.'

'Air raid? What air raid?' Mum knows Ada is stationed on a bomber air base in Lincolnshire, so her incredulity was unmistakable. 'There hasn't been a raid since D-day, not on the airports anyway. V1s and V2s is all we get now, and they land in London or the southern counties.' She follows the BBC news, which she takes as gospel, and speaks on the progress of the war with the authority of an expert.

'The air raid over Dresden last week. I got it on the Dresden raid,' says Ada, speaking matter-of-factly to the Canadian.

We're too astonished to speak. I can see the 'You bloody liar' rebuke forming on Mum's lips, but she only gets as far as 'You b—' before she checks herself and stares hard at Dad for confirmation of his disbelief.

'Go on. You're kidding,' says Mike.

'Thars a migh-tay doozer of a souvenir,' one of the GIs drawls in admiration. One can forgive his ready belief in what Ada has said; he has only recently arrived in Britain.

'Yis. I s'pose it is,' she replies with a nonchalant air.

Malcolm elbows the GI who has spoken and laughs, saying, 'Come off it, our Ada, you work in the kitchens.'

'I tell you it's the God's honest truth,' says Ada, crossing herself. 'Strike me dead if I tell a lie. I'm sworn to tell the truth.' Mum raises her eyes to the ceiling. 'Our Malcolm's right. I work in the kitchens, see, in the Flight Sergeant's Mess as a matter of fact and – well, you get to know fellows in the mess in a situation like that, don't you? I mean, it's only natural like, isn't it? I got to know one of them pretty well, Flight Sergeant Briggs, a tail gunner on a Mark III Lancaster. So I says to him a couple of months ago, I says, let me see inside your Lanc, will you? I've never bin in one of them things before.

'"If you like," he says.

'"I would," I say, so he says,

'"Right, you're on, love."

'So he gives me the grand tour and we crawl together to the tail turret with its four 303 inch Browning machine guns. It's a tight squeeze, so they put the little ones in the tail. The lanky gunners are the mid-upper guns, if you know what I mean. Sergeant Briggs is about my size, which is why we get on like a house on fire. He lets me get in position behind the guns and explains how everything works, the guns and intercom an' all.

'I reckon it's a piece of cake sitting up there firing guns and working the intercom and he says I'm right. Anyone with half a brain can do it. Besides, I'm a fast learner he says and I am, aren't I, Mam?'

Mum clicks her tongue in silent exasperation and does her usual performance of raising her eyes to the ceiling. It's obvious what she's thinking. Who could believe a word the girl said? How often has she said you can lock a door against a thief, but not a liar?

Ada continues as though uninterrupted, although she's got the message as though it had been shouted from the rooftops.

'Now you're not going to believe this, but it's the God's honest truth.' An appeal in the name of the Almighty is the ultimate confirmation of the truth she spoke. 'This day they'd loaded the bombers for the night run and had their crew briefing when Sergeant Briggs says to me in the mess, he says, "I think I'm going to die. I've got food poisoning or summat. What am I going to do? I'm deathly ill and there's no replacement. We're all on tonight."

'So I says, "Give me your flying gear an' things. I'll go instead."

'And he says, "You're ever such a good sport, Toni" – they call me Toni on base, not Ada –"will you?"

'And I say, "Course I will, give me your things. It's a piece of cake."

'So I get into his outfit and put on his helmet and strap his parachute to my bum and off I go. The crew of the Lanc don't speak much. The skipper wants everyone to mind their own business and leave him to his. Well, there weren't much to tell about the flight over, but I hear the skipper giving orders over the intercom and when he asks me, "You OK, Sergeant Briggs?" I lower me voice and say, "OK, skipper, I'm honky-dory," and he says, "Right, lads, we're approaching the target area. Watch back there for night fighters on our tail, Briggs."

'I'm feeling pretty weird, I can tell you, with my heart in my throat as I keep a sharp watch out for fighters.'

I can tell from the faint smile on Dad's face that he doesn't believe a word she's saying either, but he doesn't interrupt. He has his head in his hands, his elbows resting on the kitchen table and is listening to her with rapt attention. He loves a good story. Mum is looking into the fire. The gas light is purring on the wall. Everyone else has their attention glued on Ada, who pauses to make sure she has everyone's attention, and then continues.

'We made the run, dead level, and dropped our bombs. Then, just as we was banking away there was this bloody great explosion. The Lanc shuddered like a shivering whale. That was shock enough, that an' something smashing through the tail pod knocked me for a six. When I came to I was cold all over and in the intercom everyone was talking at once.

'Then I heard someone say above the crackling an' interference, "We've bin hit, we've bin hit, can you hold her, skipper?"

'Of course we'd been hit. The bloody explosion in the tail smashed my head against the guns and I broke my arm. I didn't know then, but they meant a hit on the flight deck. The skipper only grunted on the intercom from then on, or so it seemed.

'Gradually, we turned away from the searchlights and the flak and explosions and headed for home. I could hear the Navigator Lofty someone or other on the intercom. He was yakking to the skipper, making suggestions about what he should do and saying, "I'm giving you a hand, skipper. She's sluggish as an old cow, but she's coming round, she's coming round."

'On and off all the way back Lofty kept up his monologue, talking to the skipper and getting nothing but a crackle on the intercom. No one else was on the intercom now and all this time I'm getting colder and colder.

'Someone says, "Are you orright back there Flight'?

'And I grunt about being OK 'cause I didn't want anyone coming back and finding I'm not Flight Briggs. Then we were across the North Sea and heading inland to our base. At least, I hoped it was.

'Coming into land, the Lofty's saying things like, "Undercarriage down, skipper. Give her fifteen degrees of flap, should I? Fifteen degrees it is."

'From what I could tell, he was doing a pretty good job of helping the skipper land the Lanc. I wasn't feeling at all good myself. I knew I had a gash on my face. It hurt like a

crack on the jaw. I felt sure it was caked with blood, but I
didn't care. I think I conked out for a while from the crack
on my head. I was ever so cold an' thought I was dead and
kept drifting in and out of sleep.

'Everyone kept to themselves, questions on the
intercom I answered with grunts to show I was orright and
that's how it went on. They had to help me down from the
turret when we landed and put me on a stretcher. I was in a
terrible mess with a bloody face, and all the time they
thought I was Flight Briggs until, that is, they got me to
hospital on a stretcher.

'"My God above," says the MO when he strips me to
attend my wounds. "This ain't Flight Briggs; it's a bloody
woman. What's your name, lassie?" he asks, and I tell him
and he says, "A/C Fulthorpe from the Flight Sergeants'
mess? What were you doing going on the op?"

'"I was standing in for Flight Briggs who's got food
poisoning and couldn't fly," I says.

'"Well," he says. "You are in a mess, my girl, and the
wrong one at that. You should be in the Sergeant's mess,
not here. No one's ever going to believe you stood in for a
tail gunner. You'll be in for the high jump if anyone finds
out, so I'll tell you what I'll do. We'll put you on the sick
list and not breathe a word about it if you won't. You've
committed a court-martial offence and could be sent to the
glass house for a long, long time."

'I said I wouldn't breathe a word, of course, because I
didn't want to get no one into trouble, least of all Flight
Briggs.

'"But what about the skipper?" I asked. "He didn't
seem too good to me from the sounds coming over the
intercom. Is he all right?"

'"No," says the MO. "He's dead. Died instantly in the
explosion over Dresden. From what I heard, you have your
navigator to thank for getting you home. Got you home by
dead reckoning, which was a stroke of luck, I reckon."

'It was, I says, an' no mistake.'

So that's Ada's story as near to the truth as I can make
it, sticking to the facts as she tells them. It might seem

astounding and beyond belief, but there it is. Who would believe a stripling of a girl, our sister could stand-in to do a man's job? Whether her story's believed or not, I'm bound to say on her behalf she isn't the first nor do I suppose she'll be the last woman to masquerade as a man.

Take Christine Davis, a trooper who served alongside her husband in the cavalry at the Battle of Blenheim in 1704. Wounded in the battle, she was discovered to be a woman by the surgeons who attended her. Then there was Hannah Snell. She enlisted in the marines as a boy soldier to be with her lover and got hit by a lead ball in the groin at the Battle of Pondicherry in 1760. She wouldn't allow anyone to attend her, but removed the ball herself while still on the battlefield and cauterised the wound with a bayonet heated in a fire. She applied for a pension to the Duke of Cumberland who checked and believed her and made her an allowance of ten pounds a year. She became the only female Chelsea Pensioner. As if there aren't examples enough, what about all those remarkable women of Ferry Command who flew planes across the Atlantic?

But Mum has already made up her mind and speaks it. 'A likely tale,' she says. 'You can tell that one to the marines.'

Ada doesn't protest, but lights a Lucky Strike instead, looks at our Mum, and smiles.

'There, what did I say? You wouldn't believe me. Isn't that right? I'll just have to save it for my grandchildren if I ever 'ave any and they'll believe me.'

15   One Good Turn

STRICTLY SPEAKING, brother Malcolm barely qualifies for inclusion in this chronicle because he has yet to get into uniform by the time the war ends. That he serves his time is without question because the National Service Act is the law of the land and applies to everyone on reaching the age of eighteen, male or female. Although he does not serve under age, the fact that he is affected by the after-effects of the war is reason enough to add his contribution to this chronicle. He will also earn his campaign medal for active service even if it's for his involvement in the 1956 fiasco that will become known to the world as the Invasion of Suez.

Nor do I wish to imply that, because we others are in uniform during the world's second great conflagration, we are in the thick of it. We are not and the same is true for the majority who don a uniform because for every man who carries a rifle and bayonet into battle or who is in gun crew, a tank, aircraft or ship at sea, six or seven people are needed to support them: physicians, nurses, cooks, transportation, communication and supply personnel, to say nothing of those who tell everyone else what to do: those who serve on staff. Jack, Harry and Mary are, as they say, at the sharp end of battle and Ada May aka Toni, too, if her account of the Dresden raid is to be believed. Fred is an apprentice, while I am a sapper.

Jack steadfastly refuses to discuss the action in the Indian Ocean that has resulted in his being medically discharged as unfit for further service. All I've ever learnt is that the squadron in which he served never had more than a distant glimpse of the enemy. That must have been an unnerving experience no matter whose side you were on. Imagine zigzagging through the ocean at high speed with enemy shells exploding without warning around you and the guns of your ship letting rip into the virtual blank blue yonder, every gunnery officer relying on radar and ships of the squadron manoeuvring under radar direction against an illusive enemy.

Harry is among the first to be demobbed when the war ends. He has a problem adjusting to Civvy Street though and re-enlists, but in the Sappers not the Royal Navy. He serves for a time in occupied Germany. Mary leaves the ATS with a wonky hip for which she gets paid no disability allowance, marries and has the best that life has to offer in bombed and battered post-war Britain. Toni stays in the WAAFs for a while before getting her discharge and marrying an ex-RAF cook, not Flight Sergeant Briggs as we'd all been expecting. Fred and myself are still in uniform, because we've signed on to serve as regular soldiers; the army is adept at getting its fodder young, even in a war.

One might have thought civvy life would return to normal when peace came, but that is far from the case. There is trouble everywhere: in Palestine, China, French Indo-China and Dutch Indonesia, parts of Africa. Prime Minister Atlee and his Labour government get into power with an overwhelming parliamentary majority and struggle to cope with the massive shortage of goods while trying to develop a peacetime economy. Money is tight, jobs are impossible to find, currency restrictions mean that those who do have money are not able to move it out of the country, and the rationing of food, clothing and petrol is still the order of the day.

Were it not for American generosity and the Marshall Plan to help European enemies and allies alike to recover we would have been in dire straits. As far as the national economy is concerned, there is none. The wartime industries of munitions, aircraft, guns and tank production have fallen flat on their faces. Factories have laid off their workers wholesale, and not just those who work on the production line. Engineers, planners and aircraft designers have also got the boot. The employment situation is dreadful, which is where Malcolm's story begins.

Stationed at Cowley Barracks, Oxford, one severe winter after the war, Malcolm, a sapper like the rest of us in the military, is doing his basic training. There has been no winter like this one in half a century. No, the Thames doesn't freeze over as it used to during the time of Dickens in the mid-nineteenth century. The weather is bitterly cold all the same with blinding snowfalls, plugged roads, boughs broken under the burden of snow and power lines down. On a Friday afternoon following a heavy snowfall, Malcolm begins hitchhiking home on a forty-eight hour pass. He stations himself at a crossroads on the outside of the city hoping to get a lift. Blowing his hands, stamping his feet to keep warm, he would welcome a second great coat to fling over his shoulders. He watches other hitchhikers getting lifts in other directions, but no traffic is headed his way. Then, towards him comes an exceedingly lank, upright figure who has been dropped by a van heading for the City centre. He has bundled himself against the cold from the warmth no doubt of the van and approaches where Malcolm is standing.

'Hello. Have you been waiting long?' he asks.

'Hello, not long,' says Malcolm neutrally.

'I wonder if you could spare me a cigarette,' says the stranger. He speaks in an educated voice.

'I don't see why not.' Malcolm doesn't smoke but in his knapsack he has two packets of twenty Players from his cigarette ration he is taking home. He fishes out one packet and hands it to the fellow traveller.

'Thanks awfully, old fellow.' The stranger removes the cellophane wrapping, pulls out a cigarette, then closes the pack and hands it back to Malcolm, who shakes his head.

'No! You keep them. I don't smoke. I'm taking them home to me dad.'

'Are you sure?'

'Perfectly sure.'

'That's awfully decent of you, old man. Where are you heading?'

'Northampton on a weekend pass. And you? Where're you off to?'

'Bristol, old man.' The fellow traveller draws on his cigarette and exhales a cloud of smoke with satisfaction.

'Blimey! That's a long way in this weather,' Malcolm remarks.

'Yes, it is, rather, but I've done well hitchhiking so far.'

'Where from?'

'Beverley in Yorkshire.'

'Not today?'

'No, no. This is my second day on the road.'

Malcolm likes the man well enough. He seems a decent sort, bit of a toff from the way he speaks. He could well have been an officer, which wouldn't be unusual with the war now over and everyone being demobbed.

'I'm Algernon,' says the man conversationally, 'but my friends call me Algie for sort, old chap. What's your name, if I may ask?'

'Malcolm ... Malc for short.' No one called him Malc, but it struck him as funny; he couldn't resist a touch of one-upmanship. 'What d'you do for a living?'

Algie looked glum. 'I'm an aircraft designer. At least, I was. I've spent the entire war in the aircraft industry. Got as far as chief air-frame designer for the Beverley Aircraft Company. It's all come to an end now; thousands of us out of work. I'm on my way to South Wales. I hear there's a chance of work with the Bristol Aircraft Company.'

It occurs to Malcolm that his travel companion should be travelling by train. He shakes his head. 'That's tough. No money, I suppose.' He hopes that remark sounds casual enough not to embarrass the man.

Algie shrugs. 'I get by,' he says with resignation.

Malcolm lives well enough on army fare and is travelling 'on a full stomach'. Algie looks half starved; he can do with a square meal. Feeling rich with his week's pay of ten shillings and sixpence, Malcolm feels for two half-crowns in his pocket and offers them.

'No, no!' says Algie. 'I couldn't possibly, old chap. You've been generous enough as it is.'

'Don't be so daft. It's only five bob, and it's not going to break me. Besides, I'll be home in a couple of hours whereas you've got a long way to go. Take it. There's no one else around. Just you and me.' He laughs. 'You never know. One day you might find me down and out. Then you could pay me pay, yeah? Go on. Take it.'

'That's exceedingly kind, most generous of you,' says Algie, pocketing the five shillings with genuine appreciation, his gaunt face breaking into a smile of sincere gratitude. 'I am most frightfully grateful. If I had a way of repaying your kindness I would.'

Now it's Malcolm's turn to shrug off the older man's words of gratitude. It embarrasses him. 'Aw!' he says awkwardly. 'It's nothing an' you never know when you'll come across someone else down on his luck.' Hugely discomforted with this outburst of effusive thanks and his own dismissive words, he says, 'Why hitchhike? Couldn't you have written a letter? I mean, that's what you do proper, isn't it?'

'Not these days,' comes the reply. 'One has to appear in person.'

Malcolm is impressed. He likes that. 'One has to appear in person.' He repeats it to himself, for it shows the fellow's class and confirms in Malcolm's mind that he is in the presence of a real toff. But any further conversation they might have had is cut short by the arrival of a three-ton Army Bedford heading in Malcolm's direction. He is in luck. The driver stops, pokes his head out of the window. 'You after a lift, mate?'

'Yeah! Thanks! Heading for Northampton.'

'Hop on. I'm off to Towcester.'

The truck has someone else in the cab. Malcolm clambers nimbly over the tailboard and shouts to Algie before banging to say he is safely aboard, 'Good luck, Algie. I'll say ta-ra then. Hope you're successful.'

'Me, too, old fellow, me too. You didn't tell me your name.'

Malcolm shouts. The truck is drawing away. 'Too late now, but it's Fulthorpe, Sapper Fulthorpe, Twenty-first Field Squadron. What's yours?'

'Bentley-Lewis,' Algie shouts back. 'I won't forget you.'

Holding on to the superstructure above the tailboard, Malcolm waves. Algie's assurance that he won't forget him completely slips his mind and in the weeks to come he thinks no more about it.

A year later, walking alone in Reading, Berkshire, planning on seeing a matinee, Malcolm is accosted by an aristocratic-looking gentlemen, who touches him on the arm with the end of a rolled up umbrella.

'I say there! Don't I know you?' says the elegantly dressed pedestrian.

Malcolm, still a sapper and in uniform, is in no mood to be waylaid by anyone brandishing an umbrella, walking stick or any other handheld accessory for that matter. His hackles raised, he's not one to turn down a challenge. He stops dead in his tracks, prepared to resist the confrontation.

The man standing before him, tall and elegant-looking, wears a morning suit, pin-striped trousers, polished black shoes. He carries a brown leather briefcase in one hand, gloves and umbrella in the other and is wearing a bowler hat. He may be an officer – and some in civvies are officious with lower ranks they meet on the street. The morning suit may be an odd dress for an officer, but you can never tell.

Malcolm's hackles are up, yet he's alert enough to exercise caution. 'Know me? No, I don't think so, *sir.*' He draws out the 'sir' intentionally to show his sarcasm. If his sullen response shows, the questioner ignores the rudeness in his tone.

'But I say, old chap, didn't we meet at Oxford?'

That's a laugh. Who could imagine being at Oxford? The man must be out of his mind. Best to humour him with a display of wit. 'Oh yes, I was at Oxford, sir. At Cowley Barracks as I recall. It were in the dead of winter I was there.'

'Ah! Yes, of course. Then you'll remember me at the crossroads after the snowstorm? You were hitchhiking to Northampton. I was heading for Bristol.'

Reminded of their meeting a year ago, it now dawns on Malcolm that this is Algie who he'd met at the crossroads and it all floods back to him: his fellow hitchhiker, the snow, cigarettes, conversation, something about aircraft design. But it has gone, banished from his mind.

Breaking into a broad grin, he says, 'Well, stone the crows, you're right. I remember now. I gave you a packet of Players.'

'And five shillings,' Algernon Bentley-Lewis adds. He places the hand holding the umbrella on Malcolm's shoulder in a gesture of friendship. 'I never expected to meet you again, but here we are. What serendipity!' Algie's countenance, beaming with pleasure, clearly reveals his delight at meeting Malcolm again.

Malcolm has no idea of the meaning of serendipity, but that in no way diminishes his satisfaction with the moment.

'It's a small world after all,' says Algie. 'I never forget a face, my dear fellow, and I thank God I've met you again in more fortunate circumstances, for I've often thought of your kindness to a stranger.'

'Oh! That was nothing.'

'Nothing? On my life, yours was a consideration, a kindness I could never forget. You were the good Samaritan when I was down on my luck. God works in mysterious ways indeed, so come, my good friend, Malc. This is no place to converse, so let's find a more congenial place. I say, have you had lunch? No, I thought not.'

With that, Algernon wheels Malcolm about and heads for the George Hotel on King Street and there, with coat-tailed waiters at his beck and call, treats his good Samaritan to a full-course dinner. Malcolm feels awkward and out of place in his sapper's uniform in such magnificent surroundings with officers and their wives or companions at adjacent tables.

'Don't let these people disturb you, Malc,' says Algie, sensing his unease. 'You have as much right as anyone to eat in style. Besides, everyone can be in the carriage trade when they have the money,'

And so, with words of good fellowship and encouragement, he smooths Malcolm's anxiety at being in the elegant and stylish George Hotel with ambience of privilege and class.

Their conversation 🌀 awkward at first, but Algernon soon puts his companion at ease, asking Malcolm about his life as a national serviceman; where has he travelled since they last met? How much longer has he to serve and what is he planning on doing when he leaves the army? He is older than Malcolm by a good fifteen years, with the sophistication of a good education of one who knows how to make conversation. He asks questions and offers nothing about himself until Malcolm enquires what he is doing in Reading.

'Most fortunate,' says Algie. 'I'm working for the Fairy Aviation Company. There was nothing for me at Bristol, but their personnel department suggested I try the Fairy Aviation Company, which was looking for someone in their air-frame design department. A helpful fellow in personnel even telephoned while I was there in Bristol. After that, it was plain sailing, old chap. I've been the chief designer since the day I arrived. And today I happened to be in town for a meeting with the Air Ministry at—' he consults his watch '—three this afternoon. It's jolly good luck meeting up with you, Malc.'

It pleases Malcolm's to learn that everything has turned out well for his benefactor. When they part company, Algie presents him with a crisp, white, five-pound note, a sum he cannot hope to own in half a lifetime, and certainly not on his weekly pay of ten and six.

He looks at the note with its distinctive copperplate script and says, 'Sorry, but I can't take that, Mr Bentley. It's more than two months' pay. No, I just couldn't. Sorry, but I can't.'

'Please don't argue, old fellow. My circumstances have changed dramatically since we last met, so put it away and think no more of it.'

'Where did you get this? Rob a bank or something?'

Algernon laughs. 'No, nothing as exciting.'

And so, having exchanged names and addresses, they part company, Algernon Bentley-Lewis with a satisfying sense of having done the right thing, one would imagine, and Malcolm with manna from heaven now pocketed, to the tune of five pounds. The windfall in his fortunes make him rich by any standards and all for what? Well, nothing by his reckoning. He's only done what half his mates would have done in like circumstances.

Algernon has pressed a packet of cigarettes on him as well, more as a ceremonial gesture, he said, but as Malcolm doesn't smoke he can always give them away. Never one to look a gift horse in the mouth, he pockets the packet of cigarettes, too, and takes the bus back to camp feeling not a little lightheaded. Not once but many times on the bus he pats the fiver in his pocket to make sure it hasn't slipped out. He reckons he has to be the richest sapper in the camp.

That same evening, in the NAAFI canteen with four mates of his platoon, he puts in an order at the counter for five plates of baked beans on toast by way of celebration. But when he offers the woman behind the counter his five pound note in payment she is immediately suspicious.

'Here! Where d'you get this?' she demands. From her slightly elevated position behind the counter she holds up the note to the light to see the metallic thread to make sure it's not counterfeit.

'That's none of your business, miss. Where I got that from is mine, so just hand over the change.'

Lofty and Ginger have come to the counter to take the plates of baked beans back to the table. They have waited with him for the order to come and, as soon as the plates arrive from the kitchen, they sweep away two each, leaving Malcolm to join them with his own meal.

The NAAFI employee has meanwhile hurried away, clutching the five-pound note. She returns moments later with the canteen manager, an officious, cadaverous-faced man with a razor-thin moustache and a superior manner.

'Now, there,' he says, looking down his beaky nose, 'let's get to the bottom of this here fiver, shall we?. How did it come into your possession?' He probably intends to expose a thief without benefit of the provost corporal's assistance.

His manner infuriates Malcolm who figures he is faced with an equal here and that he's up to the challenge. 'Mind your own bloody business. Five quid's legal tender ain't it? What's more, if you're not going to give me my change I'll get it somewhere else, you skinny sod.'

'Don't you go speaking to me in that tone, young fellow,' says the manager, standing on his dignity. He knows his position and is well able to deal with lip from this low-life national servicemen; typical working-class yobs they are as far as he's concerned and he knows how to put them in their place. '

You know this is a larger sum of money than is tendered in this establishment. I suppose you know that, do you? This comes from a bank, young man.' He holds the five-pound note aloft to emphasise the gravity of the situation.

'Don't talk wet. Who d'you think you are, the bloody sergeant major or someone? Here! Give it back here.' Malcolm lunges across the counter to snatch the note, but the manager is too quick for him and moves out of his reach.

'Hey! Lofty! Ginger! The rest of you, come 'ere.'

They come as they are bid and offer their noisy support, but without success. The manager will not be moved and, firm in his resolve to get to the bottom of a suspicious five-pound note, his duty is clear. Being a man of experience, ex-Army Pay Corps, who has spent the war years dealing with scoundrels and villains in uniform making money with military stores on the black market, he knows well what to do and faces the situation with firm resolve.

'If you can't give a satisfactory answer to a civil question, my lad, it'll have to stay here in the safe until you do.'

No threat or warning of the dire consequences he faces for not returning the five-pound note or, more accurately, the change due for the order placed and given will alter his mind. The manager puts the note in the canteen safe, locks the door and there the matter rests.

Malcolm, in a manner of speaking, eats crow with his beans on toast in the company of his friends and resigns himself to what Monday morning may bring.

Come Monday morning, he obeys an order to report to the squadron office where he is marched before Captain Harcourt, the officer commanding the squadron. Also present is the squadron sergeant major, who stands majestically alongside the squadron commander. Harcourt is a reasonable man, duty-bound to investigate the unusual occurrence of the five-pound note brought to his attention by the NAAFI manager. He has all sorts of young soldiers under his command and they need a firm hand to deal with the problems they cause.

'It's all right, Sapper Fulthorpe,' he begins. 'You're not on a charge, so you may stand at ease.'

'Sir.'

Captain Harcourt opens a new file folder on his desk and extracts the five-pound note attached to a handwritten note. 'This five-pound note! Would you care to explain how it came into your possession?'

'Sir?'

Harcourt repeats the question. 'Would you care to tell me where or how you got it?'

'Yes, tell Captain Harcourt where the fiver came from, lad,' the Sergeant Major chips in, wanting to be helpful.

'It was given to me, sir.'

'Given you? By whom? A relative?'

'No, sir. A man I met in Reading Saturday afternoon, sir.'

Captain Harcourt coughs, suddenly and rather loudly.

'Oh, is that a fact, lad?' says the sergeant major, turning to exchange a meaningful look with Captain Harcourt. 'Sounds a bit of a queer case if you ask me, sir.'

Captain Harcourt raised a hand in a gesture of caution not to leap to conclusions. 'Thank you, Sergeant Major,' and, addressing the Sapper Fulthorpe again, says, 'And what, then, did you do for this five pound note, Sapper Fulthorpe?'

'I didn't do nothing, sir. He just gave it to me. He also treated me to dinner, sir, and gave me a packet of Players.'

'Very interesting, but surely you did something to get a free dinner, cigarettes and a five pound note.' The captain sounds highly intrigued.

'Nothing particularly, sir. No, I didn't do anything.'

'Anything?'

'No, nothing, sir.'

'You're quite sure, are you? I mean, you didn't go anywhere else with your new friend, then?'

'Just in the dining room of the hotel.'

'The George, sir.'

'The George?'

'Yes, sir.'

'Was this man you met staying at the hotel?'

'No sir.'

'You met him on the street?'

'Yes, sir.'

Now it's Captain Harcourt's turn to exchange a knowing look with the sergeant major, who can't resist the temptation to stick his oar in.

'This sounds almighty odd, Fulthorpe. It gets odder by the minute. Wouldn't it be in everyone's best interest if you told Captain Harcourt the story? Be truthful now and tell us what happened?'

Captain Harcourt looks down at his medal ribbons and flicks an imaginary fleck of dirt from his sleeve while he waits for Malcolm to speak. He tries to help, saying, 'What can you tell me about this very generous man you met in Reading, Sapper Fulthorpe? Was it ... ahem! ... a casual meeting on the street?'

'Oh nothing of the kind, sir. In fact it was a deliberate meeting, on his part anyway. He poked me with his umbrella, see.'

'Poked you with his umbrella?'

'Poked you, did he?' chipped in the sergeant major.

'Please, Sergeant Major.'

'Sir!'

'Yes, he did. Said he thought he knew me.'

'They often begin that way,' says the sergeant major.

'Wait a moment, Sergeant Major. Give Sapper Fulthorpe a chance.'

'Sorry, sir.'

'And what was the name of this gentleman who poked you with his umbrella?'

'I'm not sure, sir. Algernon something or other, a double-barrelled name, sir. I can't remember it exactly ... but he told me to call him Algie—'

'Algie?' the sergeant major breaks in again. 'That's a queer name, sir,' he says, uttering a quiet, hollow laugh.

'... He works at the Fairy Aviation Company he told me, sir.'

'The Fairy Aviation Company?' Captain Harcourt repeats the words slowly, ending on a rising note.

'Yes, sir. He's the chief engineer of airframe division.'

'The Fairy Aviation Company?' says the Sergeant Major, determined to get in his two-pennyworth. 'The *Fairy* Aviation Company?'

'Is he, now? In frame design, eh? Then we must find out what your manager friend has to say. Corporal Finch!'

In answer to the captain's summons, the orderly room corporal steps in from the outer office. 'Sir?'

'Corporal Finch, get me the Fairy Aviation Company on the line, please.'

'Very good, sir.'

Once connected to the Company switchboard, Captain Harcourt asks to be put through to the Chief Engineer of the airframe division and clears his throat again. 'Good morning. Am I speaking to the Chief Engineer of airframe division? Ah, good! Thank you. Yes, Mr Bentley-Lewis, you say? Would that be Mr Algernon Bentley-Lewis? (Pause) Yes, very good. I am, sir, Captain Harcourt, officer commanding A squadron of the Royal Engineers. I have a Sapper Fulthorpe in my office. He's says you ... er ... gave him five pounds last Saturday. Can you ... er ... confirm that, sir?'

Captain Harcourt spends the next few minutes listening to what Mr Bentley-Lewis has to say. Meanwhile, the squadron sergeant major eyes Malcolm with a curious and questioning glare. His mind is made up and he is intent on conveying this to the sapper standing before him. For his part, Malcolm returns his stare, wondering what all the fuss was about.

'Is that so? Is that so?' says Captain Harcourt. As the one-sided conversation continues, his expression takes on an admiring aspect, glancing occasionally at Malcolm in what seems to be a new light. At last, replacing the telephone, he says, 'Hm! Mr Bentley-Lewis confirms your story, Fulthorpe. I'm pleased. I'm even more pleased to congratulate you on your conduct. It's an honour to the Corps and in the best tradition of the service what you did. We could do with a lot more fellows like you.'

The sergeant major looks completely mystified. Captain Harcourt spares him a cautionary glance that says, 'Hold it!' and, to Malcolm, 'About this note, Fulthorpe. It is rather a lot of money, isn't it?'

'I suppose it is, sir.'

'Would you like me to put it National Savings for you, or keep it in a safe place, what?'

'I'd like to have it, sir, if it's all the same to you.'

'Why, yes, of course.'

Captain Harcourt unclips the five-pound note from the handwritten note in the file and hands it across this desk.

'You may go now, Fulthorpe.'

'Thank you, sir.'

Harcourt wishes Malcolm a very good morning before he salutes and marches out of the office, then turns to brief the sergeant major.

When next Malcolm goes home, he tells the story of his encounter with Algernon Bentley-Lewis and Mum is fulsome in her praise of him. A reflection of a sound upbringing, she says.

'You're all good children. I know I've brought you up right. There are some, mind, who could do with a bit of polishing' – perhaps she thinking of Toni Ada May – 'but they're in the minority.' She waxes eloquent on the good job she has done in raising her children before turning her attention to Margaret, who has nearly reached the age at which she would have to do her National Service.

'Are you searching for your brains?'

'I don't know what you mean, Mam.'

'Then get your finger out of your ear, or you'll be in for a nice surprise.'

'What d'you mean, Mum?'

'You'll find nothing there.'

'But Mum. It hurts.'

'Come here. Let's have a look. Potatoes! You've got a potato patch in your ears. Go and wash them. Go on. Into the back place with you.' With that admonition, she cuffs Margaret on the back of the head, propelling her into the kitchen to do as she's told.

Thinking about it, Kathleen our youngest sister may be the lucky one in the family. Perhaps Mum will mellow before Kathleen is old enough to be at the whipping end of her tongue, but somehow I don't think she will. Given her resilience and temperament, Mum will last for some time yet.

The war has gone on for five long years. Hostilities are at an end, of course, but we have a long way to go before there is any prospect of the country settling down to a prosperous peace. Rationing and shortages look like being the norm for a long time to come. Nevertheless, we have survived. That is the main thing and, given the fact that everyone has survived, we've experienced a miracle of sorts.

16   Après la Guerre

Tᴵᴹᴱ ʜᴬˢ ᴾᴬˢˢᴱᴰ – more than forty years in fact between that magical day in the war, which was the only time ever when we were together as a family, and the next time we meet. On this next occasion, two of our number are missing.

Our Dad went to his Maker years ago after major surgery for a brain tumour, which left him a virtual vegetable until he was visited by that old man's friend, pneumonia; Theresa died in her infancy, but not before Mum, with Dad's agreement, had her baptised at her Roman Catholic church.

Uncle Bill Craft has fallen off the twig too, although he lived to the ripe age of 92 and so outlasted our Dad by a good margin. Aunt Ada and Mum are still alive, both being some years younger than their husbands. They are cracking on a bit, but lively enough and they still have their wits about them. As Aunt Ada features to some extent in the marriage get together for which we've gathered after all these years, it is worth mentioning her here.

The occasion of this second family gathering has come out of the blue when our youngest sister Kathleen's eldest daughter Denise marries Tom, an Irishman from Cork. Kathleen's idea of bringing the family together once more is inspired and generous, for how she and Colin can afford such a splash on his income as a trucker is quite beyond my understanding.

Kathleen has been the dutiful daughter who stayed close to home with the exception of her Volunteer Service in the ATS, which was years ago when she was young of course. She took care of Mum at the same time as raising her own young family of four closely spaced daughters. She married Colin, a long-distance transport driver, after she left the ATS. They've enjoyed a long and happy marriage, raising their children in a house much smaller than the one in which we spent our childhood on Crane Hill. Now in the 1980s they are living near the end of Spencer Bridge Road where it forms a T-junction with Harlestone Road, which is where Aunt Ada's eighteenth-century labourer's cottage is situated, a few houses around the corner from where Kathleen and Colin live. Aunt Ada and Kathleen get on well, which is not surprising; Kathleen is cheerful in anyone's company and by all accounts a godsend in a crisis or disaster. The same cannot be said for Mum and Aunt Ada I'm afraid.

Mum moved into a ground-floor council flat at Jimmy's End, a few streets from Kathleen's place, which means she now lives but a stone's throw from Aunt Ada's. Given the close proximity of the two and the inevitability of their running into one another when they're shopping, you might have thought they'd have settled their differences and buried the hatchet, but they never did. Did I mention that? Their mutual animosity goes right back to the incident of our Gaffer leaving the house on Crane Hill in a huff. Aunt Ada still blames Mum for that, though no words have ever been spoken between them about it. If they chance to meet on the street – Jimmy's End is a small community – they pass one another by without so much as a howdy-do of recognition. We all think one was as much at fault as the other in this exercise of unending hostility. There's none like the elderly for nurturing their beefs as a miser hoards his gold, adding to the obnoxious treasure that they tuck in the back of their minds long after everyone else has forgotten what the dispute was about.

Because I left before Kathleen was born I knew nothing of her adolescent years. I left England for good at the time of the Suez crisis and immigrated to Canada. A gulf has separated me from the life I lived in England. I have had my own family to raise. Nevertheless, my work has often taken me through London en route to Africa and the Middle East, so I have frequently visited Northampton to see Mum, which means I've got to know Kathleen and her family over the years.

Like me, the rest of the family have gone their separate ways. There's no point in giving biographical details of my siblings because I know little about their lives. Ada and her family moved to Australia only to return to England; three brothers run a construction enterprise in East Africa; Jack has remained a cobbler and the women, other than Toni, have married Northampton men and raised their families in the town, but none in The Boroughs.

And so it is that with the gathering together for the marriage of Kathleen's eldest, I have found myself at the door of Mum's flat at Jimmy's End. I knock on the front door, then open the letter flap to watch Mum navigate her way with the aid of a walking stick to see who has come calling. She must have seen a pair of eyes watching her progress, though she doesn't let on she has taken notice. Opening the door, she beams with delight at the sight of me.

'Oooh! Our Arthur, I'm ever so pleased to see you' – loud enough to attract the attention of the whole street at eleven o'clock in the morning. In a word, nothing has changed, for she gives a little performance for anyone who might be watching by smoothing down her dress and looking pointedly up and the street. It's hugs and kisses for all to see.

'Come on, Ma. Let's get in. We don't have to broadcast glad tidings to the neighbours.'

She laughs. 'I don't know what you're talking about, you silly thing.'

We understand one another perfectly and I'm relieved when she leads the way inside. I carry my overnight bag in one hand – I never travel with baggage in the hold – and a bottle of brandy in a brown paper bag in the other.

A door on the right at the end of the passage gives entry to her small living room; another to her bedroom and yet a third to her bathroom. The layout of her council flat would win no competitions for use of space. Someone has used imagination to lay out the rock garden, a flower bed, a patch of grass and shrubbery that can be seen through the picture window of her room. I like that. Opposite the window is a cubbyhole of a kitchen, separated by an archway in the wall.

Mum takes some time lowering herself into the armchair that gives her a good view of the courtyard and the television set in the corner. I settle into a wooden armchair opposite her and place the bottle of brandy on the floor at my side. My overnight bag I've left in the passageway. Mum has lost none of her sense of excitement and enthusiasm, for her laughing outburst is immediate and unstoppable.

'Here! I have to tell you. It's ever such a coincidence. Our Jack and Doris come last week an' she had to slip along to see, you know, your Aunt Ada, and I said, "You must do as you has to do like, Doris. It's no business of mine," and she said, "All right, Mum. Then I'll just hop along and I'll be nippy about it. I shan't be long. There's no need for Jack to come wi' me. He can stay here and keep you company like. You know how he likes to see his dear old mum."

'So off she trots and as soon as she's gone our Jack says to me, he says – you know how he is – he says, "Mother, have you got a drop of brandy? I've got a funny turn coming on and could really do with a drop of brandy," and I said, "What are you talking about? I haven't got brandy, not a single drop in the whole house." No one brings me brandy any more. No one. Well, except our Arthur. He always brings me brandy when he comes, he does.'

'My God, Mum! You're as false as a padded bra, aren't you?'

'Such cheek. What do you mean? I haven't the faintest idea what you're talking about.'

'Oh, Mum. You have the eyes of a predatory eagle when it suits you,' I say, handing her the bottle of brandy in its brown wrapping.

She accepts the gift readily enough, but her eyebrows pucker vaguely as though caught off balance. Slowly, she removes the bottle from its wrapping, looks at me, looks back at the bottle, and says, 'Ooo! What a lovely surprise!'

'I thought you'd like it.'

'Just a minute. What's this?' she says, leaning back to get the label in focus. 'Napoleon brandy? Not five-star Courvoisier? Have you Canadians started making your own brandy then?'

'What flaming cheek. Give it back, Mother, I'll soon find—'

'No, no!' she interrupts me, sharp as a tack. 'Hold your horses. I can try it. See what it's like.' Then, with a conspiratorial glance about her, she hands the brandy back to me, saying confidentially, 'Be a good 'un, will you. Put this in the cupboard behind you. Get it out of sight of from prying eyes. That'll just do me when I'm not feeling so well.'

I stay but a short time after that. The gathering for young Denise's wedding is to begin between noon and 12.30. Mum is expecting Margaret to bring her corsage and Kathleen to take her to the hotel. Margaret arrives as I'm leaving, which is convenient because she can drop me off at the George Hotel on Bridge Street before she goes home to change for the wedding.

In the nineteenth century the George had been a coaching inn, and though now fully modernised into a four-star hotel with reception rooms and guest rooms, it is architecturally unchanged with narrow twisting stairs and steps up and down at various floor levels throughout the building. In the reception area on the ground floor with its double bar the staff have a good view of both the imposing front entrance and the rear coach entrance from a courtyard that hasn't changed in 150 years.

No one I know is around when I check in – I have arrived earlier that I expected to – so I take my time shaving, showering and getting dressed, then casually find my way back to reception. The place is now alive with an entirely different atmosphere than when I arrived. With delight, I find Malcolm and his wife Jenny.

'Hello, mate,' he says, greeting me with a brotherly embrace. 'I'm glad you could make it.'

I grin. 'I only agreed to come on condition everyone left their weapons at the door.'

'I can't unscrew mine!'

'And I'm glad,' says Jenny.

'The others are in the front parlour,' says Malcolm. 'Go in and join them. We're waiting for Mother.'

'I called on Mother when I arrived.'

'Yeah? How is she? Hello! Here she is now,' says Malcolm with his eye on the courtyard.

Two limousines have arrived in the teeming rain and parked in the dry under the carport. No sooner has one stopped than the second swings through a turn and stopped alongside the first. The doorman opens the rear door to the sound of slashing rain hitting the plastic canopy, making a deafening noise.

From the vehicle nearest the entrance of the hotel steps Aunt Ada, assisted by the uniformed driver who has opened the passenger door. Looking frail, Aunt Ada steadies herself while she waits for the driver to bring her walking frame. At almost the same time, Mum emerges from the further car, straightens her outfit and sets out for the entrance with the aid of her walking stick. We watch the progress of our elders with fascination. Neither will thank us for coming to their aid; they are both fiercely independent.

Aunt Ada has a head start to reach the door first, but Mum sees the move as a test of willpower and accepts the challenge: though she has difficulty with her legs, she puts her best foot forward as Mr Barratt of Walking-the-Barratt-Way fame long ago stepped out of the posters. The contest becomes a race in slow motion, like a pair of tortoises on the home stretch. Neither one spares so much as a fleeting glance for the other. It is neck and neck all the way with nothing to choose until the very end when, by a supreme effort of will, Mum reaches the door first and steps inside.

The two dears having arrived without addressing a word to one another, we greet them with equal enthusiasm and enter the spacious bar as a group. Everyone, it seems, is present: Auntie Jack and Uncle Doris; Harry and June; Mary and her useless husband Brian who spends his life on welfare Fred, but who has been invited for the occasion; Toni and Ken – Toni wearing a chic outfit with what her nieces and nephews later describe as a 'black rat for an 'at on 'er 'ead', which does indeed have the appearance of having been plastered into place; St Fred, a recent widower, subdued and quiet, but with ever alert eyes; Malcolm and Jenny; Margaret with current husband Geoff; Kathleen and the girls along with numerous nephews and nieces from both sides of the Dawson and Fulthorpe families. The Dawsons are on Colin's side of the bride's family and, while we're on the subject of sides, it's obvious from the strong babble of Irish accents on the far side of the bar that the bridegroom's family have assembled and are hard at it drinking good English beer.

'What would you like to drink, Mum?' I ask, for the others have agreed to fork over ten pounds each and make me the treasurer, which means of course that should I run out of funds I'll have to make up the difference for the bar bill.

'I'll have a drop of brandy, to help my heart, love,' she says, shifting her glasses higher on her nose.

'And you, Aunt Ada?'

'A Bristol Cream would suit me nicely, my ducks,' Aunt Ada, seated opposite Mum, for their chairs have been placed close together, fixes her eyes determinedly on the middle distance.

The attention being paid to them both by the others makes it obvious something is afoot. With Malcolm at the bar and amid the cacophony of noise coming from both sides of the bar, I ask, 'Who engineered this?'

'You'll see,' he says in my ear, shielding his response from the din. 'Kathleen and I thought their quarrel had gone on long enough. You'll see. We'll put an end to it.'

The rain is now bucketing down, slashing against the windows of the bar, which does nothing to help cool the room. In the smoky, hot atmosphere of the room I'm beginning to sweat. Too many bodies.

By the time we return with the drinks, a hush has descended on the room, not so completely that one can't hear the clink of pint glasses being gathered by the barman's assistant or the chatter of separate discussions going on. No, it's the charged air as, like spectators at a nineteenth-century boxing match, the company is waiting for the bout to begin. No word has passed between these two seasoned adversaries for almost half a century. One of them has to yield, but which one will give in no one could tell. The bets are even. At long last, Aunt Ada breaks the silence.

'Hello, Mag!' Her voice is quiet, her dignity intact.

'Hello, Ada!'

Forty years and a crack has appeared. Mum holds her ground for a while, then gives a little.

'It's tippling down, I see.'

'Yes, very true, very true.' Aunt Ada is in her early nineties; Mum not more than a year younger. Then Mum clamps up and gazes at the faces gathered around her. She might have guessed she's been set up. A long silence follows. We're all interested in where they will go from here. Then Aunt Ada speaks again.

'Maggie,' she says, looking at Mum with a quizzical expression. 'Have I upset you?'

Mum raises her eyebrows in surprise. 'Good gracious me! Why would you think that, Ada?'

'Oh! I don't know, only you've been a bit quiet of late.'

★

'That's it. We've done it,' Malcolm laughs heartily. Everyone joins in, with a huge sense of relief at the accomplishment.

'What are you on about?' says Mum, visibly miffed. 'I don't know what you're all standing around for like that, grinning like apes.'

'Nothing, Ma,' says Malcolm. 'It's a family trait.'

'Huh! I'm sure it is, but not from my genes.'

'It's all right, Maggie. Let them have their fun. I'm sure I don't know what it's about either,' says Aunt Ada, giving her sister-in-law support.

'Oh! They're a funny lot, Ada. Let's drink up.'

And so it is that all those years of solid ice melt in a second, allowing the marriage of Tom and Denise to begin in earnest.

Tom's family and relatives have flown over from Cork on a chartered flight. They are many and quite equal to the combined turnout of Denise's family, the Dawson and Fulthorpe families. The Irish O'Connors have found and occupied their own space and are settling down for serious drinking, but the separation of guests doesn't last long – Harry sees to that.

'The Irish might be rebellious and the English cantankerous,' he says to no one in particular, 'but we can't have this, can we?' With that, he leaves the Fulthorpe-Dawson side of the bar and steps into the O'Connor camp. The open bar serves both lounges. We can see Harry introducing himself and, moments later, ever the diplomat, he returns with half a dozen O'Connors to join us.

'Whoever said the English and Irish don't mix is either IRA or an Orangeman,' says Malcolm, bold as brass.

One of the O'Connor women, in her early forties with fine-boned features and a jaunty air, smiles and replies immediately, 'Would you mind telling us what you mean by Orangeman? I confess now that it's a new word in my lexicon.'

Loud laughter as the newcomers mingle freely. Soon, a group of Fulthorpes and Dawsons, led by the lady with the jaunty air, leaves to meet the lady's fellow Irish in the O'Connor lounge. This is, in a way, yet another historic meeting of Protestants and Catholics of which mixed company none is more in her element than our Mum, who glows with happiness. She feels, I'm sure, that she is truly among her own. Despite her legs, which still trouble her, she is up and about and putting on her fainest speaking voice and retreating to her chair opposite Aunt Ada when she needs a rest.

'How are you then, Mum? Everything all right?'

'Ooh! It's lovely, my son. I'm ever so happy with it all.'

Aunt Ada is in conversation with our Mary, so I have Mum to myself for a while. I gesture to indicate the O'Connors about us. 'Happy to be among all these micks, Mum?'

'That's quite enough of that from you, Mr Know-It-All. Here, come here.'

I'm standing beside her, so I bend down as she bids to hear the confidence I sense she is about to impart. Nor am I wrong.

'It's been a long long time, my son.'

'I'm sure it has been, Mother,' I say, sensing what she means.

With the exception of her, all of us on Denise's side are Protestants, whether Church of Chapel, but probably none of them practising. The bridegroom's family are all undoubtedly Godfearing Roman Catholics.

'You know that Denise has agreed that any children will be brought up Roman Catholic?'

'No, I didn't.'

'She's been going to the church for months, so I know all about it.'

'That's nice,' I say.

Being half-Irish, Mum can barely contain her delight to be among her co-religionists. She must have suffered extreme guilt over the years for permitting her children to be brought up even as nominal Anglicans, to distinguish them from Presbyterians and Dissenting Protestants. She has suffered the threat of excommunication and – in her own mind, at least to my way of thinking – having her granddaughter getting married in a Roman Catholic is more than a sign of forgiveness from God. It is nothing short of her salvation, redemption, her release from the threat of purgatory.

Yet here we Fulthorpes, Dawsons and O'Connors are, all mixed up like a great throng in a national celebration. Malcolm in his puckish way declares that the O'Connors are a damned fine crowd if only 'they could speak proper'.

A wit in the O'Connor clan who overhears the remark finds the Fulthorpes and Dawsons an equally grand bunch, too, apart from their funny accents.

'The English may have invented the language,' says another, raising a toast, 'but it takes Celts to show them how to use it.'

Phlegmatic English mixed with droll Irish wit signifies that all was well.

Following the service and the reception held in the church hall and served by the church ladies auxiliary, and the departure of the bridal pair, we all gravitate back to the George where we spend the rest of the evening in a convivial beer fest and all's well with the world.

★

I call on Mum the next morning to say goodbye, for I'm leaving for the Middle East this evening. I find her in high spirits, purring with pleasure like a cat that's broken a bottle of cream.

'What's got into you?' I ask.

'Well, d'you know what? Let me tell you. I got home last night, I did, an' I thought well, I thought, I'll just try a little tot of that brandy you brought me and I'll sit here and think about things.'

'Yes.'

'It was an ever such a good day, don't you think?'

'Yes, it was. Everything went off well.'

'So here I sat, thinking about things, gazing out at the courtyard bathed in warm light of the court. It was a tranquil site for sore eyes I can tell you.'

'Oh yes!'

'So here I stay in my armchair and, goodness gracious! The next thing I wake up to find the place in total darkness.'

'Oh my God!' I say, leaping up and opening the cupboard to check the bottle of brandy I'd brought her. I take it out, hold it to the light. 'I don't believe it. You've gone through a third of a bottle!'

Mum laughs merrily at the memory of it all when a noise at the front door opening sounds and the next moment Kathleen's in the living room.

'What's all the noise about?' she asks, removing her coat. 'You have the loudest laugh. I could hear it from the street.'

'It was the brandy. Mum got stuck into it last night.'

More laughter in which we all share.

'You wouldn't have found Mum so boisterous if you'd been here at seven o'clock this morning.'

'Why's that?'

'I came to check that she was all right and found her most upset. Never seen her in such a state. Moaning and groaning and carrying on she was as though it was the end of the world was here. Imagine, she was in her see-through nightdress, poking here there, everywhere with her walking stick searching for something.

'"What's the matter, Mum?" I asked.

'"I can't find it. I can't find it," she said. "I've bin searching everywhere and it's lost, it's nowhere to be found."

'"Searching for what?" I asked.

'"Me 'at, me 'at," she groaned. "I can't find my 'at."'

Kathleen speaks mockingly in the flat Northampton accent.

'"You silly devil," I said. "It's on your head."

'She was so tipsy by the time she got ready for bed last night that she somehow managed to get into her nightdress with her hat with its wraparound garland of flowers still on her head. How she managed it I don't know, but she went to sleep with it still pinned to her head. Like I said, I don't know how she did it, but she did.'

'That explains why a third of the bottle's missing,' I say.

I leave to catch the train to London shortly after that. This happy exchange between the three of us serves as a fitting end for me to this last family gathering. Kathleen and Colin have done the right thing in persuading us all to attend their daughter's wedding. What's more, the reunion has gone well. Mum and Aunt Ada are speaking to one another again and neither can remember what the fuss was all about.

Toni exults in telling anyone who will listen of her death-defying medical problems; Margaret has been taken to hospital emergency with concussion from falling down a couple of stairs, but manages to sit up on the stretcher to announce with a grin to Kathleen as she's being carried to the waiting ambulance, 'I'm concussed.'

Fred and I sit side by side at dinner and renew the companionship we shared as youngsters. We forge new friendships with the O'Connors, too, so all in all it's been a splendid affair.

Epilogue

J ACK DIED of prostate cancer two years later. He was the first to fall off the twig. In Spanish Honduras, Tegucigalpa, at the time, I was unable to attend his cremation, but the others were there. Then Harry died of skin cancer, but I did manage to visit him while he was in palliative care. My trouble is that I'm always either coming or going on business, so that meeting is a fleeting visit. I know nothing of Harry's final days until Malcolm and Jenny visit me on Vancouver Island three months after Harry's funeral. He was buried with full honours apparently.

Harry hid his light under a bush, for his wartime exploits, which he never spoke about, were legion among those in the know. Malcolm only told me what he knew of Harry's exploits while we were in Vancouver Airport, waiting for him to board his flight to London. I knew a little of it, but what Malcolm said was news to me.

Harry served on frigates during the war; that I knew well enough. Apparently, a member of the crew of the frigate, HMS *Lawson*, he made two escort runs with the Russian convoys to Murmansk. That's all in the records. A Soviet Commissar travelled aboard every Royal Navy ship, supposedly to assist with the ship's passage through the roads to dock. In point of fact, the commissars reported everything to Soviet High Command.

The reports, apparently, were filed if not read. With the collapse of the Soviet Union, the Russian Navy joined the Association of Arctic Convoys formed by the US Navy, Royal Navy, Norwegian, Iceland and Dutch navies and merchant seaman of all nations who had risked their lives on the arctic convoys.

'At one time,' Malcolm relates, 'the Russians offered the Russian Campaign Medal to all who had taken part in the convoys, but the Royal Navy turned down the offer. It

relented once the Soviet Union collapsed and allowed its
veterans to accept the Russian campaign medal after all.'

'Interesting and what—'

'Don't interrupt. We'll have to go in a few minutes. In
our Harry's case, there was more. It all centred on one
incident. His ship, K516, a frigate in the Captain Class,
made two runs to Murmansk as I said. On the second run,
a sister ship in the same squadron copped it with a German
U-Boat torpedo in the bow. The *Lawson*'s captain couldn't
stop to pick up survivors without risking his own ship.
Instead, he ordered the boarding nets dropped over the side
to give anyone in the water near enough to the ship at least
a chance to grab on to the nets. The chances of anyone
surviving for more than ten minutes in the frigid waters of
the North Atlantic were remote. With a couple of
shipmates, Harry clambered down the nets on the
offchance of grabbing one of their mates from the drink. He
was lucky, for he grabbed someone from the sea and helped
him climb aboard.'

'Good grief! Did Harry tell you this?'

'No. One of his shipmates at his funeral did. The ship's
commissar witnessed the rescue from the main deck and
wrote a report of the incident. It gathered dust in the
Russian archives for the next fifty years. Then a retired
Russian naval commander involved in the Arctic Convoys
Association chanced on the report when researching the
files for a book. The Russians, apparently, make more of
their heroes than their we do in the West. They judged the
deed of bravery worthy of an award of a Russian Navy
Medal of Valour.

'Next thing we know, a naval attaché from the Russian
Embassy arrives at Harry's bedside to present him with the
Russian "Medal for Bravery" along with a Russian sailor's
hat.'

'Go on with you. How did they know he was on his
deathbed?'

'He'd applied for his Russian convoy medal, so the
Association was in touch with him.'

'And when his name came up, the Russians connected him with the commissar's report?'

'Yep, that's the God's honest truth. What's more, the Russians turned up at Harry's funeral. I know because I was there. The chaplain, a former chief petty officer on Harry ship, draped a White Ensign over the coffin and, with a guard of honour in attendance; Harry got a good send off.'

'Well, I'm astonished. Our Harry never was one for blowing his own trumpet. What more can you tell me?'

'Nothing, except that Harry gave his Russian sailor's hat to his grandson, young Tom.'

★

I can't conclude this saga of the Fulthorpe clan without Malcolm's revelation regarding Ada's (aka Toni's) Dresden exploit. We all thought she was swinging the lamp with her tale of the raid, but everyone except me knew the truth long ago. Enquiring after her – I'd heard she hadn't been so well again – Malcolm says, 'She's all right, is our Toni, like the unsinkable Molly Brown she is. Goes under for a while and you swear she's a goner, but she pops back up and says she thinks she'll stay a while longer.'

I laugh. 'She's unsinkable, I agree, and never one to be put down. You remember the tale she told of the Dresden raid near the end of the war? I do, like I heard it yesterday.'

'You didn't believe her?'

'What do you think?'

Malcolm shakes his head. 'You never heard, did you?'

'Heard what?'

'That's the trouble with you, never keeping in touch with the rest of us. You miss it all. I was at Toni's wedding and met Flight Sergeant Briggs, ex-flight sergeant, that is. He ran a successful business after the war and kept in touch with Toni. He was at Toni's and Ken's wedding.'

'No?'

'Yes! He confirmed her every word down to the detail of the aircraft getting home by dead reckoning.'

'Good God! I never knew.'

There was no more to learn. They had to leave anyway, so I said goodbye to Jenny, shook Malcolm's hand and we promised to see one another soon, which could be in another five years if we last that long.

'See you then. I guess this is ta-ra, is it?'

'I guess it is, mate,' said Malcolm. 'Ta-ra then!'

Next thing they were through the security scanning frames and gone.

About the author

Born and educated in England, Art Cockerill enlisted in the British Army in 1943. He was commissioned in the Corps of Royal Engineers and served in the Middle East, resigning his commission in 1951 to return to civilian life.

Opposed to the invasion of Suez in 1950, he emigrated to Canada, arriving in January 1957, since when he has combined an active career in engineering with journalism and writing. Trained in power engineering design and operation before becoming a consultant to the Canadian nuclear industry, he was for ten years a member of the National Technical Committee on nuclear quality assurance and helped in writing compliance standards for the industry; likewise the national standards of accreditation for the Canadian Council on Hospital Accreditation.

In the 1970s, he worked throughout the Middle East, Africa, the Caribbean and Central America, installing equipment at the same time as writing for various international journals on political-economic themes and head of state interviews.

Art is a member of the Society of Army Historical Research and the Military History Society of Ireland. He has frequently contributed articles on military history to the *Journal of the SAHR* and *The Irish Sword*.

CPSIA information can be obtained at www.ICGtesting.com
Printed in the USA
245467LV00001B/27/P